BONESEEKER

From the Journals of Arabella Holmes and Henry Watson

Transcribed by Brynn Chapman

"I have frequently gained my first real insight into the character of parents by studying their children."—Sir Arthur Conan Doyle

"How often have I said to you that when you have eliminated the impossible, whatever remains, however improbable, must be the truth?"—Sir Arthur Conan Doyle via Sherlock Holmes

To my one and only. Famous first lines. "I could love you." And they did...

BONESEEKER

Brynn Chapman

Prologue

Philadelphia, 1910
Jacoby Manor
22 Riddle Run Road

*T*he portly man opens the door a crack, his gaze sweeping the street for prying eyes. He quickly swings it wide, ushering the tall man inside.

"Do come in Fredrick. All have gathered; you are the last to arrive."

"Jacoby." He nods and sweeps into the entryway and down the hall.

The towering man peers through the thick cloud of cigar smoke at the gathering of twelve about the round table and takes his place at its head.

He does not sit. Indeed, this situation requires he remind the others of his authority.

"Gentlemen. I shall dispense with the pleasantries and

proceed directly to the order of business."

The sound of a door opening and approaching footsteps silence the leader as his black eyes narrow in irritation and flick to the doorway.

A young, scraggly fellow pokes his head round the door, inquiring, "Is...this the meeting of the Darwinists?"

Disgruntled murmurs erupt at the use of this label.

The leader's face blazes scarlet, and all twelve men fidget in their seats, each taking furtive glances at the man at the table's head.

"That is not the correct name for this institution, but apparently you are in the right place."

Jacoby clears his throat. "My apologies, Fredrick. My new son-in-law. I invited him. Do sit down. Do not make me regret extending you this invitation."

"Sorry, sir."

The tiny man tips his bowler hat and scurries to the table. He cringes when he sees the only empty chair is directly beside the glowering leader.

The tall man's gaze scans the table, assuring all eyes turn to him before beginning.

"The Brotherhood of the Revolution stands at a crossroads today. With this unfortunate discovery our very purpose and hard work to further solidify Darwinism may be undone if this archaeological site proves authentic."

The man's eyes narrow, flitting back and forth across every face. "Miss Holmes is a growing thorn in my side, and that of our cause. If, indeed, the recovered bones prove to be Nephilim in origin, it shall greatly hinder our mission."

"Miss Holmes as in Sherlock Holmes?" the tiny man peeps.

The leader's eyes blaze with fury as he steadfastly ignores the interruption.

"Her perceptive powers are as formidable as her father. Fortuitously, the recovered hand was badly damaged and results of its examination and origin were inconclusive. Most of the team's scientists are mediocre at best, but not Miss Holmes. If the bones are authentic, and she unearths the remainder of the skeleton, I am convinced she will know immediately."

"The Nephilim?" the son-in-law whispers.

Jacoby replies, "From the book of Jude, verse six, 'and the angels that did not keep their original position but forsook their own proper dwelling place.'"

The leader sneers, "Yes. To mate with the daughters of men. If the history lesson is over, might I continue?"

Jacoby interjects, "What course of action do you propose?"

"Miss Holmes must be dealt with by any means necessary. She must be removed from this expedition."

"Beggin your pardon sir, but could you be more specific as to the particulars of how to remove Miss Holmes?"

"Did I stutter Jacoby? By any. Means. Necessary."

Chapter One

SOMETHING WICKED THIS WAY COMES

Mutter Museum, 1910
Midnight
Arabella

F ear.
The unfamiliar emotion brings a metallic taste to my mouth.

How did I miss the tell-tale signs?

The foreboding spreads; pumping its limb-numbing weakness from my heart to surge up and solidify into a ball of dread, lodging firmly in my throat.

My fingers grasp the lab bench behind me, cold, like his skin and the chill stealing into my bones.

My superior leans in close, much too close, shattering the great divide between student and mentor.

Forget propriety and society; we are beyond

unchaperoned, we are utterly alone. The drop of a pin would clatter like thunder in the stillness of the dark, stone halls of the museum tonight.

"Miss Holmes, I have a proposition."

My heartbeat floods my ears.

How dare I call myself a Holmes? I missed every clue.

My mind thumbs through mental snapshots, disregarded. Lingering glances during my cadaver dissections; his eyes stealing across me as if my body was the anatomy lesson.

His hand, draped over mine, a heartbeat too long, demonstrating precisely how much solution to add to my bubbling concoction.

Inappropriate, unacceptable touches, which I foolishly reasoned away.

"You know of my high regard for you."

His long, tapered fingers reach over to encircle my wrist. His hands restrain like icy shackles and I fight to keep my countenance calm.

I swallow. "I." And clear my throat. "I was under the impression my presence at the Museum was…off-putting."

My survival-brain wakes, analyzes, as my eyes perform reconnaissance around my lab. Two exits. My parasol lies across the room, useless.

It's past midnight—not a soul will be in the museum to hear my scream.

I stare up at Dr. Stygian. He towers well over six feet tall. I haven't a chance against him.

One word whispers, taunts.

Rape. *Is he capable of it?*

I do not know. He is overbearing and caustic, but rape...

He inches closer still, pinning me between the lab bench and his body.

"At first, I was put-upon, yes. But I've been watching, making a detailed study of you and your fastidious nature. I know of your ambitions—very lofty for a woman, wouldn't you say? I believe we could...help one another."

He leans in and his lips brush mine and I recoil—my leg twitches, at the ready to knee the soft flesh of his groin.

"Miss Holmes?"

I hear the familiar shuffle-step that I know to be Dr. Earnest, my other superior. Thank God for the old man's insomnia.

Stygian slides slowly away from me, as if savoring where our bodies touch. His eyes never leave mine.

Earnest shuffles into the doorway and his eyebrows rise when he spies Dr. Stygian's proximity.

"Fredrick?"

Stygian grants him a nod and stoops to pick up his walking stick and his cape. "Miss Holmes requested I assist with her assignment."

From behind his back, I bite my lip and give a singular, negative shake of my head.

Earnest's eyebrows knit. "Well, I must insist you off to bed, my girl."

Stygian flips his crow-black hair from his forehead and spins on his boot heel to swoop past Dr. Earnest out into the hall, disappearing without a backwards glance.

As I walk to Earnest's side, I bend to pick up my journal and parasol and hope he does not perceive the tremble in my hands.

He guides me gently, his hand on the small of my back, and out the door.

"Dr. Watson warned me you were driven. But midnight? Work ethic be deuced, one must be reasonable, Arabella."

I shiver again and vow to leave the lab by nightfall from now on.

A few months later.
Henry

The Mutter's hallways are dim and the singular window, situated high near the cathedral ceiling, permits a paltry amount of illumination as the dreary drizzle of rain relentlessly pelts the pane.

The odd combination of candles and electric light give the shadows a treacle-like, stretched appearance. Father had related the Mutter preferred to spend its funds on antiquities, so the conversion from old light to new was painstaking.

The light was indeed dim, but I was still able to discern Father's bright blue eyes turning to goad and hasten my progress.

A blast rattles my jaw. I lurch backward with the force.

My father's eyes widen in shock, his left hand shooting out to ward off the unseen danger.

"What was *that*?"

This response is saying something, for the unflappable

Dr. John Watson.

Another blast rings out; the laboratory door blows off its hinges and flies through the air, clattering against the opposite wall with a *'bang'*, narrowly missing the glass case of shrunken heads.

I pull out a handkerchief, plastering it across my nose. Black billows of smoke barrel out the doorframe to fill the hallway.

Footsteps echo behind us, and father and I turn in tandem. My soon to-be-superior, Dr. Earnest, rounds the corner, his waddle changing to an ungainly lope as he spies the smoke. His bushy white eyebrows bug to life, shooting up and under the untidy flop of grey hair hanging over his forehead.

"Arabella!" His face flushes, instantly furious. "Can she *never* act like a woman?"

"No, Alistair, she cannot. Which is precisely why she is here," my father strides toward the laboratory, "And not preparing for her coming-out party? What would you expect of a young woman raised by Sherlock Holmes?"

Dr. Earnest harrumphs, but follows obediently.

I am rooted.

Arabella. I haven't seen her since I was a gangly, love-sick eighteen year old.

I straighten my lapels. Much can change in four years' time.

"For heaven's sake, Henry, are you going to make yourself useful or stand there and choke to death?"

Father's head whips backward and his glare, a white-hot, visual cattle-prod, urges me into motion.

"Coming, father." Sweat breaks on my brow.

Stop it. He has no recollection of your feelings for her.

Dr. Earnest lowers his head, plunging headlong into the black smoke and is instantly swallowed.

I step to follow, but father restrains my forearm. "*Do you see* why you are here now, Henry?"

I struggle to keep my anger in check. "Why didn't you tell me she was here? All those months, battling over my future—you were dead-set against this appointment."

"I was. It was Holmes. Once he caught wind of your interest, there was no throwing him off—he was relentless.

You know how very disappointed I am that you've chosen…antiquities—"

"It's more accurately forensic anthropology."

Father's eyes roll. "*Such an elaborate name for dead things.* Anyway, chosen it over medicine—but at least it's proving useful. Now that you're here Holmes will stop his incessant worrying about her safety. He's normally insufferable, but since she left, he's *intolerable.*"

Even I know an idle Holmes to be a self-destructive Holmes.

I nod in agreement and step into the smoke, following the trail of barking coughs.

"Arabella, where are you, girl?" Father calls from behind me. His tone is almost jovial; as if we're headed to a bloody picnic rather than weaving our way through this acrid smelling smoke.

I step into the large laboratory; I squint and finally make out her small frame, barely visible through the dissipating black clouds.

She turns, and I marvel. Her face is a mask of calm; her dainty fingers circle a full flask of bubbling red elixir.

Bits of her hair have escaped its tidy bun and now free-fall in shocking red waves about her face. One brazen, challenging eye peers out through the mess of hair.

Between the red shock of her mane and the black soot streaking her face, it's as if I am staring down a Bengal tiger.

I take a deep, steeling breath, and my chest sears—hitching into a coughing fit.

Brilliant.

She clears her throat, blue eyes scrutinizing her superior. Her chin turns up in defiance. "Dr. Earnest. I was… experimenting—"

"You—" Earnest sucks in, his chest bloating in outrage. The result is a similar hacking fit, racking his old body in half. "Arabella. You know b-better, ever since the last incident."

"Yes, I remember."

The smoke is thinning and my eyes tick up and down, analyzing Arabella's lab.

Although I won't join father in medicine or his adventures with Holmes, I cannot help my upbringing. I've been indoctrinated to drink in every minute detail of every place I've ever stepped foot.

Bones.

Bones are everywhere, as if a graveyard platoon marched in and surrendered for display.

Patellas, femurs, ulnas, metacarpals…and skulls from both animal and humankind in various states of skeletal reconstruction, litter the walls and floor.

I look up. *And the air.*

A half-assembled, bony falcon hovers overhead, dangling from the ceiling.

All that's missing is a skeletal prey clutched in its beak.

A glass case, looking distinctly out of place among the dead, draws my attention to the room's center. Brilliant yellow, blue, orange and black bodies are strewn throughout.

It's crammed with butterflies; their vibrant black and blue wings contrast against the surrounding blanched-bones like a rainbow amidst a bleak thunderstorm.

Pins stick through their thoraxes, their wings spread in perfect display. Each one sports a label beneath in Arabella's untidy scrawl, proclaiming its genus.

Arabella's stare leaves Dr. Earnest's face, and she squints, finally registering our presence. Her eyes focus on my father and turn cautious.

Her lips twist up in a tentative smile.

He strides toward her, unflustered. Not unobserving, though, I am sure. My father misses nothing. He will have catalogued Arabella's response in his Dewey-Decimalized brain.

"My darling! It has been far too long." Father's arms wrap around Arabella, folding her in. She winces.

He pulls back, leaving his hands on her shoulders. His eyes rove quickly, evaluating her for injuries.

Her mouth twitches in amusement. Amazingly, she isn't fooled—she knows he's examining her. Knows my father better than I realized.

He can normally charm a nun out of her habit.

"John. So good of you to come. How is father?"

"Worried about you, but no longer retired, so tolerable."

They share a knowing laugh.

"Naturally, you remember my son, Henry?" Father raises his arm in presentation.

Arabella's blue eyes flick to mine. My stomach lurches.

"Of course. How could I *ever* forget Henry?"

For pity's sake. Control, man.

I nod stiffly. "Arabella. Pleasure to see you. You've... grown."

She laughs, so loud and bawdy that Dr. Earnest squirms and drops his eyes.

"Yes, children do just that. The last time I saw you—you were headed for boarding school."

"And you."

Her gaze drops with the mention of the school.

Father clears his throat. "Yes, well, your similar upbringing has bred two adventurers. Apparently Henry shares your interests. He will be working for the museum as well. Searching for medical oddities. An antiquarian."

"Will he?" Her expression molds into a most peculiar glare. Almost adversarial.

"Don't forget Henry's skills with the wax replicas," Earnest interjects, rubbing his hands together. "We were fortunate to secure him before the Smithsonian swooped in to claim him."

Arabella's eyebrows rise in interest, but the sound of someone approaching shifts her attention.

Footfalls echo through the smoke.

"What is the meaning of this?" a voice booms.

Everyone jumps in a communal start. Except father. He

straightens up, muscles tightened, ever the soldier.

His knuckles whiten as he strangles the top of his cane.

Dr. Earnest is visibly flustered. "Dr. Stygian. Arabella had an experiment go awry. Again."

Dr. Stygian towers a head taller than every man in the room. The hair on the back of my neck prickles.

Odd?

"This! This is what I mean, Earnest. "She—" he jabs an accusing finger at Arabella, "she is impulsive and arrogant and *unnatural*. She should not be considered for such an important expedition. A woman is much better suited for curation."

Father steps forward, staring Stygian full on despite the fact he's a head taller. "Sir. You've forgotten innovative and cunning and possesses her father's talent for problem solving. Is this expedition not about bones?"

"Of course."

"I dare venture no one on this eastern seaboard could match Miss Holmes's knowledge of bones."

"Arabella is a genius," I add helpfully.

I dare to glance her way. And promptly wish I hadn't.

Arabella's face is tinged purple with indignation.

She stomps forward, closing the distance in seconds.

With a toss of her head, the tumult of curls flips from her face. Her blue eyes are vicious. And beautiful.

"I am a better scientist at twenty than half your staff of port-swilling, armchair-philosophizing, smoking-jacketed morons. All debate, no action."

Earnest gasps behind me. My arms tense, Stygian's eyes go wild and bright.

Father puts a placating hand on her shoulder. "Arabella…"

She shrugs it off.

"John, you know it to be true."

His fingers land back on her shoulder and *squeeze.* "Arabella, decorum, remember? Surely all those lessons we taught in the parlor have not been forgotten?"

She averts her glare and her chest heaves, taking in huge, calming breaths.

Stygian's color rises to rival Arabella's; his black eyes murderous.

He speaks over her head, as if ignoring a naughty child's behavior. "Besides her obvious impulsive nature, she is *a woman.* Not all the men on board the steamship shall be museum employees, and I cannot vouch for their characters. She will be in danger."

Father's responding smile is wry. Arabella's head rises and their eyes lock in unspoken communication.

Father turns to Stygian. "You need not worry about her safety. Arabella is not like other girls."

"Yes, I am wholly aware," he spits, viper-like. His eyes narrow to slits as his stare bores onto her, dripping venom.

A protective surge flares in my chest and my teeth grind together.

Father interjects, "Henry will also be on the voyage. I know he would be willing to assume responsibility for her safety."

I nod, stand ramrod straight and square my shoulders. We're almost nose to nose as he unleashes the black look on me.

"Is this true, Mr. Henry Watson?"

"Of course."

Arabella's jaw pops open and snaps shut, as my father claws her shoulder.

"We will convene on this matter in a week's time. Put it to a vote with the museum council."

Stygian spins on his boot heel and exits the lab, eyeing the splintered door as he rounds the corner.

I exhale, relief flooding through me.

I turn, and smile at Arabella. "What went wrong? With your experiment?"

Arabella is not relieved. Arabella is trembling all over.

She whirls, heading for the hallway. Yelling over her shoulder, "I. Don't. Need. Protection. *From any man.*"

She stomps out the door in the opposite direction as Stygian. And is gone.

The lingering black smoke is the only proof she was ever present.

All three of us stare at the spot she's vacated.

"Boldness, be my friend," father murmurs.

I keep my gaze straight ahead, but can't help my smile. "It will have to be."

Chapter Two

BELIEFS, SHAKEN

Bella's Laboratory
Arabella

I stiffen as footsteps draw close, echoing down the hall. My eyes dart around the state of blackened, sooty chaos that was once my lab. Two hours later, at least the smoke has cleared.

I extract a tiny femur from the box of bones, spinning it round through my fingers and sigh. "At least the specimens were spared."

I force my eyes from the partially erected skeleton and toward the entry.

Footsteps echo off the hallway's high ceilings and stop, as if the visitor is pausing.

His tall form steps through the doorframe, overcoat drenched from the downpour lambasting my windows.

Henry. My heart does a strange little flip in my chest,

resulting in a cartwheeling rhythm of beats.

I've never been apt with words. I think in pictures, as my father before me.

Since my unusual childhood, my mind visualizes my feelings as the organ of my heart, sequestered in a metal box. Its outside covered with countless locks and bolts.

To keep everyone out. To love is dangerous.

It now throbs against the confines of its chamber.

Henry removes his hat, spinning it in a self-conscious circle in his hands. His hair is darker than when we were children. It was almost white-blonde. And his eyes....

"Your eyes. I don't remember them being that color, Henry."

His eyebrows rise. "Still blue. Like my heart."

I roll my eyes. "*Please*, Henry. I know you, remember. Or at least I did. Your poetry will have no effect on me."

I flush.

I've done it again. I can never discern polite conversation from taboo. I speak my thoughts, directly. Which is why I lasted all of four months at boarding school. And why I was expelled for fighting.

Practically the societal kiss-of-death for a woman.

Henry's mouth curls up on the sides into a closed lip smirk. "Poetry has no effect? Pity, that. I find it most effective with the female persuasion. Arabella, you've changed quite a bit, as well...."

Henry's hands fidget and the motion triggers images.

My mind time-travels. A tinier, happier version of us darts through my memory and across the English countryside, dirty and mischievous.

I'm instantly at ease. It's as if we've never parted. Our four year estrangement melting away.

How easily I forgive him. Too easily.

I see it too, in his eyes.

Same old Henry.

Except even larger and strikingly more handsome when last I saw him. My mind replays our final goodbye as he stepped onto the boat, bound for boarding school. The very-rare pain that had gripped my heart.

He steps closer and gently wraps his fingers around my elbow and the images flicker away.

Little shocks of excitement spark up my arm, and the heat spreads as my flush deepens. My face might catch fire at any second.

His voice drops an octave, his face becoming all seriousness. "Listen, I know you were offended by father's offer of my protection. He was merely placating Stygian. I haven't forgotten your mind, your brilliance. You thrashed me in almost every subject, so please, friends again?"

I am staring. *Stop staring.* The words, *spontaneous combustion*, keep popping in my head.

I shiver and hope he doesn't notice.

My mind flicks to our singular kiss…which changed everything.

I'd grown to detest that fateful kiss as it had wholly altered our comfortable, easy friendship into…something else entirely. Ironically, the coming together of the kiss, kept us awkwardly apart till the day he stepped on the boat. Wasting our final days together.

I shake my head, banning the memory. "Yes, Henry. I'd like to be friends again. I thought we still were."

He smiles. "Good." His eyes pick through the piles of bones. "Tell me more particulars about the expedition. I have only heard the basics. It's been a whirlwind since our arrival."

My mind sharpens. The blazing fire of obsession burning off all other thought.

I think of father, huddled over a singular piece of paper, unmoving for hours, working through a problem.

I cannot help my smile.

Henry smiles back; his eyes squint playfully as he bites his bottom lip.

I catch my breath, distracted.

This is a first. Once aboard the obsession juggernaut, I never swerve or falter. A deductive automaton. Just like father.

He clears his throat. "Arabella, the expedition?"

My mind clicks as a litany of images invade my cortex. "Remember the massive storm a few months prior; the one that snapped off tree tops like matchsticks?"

"Yes, I read of it."

"It unearthed a hand in upstate New York, and the museum acquired it. It is currently locked safely away in Earnest's office. It's twice the size of your own, Henry. And you are a tall man."

He worries his lip. "Ape?"

"It has 27 bones, the same as our hands. The sheer size; it would be larger than any ape I've ever seen. I've spent hours examining it."

"Yes, I'll wager you have."

White-hot anger flashes. I'm quite used to men having no idea what to do with me and my mind.

"The results are inconclusive. That comment was very droll. So you suggest more feminine pursuits, Henry? Has boarding school narrowed your thoughts about women? Expect me to knit, to play an instrument and speak when spoken to?"

My eyes flick to challenge his, but he merely smirks and my anger dampens as quickly as it flared. My cheeks flush at my outburst.

His eyebrows rise, but his expression is unaffected. "Your temperament still matches that hair, Bella. Well, that's a relief. I know how I may be of use."

"How's that?"

"Your sense of humor, my dear. You've lost it. Finding it will become priority. I can only assume the lack of my presence contributed to its demise," he pauses, blue eyes scrutinizing.

I feel like one of my specimens, I'm the one under the microscope.

"Yes, well, father has a very—"

"Dry sense of humor, I know. I was around him as a boy, too. It's just, in order to survive amidst these egomaniacal men of science—you must learn to control it. Stygian obviously doesn't want you on the team, then?"

"No. He was vexed that I was actually granted a curation position. He doesn't believe in women venturing out of the home. Or being worth more than child-deposit-boxes."

A memory flashes. Stygian's hands, rough against my bare arm.

The hot color on my face deepens. I turn away quickly,

but he catches it.

"Arabella? What aren't you telling me? It's more than that. Did he try to woo you? And you spurned him?"

I laugh, and almost taste the bitter. "*Woo* is a very interesting way to put it."

Henry goes rigid, clutching my elbow again. He spins me to face him but I cast my eyes to the floor.

Father warned me of my eyes. How they never, ever lie.

Henry's warm, large fingers grasp under my chin, turning my face up to force my gaze. "Did he—? What happened?"

Henry's face glows a furious red, a muscle bulging in his jaw.

"I'm fine." I blush when I realize what he's asking. "It's nothing, it's over. He is not worth the worry. I'm sorry Henry. I just, well, I'm sure you remember. I don't—I'm not like other girls. I just can't be. I gave up trying."

Especially after the fiasco that was our kiss.

He nods, nostrils flaring as he exhales through his teeth. His long body eases, his thigh brushing mine as he relaxes against the lab bench.

His hand slips too slowly from my cheek. His eyes skip across my face, trying to read me.

"I remember. But I also remember you were my favorite playmate. I never knew what adventure you'd dream up."

I smile. *I must get him off the Stygian subject.*

"One side has proposed the skeleton is a Nephilim."

"From the Bible, the book of Jude?"

I nod, feeling the hair on my arms rise. I rub furiously, trying to quiet them. "Yes, the angels who forsook their dwelling in the heavens—"

"To mate with women. Their offspring were giants."

I nod. "Nephilim. The mighty men of old. I plan to write a paper disputing it. Proving the bones are Neanderthal."

Henry cocks his head, frowning. "Really? Without any data, you're already forming a hypothesis? That does not sound like any Holmes I've ever met."

"I believe in *science*, Henry. And in myself. Nothing else."

"Ah."

His expression is so smug my hands ball into fists.

"What does *that* mean?"

He shrugs.

I begin to pace. "This position at the Mutter…is everything. Father called in a myriad of favors to secure this placement. I've never fit in. Not in sewing circles or with giggling girls or with anyone, anywhere. But *here*." I stare up at the bones, with more affection than I know to be acceptable. "The museum is a home built of science. This I understand, nay I *excel* in. And if I was forced to leave…"

Henry's gaze is rapt, never leaving my face and he swallows. "I recall one other place you always fit perfectly."

I bite my lip, perplexed. "Your father's morgue?"

He rolls his eyes and steps closer once again. "With me, you intolerably obtuse girl."

Heat and fear for my heart flush my cheeks.

"As for science, I have witnessed events without explanation," he says quietly.

"Preposterous."

My embarrassment fizzles to dread as I see it, over his shoulder, on the windowsill.

The black Swallowtail butterfly should not be out. Out in the rain. And it's almost too late in the season. The coppery taste of fear floods my mouth.

The butterfly alights from the sill, coming to rest on the case. Its wings beat slowly, as if mourning its fallen, under-glass comrades.

Henry registers my expression and follows my gaze. "What is the meaning of all those butterflies? I thought you were strictly a bone collector?"

A chorus of voices silences my reply. A small crowd approaches, their laughter growing louder as they draw near.

Henry's face drains.

"What is it? What's wrong?" I raise my hand, and it hovers above his arm. I want to touch him, to be bold.

But the opportunity passes as Dr. Earnest, Dr. Watson and two women enter; their raucous laughter ringing in my ears.

My hand drops back to my side.

The women's glares simultaneously rove over my unfashionable dress, my ink-stained fingers and bestow identical cat-like challenges disguised as smiles.

Women, as a rule, hate me.

John motions to Henry. "Henry, may I present Dr. Earnest's daughter, Priscilla."

Priscilla bats her eyelashes at Henry, tapered fingers playfully twisting a perfect blonde spiral.

"So wonderful to meet you, Henry. Will you be accompanying us to dinner?"

Henry's eyes find mine. "I was going to help Arabella—"

Dr. Watson cuts across him. "Of course he will. Arabella won't mind, will you dear?"

John leads the women, one on each arm, toward the door. He launches a death-stare and a stiff nod over his shoulder for Henry to follow.

I quickly turn away and bend down to sweep the soot and broken glass from the floor to hide my expression.

"Arabella...I shall see you tomorrow."

"Of course."

When I hear his footsteps fade away, I turn to stare at the butterfly, still batting its wings at a maddeningly slow pace. As if it languishes to torture me.

"Go. Away."

It takes flight, soaring through the air, weaving in and out of the suspended skeletons, and rebelliously lands two feet from my hand. I blow, hard enough to flutter the black wings and it finally retreats toward the window.

I track it, boots frozen to the floor, until it finally slips out the window.

"Henry, Henry, you are a show dog to be trotted about."

What concern of it is mine, what Henry thinks, or about John's matchmaking schemes?

A worry, heavy as a granite ball has lodged in my throat. My muscles convulsively attempt to swallow it.

Father's voice echoes; burned into my memory, after a particularly awkward ball. Delivered in his usual take-no-prisoners, way.

"Arabella, a *wife-in-the-making*, you are not. But science, perhaps that may be your beau." And then quietly, as he walked away, "I hope it will be enough."

I jam my eyes shut. A foreign feeling wraps around my windpipe, threatening strangulation. My hands cover my mouth as I struggle to master my breathing.

A sharp pain throbs in my chest as if the glass shards have spirited off the floor and embedded into my beating heart.

I feel color heat my face as I replay my confession to Henry, about this place...and his response. I'm struck with the urge to find him—to tell him more.

I sit still and close my eyes and inhale deep breaths. I never, ever reveal the inner workings of my mind.

But this was always the problem...and *the draw* of Henry Watson. He made me confess my heart.

I picture it rattling its accession that I find him, tell him, hold nothing back.

"Be quiet."

The tittering girls on John's arms fill my head, mocking me.

I thought I was sensible. I struggle to name this unfamiliar emotion.

Jealousy. I am jealous.

Chapter Three

Henry

I match father's quick strides as we hurry across the Mutter campus toward the museum proper.

"Are you ready then, Henry?" Father's voice is light, but his eyes are serious. "Stygian is not to be trifled with; all the months studying in Paris come down to this..."

"I know," I snap. I clear my throat. "Sorry. Nerves."

"Of course."

The molds. The doctors here are mad-keen for them.

Moulage is the more civilized name for my wax figures which capture the shape and size of disease, so that physicians may more easily classify the afflictions.

The Philadelphia Indian summer is fading and I shiver as a breeze ruffles my hair.

We pass through the black wrought-iron gates

26

surrounding the Mutter and climb the stairs to the entrance. I swallow as father heaves the massive wood door open. It's as if their towering architecture was designed for the Nephilim.

I give father a wry smile and exhale through my teeth. We pass behind the large marble staircase, into the top floor of a double-decker room.

The first floor is littered with glass cases in various states of repair while the ceiling is yawning open, allowing those on the second floor to peer down.

I stare over the edge and catch a flash of Arabella's auburn hair and a young man's stooped posture. I recognize Jeremy, my fellow antiquarian; the only man in the Mutter with whom I could possibly tolerate sharing a pint.

We walk slowly down the staircase and the sight gives me pause. It's the strangest room I've ever seen.

Like Poe's nightmares have materialized and then been neatly categorized for humankind's education.

Wall to wall oddities, each more horrifying than the last. Brains, suspended in fluid, plaster molds of a pair of conjoined twins, fused at the torso.

Arabella completely ignores us. She lifts a skull from inside a box and holds it aloft, her eyes roving across it.

Jeremy hurries over, extending his hand. "Wonderful to see you again. Welcome aboard, Henry. So, they hired you for your *'moulages?'"*

Father is trying not to smile. I try not to pummel him.

The room is suddenly a blazing inferno. I force the fidget from my hands.

Arabella's intense gaze fixates on us. "But I thought the

European masters were very secretive?" she prompts. "That's why we've had to ship all of our models in from abroad."

When it becomes apparent I am mute, father answers for me. He gives me one more *last-chance* glance and rolls his eyes.

"They are. But...Holmes and I have *contacts* across Europe."

Arabella nods. "Of course." Then in a lower voice, "People who owe you favors." She mumbles as she walks away, "The very reason I am here as well."

In seconds, her focus is back on the skulls; placing one on a shelf and plucking another out of the box.

I set down my box and extract two wax figures surrounded by bell jars; the first of a child's arm with smallpox, the other of a gangrenous lower leg.

Father checks his watch. "I'll leave you to it then. See you this evening Henry. Don't forget to prepare for your presentation," father says.

Now I roll *my* eyes.

"What presentation?" Arabella is all eyes again. She spies the molds and hurries back over. Her inability to remain in one place for more than ten seconds is giving me vertigo.

"Dr. Stygian and I are giving a phrenology lecture tomorrow if you'd like to attend."

"I have to be moving, too, or I'll be Stygian-meat. I'll be at the lecture. It sounds fascinating," Jeremy interjects over his shoulder. He's walking across the museum floor, into the adjoining room. He disappears as the door clicks shut.

Arabella scoffs, "Psuedo-science."

She bends to stare at the molds. "May I?" She nods

toward the specimens.

"Of course."

Her dark blue eyes squint and scrutinize. After a moment she nods. "They're quite good, Henry. Dr. Earnest chose well."

She spins, heading back to her categorization.

I walk over to her pile of bones. She's particularly lovely today without the frills, in trousers, black boots and a white shirt. They hug and accentuate her every curve. I swallow and avert my eyes, which dart to a glass case and a very long...*colon*.

I shrug. "I'm not sure I put much stock in phrenology either, but I did do the coursework, so figured I'd assist Stygian. It was before...we talked."

About him. About his need to acquire you like some artifact.

She waves the words away without pulling her eyes from the skull.

"Quiz-time, genius. Pray, tell me, why do we have this skull?"

She's asking me to identify abnormalities. A test.

I force myself to examine it, not her. I squint and rub my chin, considering.

A long jagged line puzzles across the forehead, cutting it in half. I estimate the age of the specimen by the size of the head.

"Persistent frontal sutures. They should've disappeared with the fontanelles as a younger child. It results in the egg-shaped skull."

Her face lights up. "Very good. You may be after my job."

She flips up another. "This one?"

This head is gruesome. Porous holes have eaten into the forehead, trickling down to distort the nasal area. "Syphilis damage."

Arabella drops it and claps her hands. "You *have* studied."

She manages to be condescending and charming. Just like her father.

I smile. Arabella's reaction to science is like Priscilla's reaction to a new gown.

"Did Stygian give you the tour?"

My teeth grit together. I can't stop imagining him touching her hand, her back ... it's more than I can stand.

Angered revulsion bubbles in my chest.

She's staring, her lips pouty and perplexed. My grimace is reflected in the mirror behind her.

"Sorry." I banish the thought. "No, I've not had a proper tour. Would you do me the honors, Miss Holmes?"

"Delighted, Mr. Watson."

To my great happiness, her arm slides through mine. Attraction tingles up my spine and my collar's suddenly three sizes too small.

I lose focus. She's talking. I struggle to pay attention.

I thought four years away would lessen her hold.

She drops my arm and turns to stare. "Henry! Really, are you always so distractible?"

Only in your presence.

I hear father's words regarding Arabella, and my feelings toward her, delivered on the day of my departure as she walked away.

"Some distance, Henry, and you will gain perspective.

You are very young. I am sure this trip to France shall expand your horizons."

I clear my throat.

"I'm sorry. I've much on my mind. I promise to be a better pupil. Continue."

She sighs like I'm one of her charges.

I stare up at the loft above. The entire perimeter of the square is lined with cases and the smell of formaldehyde stifles the air.

"One of our duties is to venture out and secure the specimens when the calls arrive?"

She nods. "Yes. You, I, and Jeremy Montgomery."

She walks ahead and halts in front of the first case. Several bits of brains float and bob in glass bell jars.

"The brains of murderers. This one killed all three of his wives. They dissected them—"

"To try to determine what constitutes a fiend?"

"Essentially."

Skulls of various species sit in a row: orangutan, capuchin monkey, crocodiles, cats and dogs. "These need no explanation."

I halt at a picture of a young woman I instantly recognize.

"Laura Dewey Bridgman. The first blind-deaf mute to learn to communicate." A flash of memory skips through my head. "Didn't you have a doll with the eyes poked out that you named Laura?"

She smiles. "I and every other small girl of my age. We were all inspired by her."

Arabella gestures to a partially full case. My eye twitches. Stillborns inhabit the glass jars, each suspended in their fluid filled coffin.

Arabella's normally smooth face pinches. "Conjoined twins, tethered at the cranium." She averts her eyes and gestures without looking. "Anencephaly—born with portions of the cranium and brain missing. Well, you can read them. They're all labeled." She walks away and very quietly adds, "*By me.*"

She turns to leave, headed back toward the comfort of her beloved bones.

My head whips toward a tumult on the staircase.

Montgomery is taking the stairs two at a time in a gangly whirl of arms and legs. A man-sized spider.

"Arabella, a stillborn call has arrived." He shoves a piece of paper into her hand. "Stygian says to make it a priority, and that only you should go. Sorry."

Arabella stiffens, holding the paper in the tips of her fingers as if he's handed her a serpent.

She presses her lips white and nods.

Montgomery hurries back up the steps, shooting me a salute. "See you at dinner, Henry."

Arabella's frozen, staring at the paper. It begins to rattle in her hand.

I hurry to her side and gently touch her arm. "What is it?"

She whirls, her mouth contorting with dread. "*He knows* I do not wish to acquire the stillborns. It's the singular request I've placed in the year since I've been here. I stay later than the others and I'm more precise and I work harder. It's never enough."

Her eyes widen and fly to the case. Her shoulders shake

as if stricken with palsy, her fingers splay against the glass.

"They—they *affect* me, Henry. Stygian does it to grind in the point. That I am a woman and do not belong here. That my feminine constitution is not compatible with science."

I take her hand and fight the haze induced with touching her and extract the paper.

"I'll do it, Bella."

"No one ever called me that but you." She squeezes her eyes tight, fidgeting with a baby-blue ribbon around her neck. She gives it a compulsive tug, and I glimpse a small silver key. She drops it and stares me full on.

"He will be cross." She shrugs, "Like any other day. Henry... thank you. I will come, however. Stygian is perpetually searching for a cause to dismiss me. How might I repay you?"

I move across the room, shrugging on my coat. "Come to the phrenology lecture."

She sighs. "Fine."

Henry

The carriage rattles through the night. I glance at my pocket watch.

Bella is as silent as Laura Dewey-Brigman. She hasn't uttered a word since we departed the Mutter.

I have seen this...*stillness* before, in Holmes. When in

pursuit, his body could remain immobile for hours; a sure sign his mind performed mental acrobatics.

It was disturbing. One without knowledge of the Holmes family might've thought him, or her, catatonic.

Bella's hands suddenly jerk to life, and absently stroke the black and white dog between us. He cocks his head to stare and whines.

Words fail me, too. What might I say to calm her? This horrendous deed must be done.

We arrive at the address, 22 Riddle Run Road.

Jameson, the museum coachman, opens the door, extending his hand to Arabella. His concerned, ancient eyes sweep across the sprawling brick home and then back to Bella's face.

I suspect he's accompanied her to past acquisitions.

Arabella steps out to stare at the building as resignation blackens her features.

She squares her shoulders. "Henry. I will do it. Just... wait in the carriage."

I open my mouth to protest, but she's halfway up the walk.

Newton, her dog, follows, his tail tucked between his legs. She traverses the walk, backlit against the yellow light. The dog halts, sitting to wait, without a word from her.

Fear for her closes my throat. A primal need to protect her.

"Blast. I cannot sit in this infernal carriage."

I scramble out to wait beside the dog.

She hesitates, fingers tracing the knocker; a horrible

gargoyle. Her shaking fist raps on the door.

The tremors intensify; up her arm, through her shoulders, till her whole body quivers.

I hurry to her side and glance down, expecting her fury.

She meets my eyes, and I don't see anger but instead, a gratefulness.

I raise my fist and knock hard on the wood. Mid-rap, the door opens and a squat, red-faced man appears, dabbing his forehead with a handkerchief.

The man extends a fat hand, pumping mine unconsciously. A large round ring, sporting an *R-* bumps against my finger.

A feminine wail pierces the hall, like a woman being murdered. Hair stands to attention all over my body.

I nod. "Sir. We received the call to come to collect the child."

"Children, actually. Thank you. My wife is upstairs. Nasty business, this. Triplets. Two dead, one still on the way, God willing."

He hurries up the stairs, and Arabella and I follow.

Her shoulders hitch as she fights to maintain her breathing, but her face is chiseled from stone.

"In here." He motions into a room adjacent to the birthing room.

We step inside and my mind reviles in horror.

Blood, so much blood.

Stained white sheets pile on the floor, blood-filled basins and forceps litter the table. I jam my eyes shut to reorient myself and feel my nostrils flare.

The salty-copper smell saturates the air and fills my

mouth. The sanguine smell of death.

Arabella curtsies to the midwife, bowing her head in reverence for the dead. "Madame Cutler? We are here for the babies."

The gray-haired midwife sighs, pressing her chalky lips tight. She wipes her brow with her blood-stained fingers and it leaves a macabre streak. "We tried, Miss Holmes. But sometimes—"

Arabella holds up her hand. "I know. I know you've done your best. You always do."

A feminine howl erupts from behind the closed door. Bella and I start at the sound. "There is still one child on the way?" I prompt.

"Yes."

A small housekeeper bustles around, gathering the bloody sheets, her face is ashen as she mumbles. "I say the mistress is better off. She looked at the moon, she did. If this baby lives it will be at best a sleepwalker, and worst, a lunatic."

I harrumph. "Absurd. Might I be of assistance, Midwife Cutler, is it?"

"That's quite enough, Fanny." Madame Cutler rolls her eyes, lowering her voice. "She's new, and we're down two maids. Ignore whatever comes out of her mouth."

Another wail. But this one is made of melancholy and seeps around the door, as if the woman's hope is fading.

"What do you know of birthing?" The midwife's face is skeptical. "The town doctor is indisposed at present. An how old are you, boy?"

"Only a score and three, I'm afraid. However, my father

is a doctor and insisted I be instructed on as many areas of medicine he could squeeze into my school breaks. I am by no means a physician, but have seen my fair share of births."

"Against my will," I add, low enough so only Bella may hear.

The midwife turns, conferring with the maid.

Arabella whispers, "Liar. You are not yet twenty and three."

"Only off by weeks." I raise an eyebrow. "You aren't helping."

Another wail and the midwife whirls. "Fine. I need any help I can get."

Arabella's eyebrows have disappeared beneath her fringe and she's shaking all over.

I turn around to stare at her. "You don't have to come in."

She quickly shakes her head. "No. I'm coming."

We follow the matron into the room. Bella leans against the wall, her face a blank, white slate.

The midwife steps quickly back into position between the mother's legs and I slip in beside her.

"The baby is crowning." A brown tuft of wet hair appears.

"Ahh! Please, please Mrs. Cutler, save this one." The mistress of the house is gaunt and haggard; her pale complexion proclaims her time is fading.

"Shush now, Missy. Save yer strength."

A contraction rocks the protruding belly but the head doesn't budge.

"You see?"

My eyes drift up the woman's unnaturally small waist;

undoubtedly corseted till her innards were hour-glassed.

"Like a camel through the eye of a needle." I sift through my deliveries with father. A spark of hope lights and my mind fans the flame. "Might you have any chloroform?"

"Aye. Just a spot left. Susie, attend her." The nurse bustles to the woman's head as the pungent smell floats down to the two of us.

"Do you have scissors?"

"Yes."

"Clean them."

"How?"

"Scorch them over the flames." I gesture to the roaring fire. "Hurry, please. We haven't much time."

The nurse returns and I feel the still-warm metal slide into my palm.

"What are you doing?" The midwife is horrified.

"I am going to make an incision...to widen the birth canal. I've seen my father do it on several occasions. And I've... done it once."

"Let him try! Look at her!" Arabella's normally-low voice is high with fear.

The woman's respirations are slowing. Her chest barely rising and falling. "She's lost a good deal of blood."

The midwife notices, too. We will lose the mother as well.

"Alright. Go on then."

I slide the scissors to her perineum. The next few moments are like an automobile ride, with time streaming too-fast, leaving me slightly dizzy.

The hard muted click of metal through soft flesh.

A wail; a rock-hard contraction. "Bear down Missy! Push with everything ye got!"

The lodged head depresses into the fleshy crease I've created, sliding beneath her pubic bone.

A gush of amniotic fluid and blood and soft-baby-skin slide into my arms. *A boy.*

I smile so wide it's painful.

Hands slide around him as the nurse whisks him away.

'*Thwack*'. The nurse smacks his tiny bottom.

I hold my breath, thinking of the stained sheets in the adjoining vestibule. *Please let him live, please let him breathe.*

A lamb-like cry fills the air, breathing life back into the room.

My heart slows and I feel the relief flooding my arms and legs, weighting them. I move alongside the midwife, showing her where and how to stitch up my incision.

I turn to Bella. She clears her throat. "Well, well done Mr. Watson."

I nod.

The midwife calls over her shoulder, still tending to the afterbirth. "That was quite a trick, Mr. Watson. I will be in touch. I want to hear all your father has taught you. It is a bleedin shame you aren't deliverin' babies. The...poor lambs are in the adjoining room."

The mere step over the threshold is like a journey cross the River Styx.

I shiver and the nurse hurries to our side. She eases a misshapen bundle into Arabella's arms. Her chin trembles once and she swallows.

Arabella nods and we turn without another word. I tip my hat to the nurse and hurry behind her.

Bella cradles the bundle gingerly, as if not to disturb the babies of their rest.

I feel my eyes sting and the protective fury ignite.

Angry at this grim life, anger for their tiny, snuffed lives and anger at that pompous, in-need-of-a-thrashing moron for putting her through this punishment.

Bella's breathing is ragged and she's already ghosted down the steps, moving so fast I wonder if her feet are touching the floor.

She nods to the master of the house, and without a word, steps out the door.

The night air is a welcome relief and I gratefully suck it in; its clean smell washes away the toxic thoughts clouding my head.

Arabella hurries to the carriage. She places the bundle in Jameson's hands with such gentle care; I have to swallow the thick tightening that's suddenly in my throat.

Their brother's wail drifts out through the open window as if lamenting their loss.

Jameson lumbers to the back of the carriage, depositing the corpses in a specially-designed box.

Arabella scrambles into the carriage without looking back, Newton at her heels.

I peek in the window. Head bowed, eyes closed, she could be praying beneath the hood. She bends to pick up her bag from the floor. The dog wiggles his way under her hand, nudging for affection.

Stygian is a monster. How many times has he forced her to face this—to prove her worth? To torture her for spurning his advances or to reinforce her place is home and hearth?

I've crafted moulages of smallpox, elephantitis, and even a woman with a horn growing out of her forehead.

Dug through troughs of dissected arms and legs to memorize the human physick.

But *this*—these innocents.

Their lives over before it has even begun; they've had no chance at all.

The carriage rattles forward but Bella will not meet my eyes, her hands aimlessly fidgeting with the dog's collar.

Her head suddenly whips to stare at me directly, and her lips move, but no words issue forth.

"Something on your mind?"

Her head drops and she stares at her lap, appearing to wrestle with her thoughts.

"I." Her face puckers, like the words cause her physical pain.

"Yes. I'm listening." I sit stock-still, waiting.

"I find it very hard to put my vexations to words, Henry."

I nod and smile, trying to ease her discomfort. She sighs. "I. Had a sister. A stillborn sister. I only found out a few years prior. Ever since…I have nightmares about her. And these calls—"

"Make them worse." The smiles slips from my face and I reach over to grasp her hand. "I didn't know. I'm sorry."

She nods, and stares out the window once again.

Chapter Four

A Master of Disguise

Outside The Mutter
Henry

I just finish mopping the blood from my waistcoat as the carriage rattles in front of the Mutter's wrought-iron gates and Bella's hand is on the door before it has come to a stop. She hops out and a surprised Jameson ejects, "Miss Holmes?"

She spins. "Henry, could you be a dear and deliver the bundle to Montgomery?"

She eyes Newton who is trotting happily at her heels. "Newton, home."

The dog whines, but obediently turns, tail between his legs to slip through the open gate.

I scramble out, trying not to let Bella out of my sight, but she's almost at the corner. "Jameson, could you..."

The older man sighs. "Yes, Mr. Watson. You best hurry.

She's a crafty one."

"I am well aware."

I bound after her, but she's managed to turn the corner into a darkened alley.

"Blast."

I follow suite, eyes sweeping the dark street. *How far could she possibly get?*

I don't see her anywhere and I feel my heart thrum in my mouth.

The dirty sideway is strewn with a few vagabonds, assorted trollops and drunken couples who nuzzle under shadowy gaslight.

My hands fidget and find my hair. Twirling it nervously. "Bella. Bella. Where are you?"

A gaggle of street-walkers flirt with a pair of Johns.

I see one alone.

Ah. They always travel in pairs, for safety.

I pick up my pace, heading toward the bustling woman.

My eyes narrow. Her dress is hiked to reveal stockings and shapely calves. Her curls are piled on her head and…my eyes flick to her boots.

A flash of recognition: my eyes snap back to the nape of her neck. *A baby-blue ribbon.*

My mouth pops open. Desire pumps through my veins and I allow myself the luxury of taking in her every curve.

Ten feet. Her calves look impossibly strong yet feminine.

Five feet. Her tiny, tiny waist. I envision my hands wrapping around it, pulling her flush against me.

It's so small. She looks so fragile.

My thinking brain overrides my animal brain with a whip-snap and I hear my father's refrain in my head. "Focus, Henry."

I fall into step beside her, synchronizing our footfalls.

"I'm done for the night, sir." Eyes painted black with liner flick to mine. They widen in surprise then tighten with anger.

"Henry. What are you playing at?"

"Bella, what *are you* playing at? And how in the world did you change so quickly?"

My mind flashes to the oversized bag on her lap in the carriage. Then to my childhood, to Holmes's myriad of disguises. She's learned from the master.

Ahead, two policemen walking their beat cross the road, heading directly toward us.

She grabs my arm, tucking me into the alley's cranny.

She pushes her body against mine and I instinctively return the favor.

"Henry," she chastises.

I hear the footsteps. She grabs the rim of my hat, tilting my head to hers, hiding my face. Our lips are inches apart. Her breath puffs hot against my chin.

"Bella." My voice sounds gruff.

I'm certain it sounds thick with anger, but that could not be further from the truth.

"Just bloody hold still till they pass. Pretend you desire me."

I almost laugh aloud at this irony, but quickly assume the position as the footsteps halt, linger and shuffle, then proceed to walk on.

She backs up, giving me space and spins away, peering 'round the corner.

"They have gone. I must go. Go back to the Mutter, Henry."

The rage returns. "Are you mad? I am not going anywhere."

She stamps her foot. "You are so very frustrating. Fine. Here." She jams the bag into my hand. "For the love of mercy put something on so your face isn't screaming, 'I-don't-belong-here.'"

I rifle through the contents and slide on a battered bowler and a scarf. She eyes me, evaluating, and proceeds to stoop and scoop a handful of mud which she promptly flings across my boots.

"Hey!"

"There. Not perfect, but it shall have to do. Time is of the essence."

We're walking down the street again and the only sound is the slur of drunken voices and songs emitting from the corner pub.

A tall man turns onto the street and Bella misses a step.

The man's physique forcibly reminds me of Stygian, but as I look closer, I confirm his clothes too shabby and his demeanor too meek.

Still, she too, was thrown by his appearance. A revelation hits.

"You are following Stygian, aren't you?"

Arabella purses her lips then exhales. "No, that would have been a happy coincidence," she says wryly. "But he is up to something. I think he had another reason to send me on the call tonight, aside from torturing me, that is. I believe he wanted me occupied and away from The Mutter."

Ahead looms a factory, a brothel and a church.

"Please be the church," I mutter.

I see her lip twitch as she fights a smile but she doesn't respond.

I follow as she veers toward the factory, where a ramshackle sign proclaims, 'Bane's Meats'.

She ducks around the side of the building to where a door stands ajar and a sliver of light cuts the darkness of the alley.

A young, fresh-faced man of just-eighteen appears at the door. His eyes light upon seeing Arabella. "Hello, beautiful."

"Allo, Jimmy." Arabella's cockney is impeccable. I fight my jaw and manage to prevent its gaping. "Did you find what we discussed?"

Jimmy registers my presence and scowls. "Who's he?"

"'E's just me brother, never fear. Streets ain't safe nowadays. He insisted on coming."

Jimmy straightens his tie. "Alright then." He slides a long folder from beneath his jacket and presses it into Bella's palm, letting his fingers linger on hers.

She gently extracts them. "Thank you. I'll be sure you get the money. Be careful, now, and keep your ear to the ground."

Bella turns to me, but is whirled back by his grasp. "I'd much rather have a romp with you. You can keep the money."

"Perhaps another time." Bella slides her hand away but gives him a smile that would scorch any man's soul.

I unclench my jaw. When we're out of earshot, I whisper

pointing to the envelope. "What is it?"

"An inventory list for the meat company. For the prior three months."

"Why?" I prompt.

She quickens her pace. "We haven't the time now. Later."

"I shall hold you to that. Has Stygian mentioned if you are approved for the expedition?"

Bella shakes her head. "No. Not a word. I shall have to wait for the committee to decide my fate."

The Mutter is two blocks away and Bella halts so quickly I step twice before I can stop.

"I will duck in here and change Henry. I will see you tomorrow."

And before I can protest, she is gone.

###

Arabella

I stare out my cottage window. Anxiety twists in my gut and can no longer stay still. I pace as my stomach churns—too many changes, too much hanging in the balance. I detest change. The rhythm of routine soothes me.
I force myself to halt and take a deep breath.

Math problems scribble and erase in my mind, calming my wits. Their never-changing nature an anchor for my mind.

I close my eyes and press my head against the cold

window pane.

Calculations and written words appear and disappear like cognitive fireflies in my mind; but they scatter as Stygian's scowling face appears.

I ruminate, murmuring the inventory list over and over like a chant. The one ingredient's use escapes me.

My mind is normally photographic with text; I may bring up a page just as I saw it, almost automatically.

However, when I think on this particular ingredient—I merely get blurry flashes. I stamp my foot in frustration.

I wish fervently for my father's mammoth library. I recall the smell of leather and pipe-smoke, and deeply associate their presence with books.

I could only bring so many volumes on the vessel from England.

I remember there is a comprehensive compilation in the Mutter…in the study between Stygian and Earnest's rooms.

In my childhood, John and his family were forever the balance of my life. I visualize my two influences as scales, tipped one way or the other. John's family, warm and social, and my life with father—a whirlwind of science and study and silence.

The memory of Stygian's hand on my cheek and his breath on my neck stays me. I fight the compulsion to act. To go and find the book this moment.

"Be reasonable."

I hear John's voice warning against my impulsive nature. Father and I were much too similar—he often encouraging my little jaunts as '*brilliant*'.

I pace faster and step onto the porch, whistling for

Newton once again. The Mutter's black bricks appear more foreboding in the night. I check my watch. Newton has been gone for over an hour.

"That isn't like him at all."

A tickle of worry bids me rub my arms. I permit them to wrap around my waist. That dog, all my dogs, mean so very much to me. They lavish me in love, asking for little in return.

Quite the opposite of my experience with humans. Who seem to take, take, take and are rarely satisfied.

I cup my hands and whistle again and scan the courtyard. No one. Quiet and still as the cemetery across the street.

"Newton, come!"

I pause, listening for the tinkle of his silver bell. Nothing.

"Blast that dog."

I turn to grasp my boots but a bark stays my hand. Newton is bounding across the lawn, dragging…I squint.

Dragging a very long bone. "Come Newton."

Intuition, like the whispery touch of a spider, prickles up my spine.

His claws click on the wooden steps as he hurries inside to hide his treasure.

I quickly shut the door and lock it and stare. I walk to the kitchen and return with a bit of meat. He drops the bone, wagging his tail.

I stoop and hold it in my hands, tracing the ridges. The end that is intact is slanted. "That is most definitely a femur."

The other end is cracked off. I spin the bone to peer inside and I stoop and hold it in my hands, tracing the ridges.

I walk to the fireplace and snatch my monocle from the

mantle, hastily jamming it over my eye.

I suck in my breath.

The compact bone in the center is one-fourth full. The walls suddenly seem to be lurching toward me and are squeezing my last bit of breath.

"It's human."

My mind races back to the list of ingredients from the factory.

I return to the door and fling it open, jamming the bone beneath Newton's nose. "Find."

His tail tucks between his legs and he whines. "Newton, I said, *Find*!"

He pads off the porch and I follow, already certain of where he will take me.

Chapter Five

Mutter's Catacomb of Hallways
Next Morn
Henry

Even in broad daylight the Mutter manages to cast an eerie atmosphere. My eyes flick across the glass cases; the first filled with humans skulls showing a smattering of mankind's pestilences and in the second, three fully erected skeletons are wired and stand at eternal attention.

I cock my head and note that the man's skeleton rests a bony hand, bracingly upon the child's shoulder. I purse my lips.

Perhaps Bella does have a tiny, tiny sense of humor.

I have no reason to be wandering the Mutter. I am supposed to be unpacking. When father arrives and happens on my belongings, piled in the center of my cottage there will be a minor skirmish.

I walk further down the hall and my paltry collection of moulages now sit behind their own glass encasement for the world to view. I experience a fleeting prideful moment before the crush of further responsibilities smothers it.

I need to begin again—I have many more to sculpt before the team departs to search for the rest of the body. But a nagging need refuses to leave me; I must see her before I begin.

She was once in my every thought. Till I departed for boarding school.

With every year, every girl, every ball, I hoped her hold on me would lessen. And it had.

Before arriving at the Mutter, I only thought of her several times a week, rather than a day.

Images of all my crumpled letters, overflowing my bin at school, taunt and remind me…she never really vacated my mind. She just moved to the back corner, waiting impatiently to re-introduce herself.

I walk past the display of shrunken heads and realize, "I am utterly lost."

Nothing looks familiar; I haven't yet memorized the Mutter's catacombs.

And then I hear it. A woman's voice humming, *Let Me Call You Sweetheart*.

It's her. I swallow and follow the sound.

It's surprisingly close to pitch-perfect.

I stand outside the door, collecting myself.

As I turn inside, I feel my smile falter. "What the deuce?"

Arabella's eyes are wide. "Henry?" She stares around the room, looking embarrassed and stands to brush off her pants.

A few tiny bones sprinkle to the floor and she bends to scoop them into her palm.

The room is a veritable stable, albeit, a frozen one.

My eyes skim left: badger, bobcat and a bear, rearing on skeletal hind legs are the welcoming committee. Even without flesh I'm able to identify them.

I walk toward her, passing a deer, elk and..."Is that a bloody alligator?"

She smiles timidly. "Yes."

"How? Why?"

She launches. "I was corresponding with an anthropologist and he explained the only real way to distinguish between animal and human bones would be to study and re-assemble them so I've been collecting them since I arrived—"

"How did you obtain them?"

"Many ways. Hunters, the police inspector. Once they heard what I was doing everyone has been ever-so-helpful and—"

"And those?" My finger points behind her to another freakish scene of animal-suspended-animation.

She shrugs. "Taxidermied ones. Jeremy has been helping me. And a friend from town."

I try to picture any other female assisting Bella and almost laugh. "I assume this *friend* is a male?"

"Of course. He has been ever so helpful."

"I'll bet he has."

"So." She cocks her head, looking awkward, my implications completely lost on her. "What did you need, Henry?"

I battle my expression—trying for care-not, but most

likely only achieving awkward.

What did I want? To say this is my dream appointment but now that I'm within five feet of you I cannot bloody-well think of moulages or anything else?

"I. I thought we might have dinner. To discuss your thoughts on the Nephilim versus Neanderthal controversy?"

Her face blushes as scarlet as her hair. "I don't know if we'll have time. The expedition departure is looming and I don't even know if I've been approved yet. You know how Stygian feels—"

"Has Stygian dropped any hints, one way or the other?"

Bella shakes her head. "No. Apparently the decision will rest solely on the committee's ruling."

"Miss Holmes." Stygian's voice is grave.

He sweeps past the petrified menagerie as if the presence of skeletal animals are as ordinary as the sun's rising and setting.

His eyes only see Bella.

I clear my throat.

He regards me for a mere second and nods. "Mr. Watson."

His attention snaps back to her.

She squares her shoulder slightly? "Sir?"

"Have you finished cataloguing the new shipment?"

"Not yet…"

"Might I suggest you return to your lab and do so? Surely Mr. Watson and these…specimens, can spare your attention?"

Stygian eyes me warily. "And you, Mr. Watson. Settled in, all unpacked, are we? Prepared for departure?"

"Erm." I step backward, heading for the hallway. I make eye contact with Bella from behind his back. She gives me a scarcely perceptible dismissal.

I hesitate—but her eyes narrow.

"Not really, sir. I'll just be going there now."

Henry

Darkness has swallowed Philadelphia whole; I am considering a walk because my frayed nerves would not even consider permitting me rest, but the stench is so overpowering tonight I've settled with hovering around my window.

It's only been a day since we left Riddle Run Road and the mysterious meat factory but Arabella and the poor babies refuse to vacate my head.

And that bloody list. What items on an inventory sheet could be worthy of a disguise and a stroll through Philadelphia's most dangerous district?

Stygian has seemed almost deliberately keeping Bella and I so very busy I haven't had a moment alone with her to discuss anything at all.

I stand at the window, resting my forehead against the cool pane. My assigned cottage is in view of Arabella's.

There's no movement next door and dread does a little dance up my spine as I chew my cuticle.

I sigh and stare around the room. The museum certainly doesn't invest its money in housing.

A threadbare rug covers the hardwood floor. A great fieldstone hearth rambles to the ceiling. It's only four rooms, but since arriving, I live at this table…by the window.

I'm embarrassed to admit I spend most of my time staring out of it.

Directly at Bella's cottage.

Like tonight.

Her bedroom is the second window at the back of the cottage, and each and every night since my arrival, I wait. Wait for her to turn in for the night.

I am unable to retire until she dims the lights. It gives me some sort of odd comfort, knowing she's safe in her bed. I imagine the black and white dog standing sentry beside her.

I slump into the chair and fiddle with the teacup; I grit my teeth against its tinny rattle.

It's only natural to be concerned for her welfare.

My face flushes at my denial. The longing stirs and I close my eyes.

I think of Priscilla and father's matchmaking schemes, disguised as balls—and all the whirling, flirting faces of the past few months. Their beautiful, feminine bodies waltz through my imagination. I could be with any of them tonight.

All accomplished, all connected, all in love with me. Or at least the idea of me.

But I. I love none of them.

It's Bella I want. It's always been Bella.

I tilt back on the chair, balancing.

"You must forget her. She doesn't see you that way."

My voice bounces off the exposed beams, ricocheting

back in my ears.

A sharp bark then a growl cuts through the night. I snap the chair down to the floor and whisk the drape aside.

Two police inspectors, by the looks of their uniforms, are tramping up Arabella's steps and pounding on her door. "Miss Holmes? Miss Holmes, if you please?"

"What the...?" I shoot to stand, reaching for my overcoat. I debate the tiny pistol, but leave it lie.

I'm out the door in seconds, striding across the wet grass. The city smell burns inside my nostrils as they flare.

The two men turn to stare; the younger officer's hand straying inside his slicker.

"Sir, this is official police business. Move along."

"If it involves Miss Holmes, it is my business."

The smaller man grimaces and pulls out his Billy club, tapping it against his open palm in warning. His pale, pockmarked face, begs me to cause trouble.

The door opens and Bella appears in the doorway, fully clothed. She nods, nonplussed at a uniformed officer on her porch after midnight.

"Inspector. How might I be of service?"

Her eyes dart to me and back to the inspector. Her expression is smooth and unreadable.

The man hesitates. "What about him?" The inspector nods at me.

"*That* is Mister Henry Watson."

"A relative of Dr. John Watson?"

She smiles. "The very same. Henry is his younger son."

The prodigal son. The obstinate one. The one who did

not go into medicine.

"So you don't mind if he…?"

"No, it's fine. Henry is all discretion." She steps outside, shooing the dog back in. "Desist, Newton." She shuts the door on the dog's growling. "I assume you require my assistance?"

"Yes, the hansom is this way, Miss Holmes." He gestures toward the waiting carriage.

I attempt to make eye contact with Bella, but she is wholly engrossed with the inspector and the task at hand. I follow behind them, grateful they are not protesting my presence.

We whisk down the main thoroughfare, whizzing past a mixing-pot of humanity. Ladies of the evening, drunken lads and the occasional dandy up to no good, fly past on either side.

Arabella stares straight ahead, not meeting my gaze. Lost in thought.

The carriage careens, speeding toward the river. It rumbles to a halt and we depart.

The river comes into view. My scalp tightens, shriveling against the chill and what skullduggery brings us to the water.

We step from the carriage and the inspector waves us forward.

The gurgle of water dominates the night, leaving the city noise a mottled undercurrent of sound.

The riverbank is a steep drop-off, but the inspector makes no apologies to Arabella. Never would a lady be asked to endure such a task.

They must be well acquainted.

We ease our way down the slope in a diagonal line.

We reach the shore and Arabella steps forward, but the

inspector raises his nightstick, halting her.

His black eyebrows pull together. "Miss Holmes, it's rather gruesome."

"Inspector." Her tone is chastising. Her eyes are electric, searching the riverbank.

"I know. I know." He tips his hat compulsively. "I still feel the need to warn."

Down in the shallows, I spy our destination.

Bodies. And some parts to spare.

Three at first glance, but I quickly realize one has been rent in two. The torso lies surreally spread-eagled, separated from the legs. And a smaller body, with very little flesh on the pelvic skeleton, lies beside it. The shallow waters lap against the legs and the other is half-hidden in the grass.

Arabella ducks under the nightstick and strides across the shore of wet stones.

She knots up her dress, wading in, oblivious to the appreciative stares of the policemen. I arch an eyebrow and they both avert their eyes from her perfect, ivory skin.

I *force* myself to look away.

Bella bends forward, holding up a lantern.

"This one is a woman." She gestures to the halved remains.

"How do you know?" The younger policeman says quietly.

"The shape of the pelvic bowl." Her finger traces its outline above the body. "Men are more heart shaped, women, more round, to allow for childbirth."

"Ah." The chief inspector steps closer. "What about this one. Murder? Dismembered?"

Arabella squints. "This body has been moved." She

points to the blue and black pooling on the corpse. "He died on his back, thus the discoloration—but now he's facedown."

"What about the dismemberment?"

Bella rubs her temples. "Difficult to say. It is a rather jagged perforation…"

She turns to hand me her lantern and proceeds to open a bag hanging on her elbow, which looks like any ladies satchel and pulls out a pick.

If the night weren't so gruesome, I'd have laughed.

Only Arabella.

She carefully lifts up the flap of skin on the torso. "And a significant portion of his organs are gone."

"Sacrificial death?" The inspector suggests.

She shrugs. "Not enough evidence."

"One more item, if you please, Miss Holmes."

Arabella follows the chief inspector to the higher grass and points. I hold the lantern closer and she pulls out a magnifying glass. Her face screws up in concentration.

She plucks a huge bone from the earth, with one end sheared off.

"It's a femur." When the younger detective looks confused, she adds, gesturing, "The long bone of the leg."

She turns it, examining the hollowed core of the bone where it's been sheared.

"Yes, but is it man or beast?" The inspector holds his breath.

Bella sighs. "Man."

She points, speaking directly to me. It's a lesson now, not a crime scene. Her eyes beam with an obsessive flame. The police have momentarily disappeared from her perception. Her hand quickly dips into the bag and extracts a peculiar-looking monocle. She fashions the stem of it behind her ear and locks the glass in place over her eye and stares into the bone.

It's like none I've ever seen; multiple lenses swing in and out for various magnifications.

"What, pray tell, is that?"

She waves my comment away. "New-fangled magnifying glass, courtesy of our fathers."

She tilts the bone so that I may see into the center. "First, the slanted angle on the top indicates the bone's owner walks upright." She tilts it, so I can see inside. "If the hollowed-out center is filled with one-third bone, it's a large mammal. One-fourth filled, a human. One-eighth, a bird. For flight, the bones must be light."

"Excellent, Miss Holmes. Your knowledge is indispensable."

Other policemen are now trickling down the bank. Arabella's face twists with anxiety. Not all will value a feminine opinion, especially on a subject so serious as murder.

The chief notices. "Thank you, Miss Holmes. Just like your father, you truly are helpful. Please give him my regards." He tilts his bowler in dismissal.

"Thank you, I will, Inspector Giamatti."

"I will escort her home, sir. I'm sure you've much more to do." I nod toward the oncoming onslaught of uniformed officers.

He tips his hat again. "Mr. Watson. A pleasure."

Chapter Six

Mutter Lecture Hall
Phrenology Presentation
Bella

John sits down beside me, bestowing his 'let's make the best of it' smirk.

He leans in and whispers, "Do you remember our case where Holmes employed phrenology?"

My mind whisks through a litany of images, like thumbing through a mental photo collage. I think in pictures and after multiple conversations with John, have discovered this is not necessarily the norm.

"Yes. Father occasionally used it on me, and my unknowing playmates."

I picture father, his long fingers probing through Henry's tousled hair after he'd caught us blowing up the mailbox. *Again.*

"However, his deductions were completely at odds to *my* opinion of the person."

Like telling me Henry was not a good match for me. Even as a friend. Which simply. Wasn't. True.

Henry was the best friend I ever had; then or now.

Father thought his intellect beneath me. What he failed to realize was that no man, from any race or continent, would ever rise to his impossible-to-meet qualifications for my husband.

John raises one telling eyebrow, indicating he knows there's more to this story than I shall ever divulge.

"It's only an hour, Arabella." His smile is bracing.

Henry has taken the stage with Stygian. I suck my breath in and bite the inside of my cheek.

I hate how he affects me. I am powerless to the attraction.

Henry's beauty is staggering. His thin lips, deep set eyes and perpetually tousled hair gave him a permanently just-risen-from-bed appearance that no amount of coiffing could tame.

John tsk's beside me. "That hair. I swear we should just shear it."

I feel the laugh rising in my throat.

"Like a sheep. Honestly, his hair is like a horsetail." John sighs.

I cover my mouth to hide the smile and feel the heat on my cheeks.

I know my face to be as red as the ridiculous feathered hat, blocking my view.

And the flush deepens.

The woman beside me stage-whispers to her daughter, "Wilhelmina. That man is an English thoroughbred among

Philadelphia nags. You *must* attempt to speak to him after tonight's presentation."

John leans in and whispers, "Do you see? Even that woman agrees with my equestrian comparison."

At this, my loud laugh breaks free.

I bristle as the woman in front of me fans herself; her wide eyes follow Henry's every action on the stage.

Feathered-hat-lady, who blocks my view, finally removes the poor taxidermied creature, mercifully placing it on the seat beside her.

I once again vow never to become a lovesick, pandering female. This auditorium is bursting with them and seems to expand and contract with their every sigh.

I glance around. Every woman in the audience is glued to Henry's every twitch. His attempts at taming his dark blonde hair have failed, as it is slowly rebelling to its normally chaotic state. His cheeks are high with nervous color.

His smile could incinerate any woman, like Medusa's power in reverse, channeled through those smirking lips.

The sheer number of interested fools makes my skin prickle and I shift in my seat. I detest crowds.

So many people asking so many things at precisely the same moment.

I hear snippets of every conversation within five rows—and am unable to block them. Another inherited Holmesian trait. It's useful for detective work, but not for living.

One row back. "Do you see him, my stars; I've never seen a man so very handsome—"

Two rows to my right. "Is he married? Engaged, then?"

I sigh.

My brain spits fireworks with the excess sound. A woman's high-pitched cackle makes me jerk, raising every hair on my arms.

John's hand pats mine. The man notices everything.

So does Henry. *It's unnerving.*

For all of father's genius, and deciphering the slightest change in surroundings, he rarely noticed when I was upset.

I picture my tiny self, weeping amid taunts of, 'Where's your mother, Arabella? Did she think you odd—so she left to find a normal girl?'

No hugs from father, no confidential talk. Instead, he bought me a new dog.

I shake my head, banning the memory.

Or perhaps father did notice, but not having the slightest idea how to handle the female persuasion, chose to pretend otherwise?

"Welcome."

Stygian's black eyes and booming voice immediately hush the low thrum of the crowd.

My eyes narrow on the stage.

"Our demonstration this evening will focus on the controversial science of phrenology." He gestures to a chart beside him. The title at the top of the poster proclaims, "Know Thyself".

Henry's eyes dart to the illustration of the human skull, sectioned into parts.

"From the size and shape of one's cranium, many deductions may be drawn," Stygian continues. The yellow stage lighting casts shadows across Stygian and Henry's faces; the black bruises beneath their eyes, reminding me of corpses.

Stygian's voice commands attention. "From one's instinct for reproduction to predicting a person's pride and vanity—to whether one has the heart, or mind, rather, of a murderer."

A murmur rushes through the crowd like a wordless ripple.

Chills lick my neck. John uncrosses his legs at the inference. Apparently it makes him nervous, too.

I whisper, "This *science* is more like voodoo. But that hasn't stopped people from arranging marriages around it, or hiring or firing staff based on its *predictions*." The disdain coats my voice. I hear my tone rising and rising, like one of my blasted butterflies. "Perhaps we might employ fortune tellers to predict our next scientific discovery."

"Arabella, quietly!" John blurts in a harsh whisper.

Feather-lady glares at me.

On stage, Henry has extracted a large caliper.

"We need a volunteer. Two actually. Miss Holmes, perhaps you might grace our stage?" Stygian's voice drips sweetness.

Three rows of jealous feminine eyes turn to glare.

My eyes meet John's. He cocks his head slightly, his eyes screaming a silent message—*m*anners, Arabella.

I stand and walk up the aisle, which appears to have magically elongated, as several females shoot envious scowls overtop their fluttering fans.

I resist the urge to snap them in half.

Time seems to have slowed and I focus on not kissing the

carpet as I pass the staring crowd.

Henry and Stygian both study my face. My breath quickens, and the back of my neck prickles with panic.

"And Miss Earnest, if you please," Stygian says, staring over my head.

Priscilla.

Stygian is orchestrating a scene, baiting me. He somehow knows of our convoluted triangle.

I raise my chin in defiance and stop at the foot of the small staircase. I force myself to meet his gaze. Stygian quickly walks down, extending his hand to assist me.

The heat of a hundred sets of eyes sears my back as convention forces my hand into his.

I sneak a glance at Henry. His eyes are forward on the audience, but a muscle bulges in his jaw.

Stygian gestures me toward the plush, crushed-velvet chair.

"Please, sit."

Says the spider to the fly.

I sit carefully, almost expecting nails to jut out and impale me to the thick fabric.

Priscilla arrives; all flounce and bounce as Henry escorts her up the stairs. She shoots me a smug little smile before arranging herself and her skirts before him.

Priscilla's whole body trembles; her long neck and face remind me of a high-strung greyhound, quivering in anticipation of his touch.

Montgomery lopes up onto the stage, long fingers outstretched. Stygian slips off a heavy ring, placing it into his palm. I catch a glimpse of it before it disappears into Montgomery's pocket. Gooseflesh rises on my arms along with a flash of recognition.

I have seen a ring like that before, but where?

Henry's arms bend theatrically, referring to the diagramed phrenology head. His warm voice carries into the crowd, "Different parts of the brain perform different functions. Phrenology is based on the premise that when part of the brain is used more fully, the corresponding spot on the skull will rise to accommodate the growing brain beneath."

"May I?"

"Of course Dr. Stygian." Priscilla flashes the audience a winning smile.

Stygian's fingers slide through her blonde locks as Priscilla's eyes drift closed. She exhales softly.

"Miss Earnest lives up to her name. Her skull shape is indicative of perseverance and passion."

Both of their eyes flick to Henry. He looks aghast.

Stygian continues, "Her child-bearing map is ample and her musical ability very prominent. I say, do you play, Miss Earnest?"

She bats her eyelashes, "Why yes, I do. Amazing Doctor. Everything you've said tis too true."

I turn my head so only Henry might see and roll my eyes. I'm forcibly reminded of snake-oil salesman and traveling medicine shows.

Stygian mumbles, "Henry, you must be thrilled to hear of that child-bearing map, eh, my boy?"

Henry squints incredulously, but says nothing.

Stygian removes his hands from Priscilla's hair and

strolls to my side.

He tugs the singular stick from my hair, sending an auburn curtain tumbling into my face.

His thick, heavy fingers thrust into my hair.

I suck in a breath.

Out of my peripheral vision, Henry takes one protective step closer. His fists ball at his sides.

The audience is hushed, waiting. The expectation is palpable, as if every patron is holding their breath.

The gaslights lining the stage suddenly seem to blaze like the sun and I fidget against their heat.

Stygian's fingers massage every bit of my head, from behind my ears to my forehead and back again.

"Easy Miss Holmes," he croons. "Mr. Watson, might you perform the measurements?"

Henry steps in front of me, and I shiver as the cold metal of the calipers touch either side of my temples.

He slips his boots alongside mine beneath my dress, and gives a little squeeze with his legs. Trying to reassure me he's right there.

My heart. How it twists when he's near.

I want to pull it from its protective box, still beating, and place it in his palm. To be done with it; give it to him.

In the space of a breath, the caliper and his reassuring touch are gone. His fingers scribble down the measurements. He hands the clipboard to Stygian, stepping out of the way.

"Mr. Watson, record my observations, if you please." His eyebrows rise, and he pushes the clipboard back to Henry.

Stygian's fingers probe again and I shiver, remembering

the unmistakable lust in his eyes as he cornered me in the lab.

His fingers locate a lump on my skull and hold, palpating back and forth, back and forth.

The world swirls and blackness presses against my wits. I inhale deeply, trying not to swoon.

Quietly, so only we on stage might hear, Henry whispers, "Bella. Are you alright?"

Stygian growls, "She's fine, Henry. She's just not used to masculine… contact."

Priscilla quietly snickers.

I am very poor at discerning people intentions, but not so with animals. I am seized by the impression that his behavior is like a dog's, marking his territory.

I swallow compulsively, again and again. Trying to maintain control.

Tension *rolls* off Henry. His legs bend and tense, reminding me of a tightly-coiled spring, ready to explode with the slightest nudge.

He steps toward me, as if to strike Stygian, right now, right here on stage.

I give him a quick look. His chest is heaving. He's furious.

I picture the headlines in the Philadelphia Examiner.

Dr. Watson's son assaults Mutter Professor.

He'll be fired and publicly humiliated in one impulsive punch.

His life and promising career over at the ripe old age of nearly-twenty and three.

"I'm fine, Henry. It's alright."

Priscilla's eyes flit back and forth, watching our exchange, and her full pink lips draw into a scowl. She flips her blond curls forward, huffing and crossing her arms like a child.

Henry steps to Stygian. "Miss Holmes doesn't look well. Please hurry so that she may return to her seat. If she loses consciousness, you'll be hard-pressed to find more willing victims," Henry forces between his gritted teeth.

Stygian turns away to address the audience. "According to my assessment, Miss Holmes has a good deal of pride, a greater deal of intellect, and an extraordinary memory."

Henry points to the map of skull attributes as Stygian ticks off my proposed personality. His nostrils flare and his fingers tremble slightly where he touches the poster.

The audience applauds. I search and find John's pinched face embedded in the crowd. His walking stick is propped and he's leaning forward as if he's prepared to stand.

"She also seems to have no inclination in the child bearing map, a serious lack of forethought, but is gifted in music."

My chest flushes with hot-red embarrassment. So far, he's spot on, except the musical predilection. He has confirmed my own suspicions, but to have him proclaim I'm not fit for motherhood, though, to an entire assembly is…

Flashes of sneering boarding school girls detonate in my mind. My breath rattles in and out and I try desperately to maintain control.

Their taunts are spatial whispers in my ear, coming and going as if they're in the room.

"Babbage's adding machine. That's how warm you are, Ar-a-bellllaaa. Is your heart made of coal, Ar-a-bellla?"

Stygian finally looks alarmed; I know for his lecture, not my welfare.

"You are dismissed, Miss Holmes. Mr. Watson, would you like to choose more volunteers?"

Henry's eyes are slits. "No. I think you should do it, *sir,* as you have so much more experience. I'll escort Miss Holmes from the stage."

Priscilla scoffs, muttering her displeasure.

Henry takes my arm and motions to Montgomery to take his place.

I lean on Henry as the audience applause bombards my ears. I wince. The loud voices are physically painful; as if someone is jabbing a fiery poker in the center of my ear.

I fight the urge to cover them. As a young girl, I would've bolted. I grind my teeth.

Just make it out of the auditorium.

Henry is staring at my expression, his mouth contorted with worry.

We mercifully exit, stage right, and my breath exhales in a whoosh.

The world upends and I'm disoriented and I'm blinking, but it feels slow and deliberate.

Henry has scooped me into his arms. His heart pounds against my arm.

"What are you doing?" I try to sound incensed, but I'm honestly too weak to care.

"Taking you to your cottage. No arguments."

Chapter Seven

Six Impossible Things

Henry deposits me gently on the bed, shooing Newton onto the floor. As soon as he stands, the dog leaps back up, draping his black and white body across my legs. He rolls on his back, pink tongue lolling to the side.

"Good boy." I scratch behind his ears, avoiding Henry's eyes. "Don't you have to get back?"

I finally look up. His intense stare elicits a falling sensation.

"No. I'm staying till I'm satisfied you're alright."

He walks around my room, fingers dragging across the furniture tops. His eyes skip across my bookcase, and halt...and squint.

I hear my heartbeat in my ears. *The Antiquarian Journals.*

He turns to face me with narrowed eyes. "I've read those journals. You've been studying—"

"Yes, the oversized skeletons found in different regions

of these states."

His lips twist into a triumphant smirk. "Pray tell, how long have you been mad-keen for oversized skeletons?"

"Speak plainly."

His expression turns black; I envision dark thunderclouds rumbling across his forehead.

"You are researching the Nephilim. Admit it."

I sigh. "Science makes sense, Henry. Please quit ruining my world."

He steps closer. "You mean your very structured, barricaded, do-not-touch-my-heart-world, makes sense."

My heart gives a violent pitch; my hand strays to my chest before I can stop it. My heart quivers inside its metal case, rumbling like a kettle drum. I swallow and admit, "Rules are my comfort."

The bed depresses as he sits, blue eyes boring into me. "Rules are made to be broken."

A foreign wanting stirs in me. I picture my hands entangled in his thick, tousled hair.

I clear my throat. Terrified I will do it. My heart is a wild-bird in my chest.

"For instance, women permitted on expeditions. One rule that should be broken."

He slides so close our legs are touching, my skin burning at the contact. I don't answer so he prompts again. His eyebrows pull together, creating a deep furrow between them. "The best parts of life are the sticky parts, Bella. The ones you're strategically avoiding."

He stands abruptly, and I'm ridiculously out of breath.

Stygian was right. I am not used to human contact.

Affection was the exception rather than the rule in my household.

There was love, after a fashion, but not affection.

Henry is still and staring. I follow his gaze and brace myself.

He's spied my map, stuck to the wall.

He strides across the room, head whipping comically back and forth, his mouth agape.

At least twenty sets of pins jut out in clusters from the map. His fingers trace over the pinheads in wonder, starting with the grouping in Ohio, to Tennessee, all the way to Arizona and California.

He whirls. "Out with it."

I cross my arms and defiantly shake my head.

His eyes narrow. "No. No. This will not do. You've obviously been doing even more digging than I, despite your protests of the impossibility of such creatures. What do you know?"

His face changes abruptly, his voice lowering; apparently changing tactics.

His voice suddenly drips like honey. "If I am to accompany you, would you place me at risk, without all the data?"

I bite my lip. "Fine." I chuck a book at him.

He deftly deflects and flips it to examine the spine. "Life among the Piutes. I don't understand?"

I slither out of bed and walk to the map, pointing to the congregation of pins in Nevada.

"A woman named Sarah Winnemucca Hopkins wrote

that book, chronicling Indian histories. Piute legends describe very large visitors with flaming auburn hair, and double rows of teeth. At this site, twenty-three skeletons were unearthed in 1883. They were discovered in Lovelock Cave and all were between seven and eight feet tall. The Piute called them, Si-Te-Cahs."

Henry's jaw drops. "Really?"

He begins to pace, hands twisting furiously. He whirls. "What do the different colors signify—the red and green pins?"

I smile. Only he would notice my classification system in one minute flat. "Red are for double rows of teeth. Green is for six toes."

He steps back for a wider look, as if seeing the map for the first time. His mouth works furiously.

He gesticulates, rapid-fire at the states, first to Arizona. "This one?"

My mind rifles through the files. I see the pages perfectly, just as I read them. "Stone sarcophagus housing a twelve-foot, six-toed skeleton."

He touches the one in Tennessee. "This one?"

"Human footprints, preserved in rock, measuring thirty-three inches, and six toes."

"I must see your notes."

My eyes open wide, my hand shooting to my hip. "I don't have notes."

"Of course you don't." He sighs. "Would you write some for me?"

I walk back to the bed and sit. "I suppose."

"We lesser mortals appreciate notes. Besides, you will

need them for references in your paper."

I tap the side of my head. "Easily transcribed."

He rolls his eyes and half-smiles. He reluctantly turns from the map, heading back toward me.

He reaches my desk and picks up a paper.

It's my Neanderthal thesis. I can tell by the pinched look on his face.

Our eyes lock again. "Arabella. Do you really assume we are the greatest creation? Even after… all those pins? Doesn't that seem arrogant to you? I mean let's consider the laws of gravity—up, down. We've witnessed evil, surely there must be good."

I shrug. "I don't know what to think, Henry."

"That's a first."

We both laugh out loud.

He walks back to my bookshelf, fingers tracing the titles. He lifts *Alice in Wonderland* and cracks it open.

"Do you remember—?"

"Reading it in the barn, acting out the scenes by candlelight? Of course." My smile is so wide it's painful. It's as if I am bearing my soul.

But I love this memory.

It lit so many lonely, dark days while Henry was away at school.

I've had so few friends, and the ones I did were mostly male.

To women, I'm a foreigner, unable to speak their language of pin curls and parasols. I must pretend, pretend to be normal.

He sits beside me on the bed, much too close.

I smell him; woods and musk. I feel my stomach pitch and bite my lip again.

My mind shifts, slowly, deliberately; like emotive clock-cogs, from data…to him.

His fingers brush the back of my hand in a singular stroke.

"What about six impossible things before breakfast?"

"That's child's play, Henry."

"Is it? How amazing is it that we're both here, after all this time? That can be one."

He grasps my hand out of my lap, gently pulling up one of my fingers.

I shake my head, but can't help the smile that breaks through. Can't help being pleased. *How* does he always convince me that the world might hold more than my eyes can see?

We shall be dismissed if we're caught alone in my room. And him sitting on my bed. Touching me.

Not to mention the chastisement from father and John.

But my heart throbs with raw, unfamiliar demands.

"This possibly-preternatural hand shall be two." He flicks up another finger. "We shall see what else transpires. I expect we'll make six before a fortnight."

In a blink the teasing is gone; he's deadly serious. His hands fidget, twirling his pocket watch, considering.

I sigh. "Go ahead. I know you wish to ask me something. Something dreadful by the way you're mucking about."

He smiles. "You honestly don't know the meaning of small talk, pleasantries—"

"Wastes of breath. Speak, Henry?"

"Your mother. I've never asked about her, not in all this time. Do you know who she was?"

My face boils with heat. "I believe your father actually knows more than I. I know she was…an opera singer."

Henry's eyes widen as his brows disappear beneath his hair. "Really?"

"Yes. Apparently I was a burden, so off to the Holmes's I went."

Henry's fingers steeple. He's lost in thought, staring past me.

"Ahem?"

His blue-green eyes flick back. "So, *do you* show musical inclination?"

I know what he's thinking. Stygian's predictions from my skull, and now, the revelation I'm descended from musical blood.

"I never had much time to find out. All science and math and Latin and—"

"Yes. Well, perhaps we should find out."

"You only want to test the phrenology's prediction. That I'm gifted in music."

He shrugs. "Perhaps. We will go to the theater, when the expedition allows."

He leans forward plucking up my journal, my locked journal, from the bedside table. "What secrets do you keep in here?"

"None of your bloody business."

His fingers trace my neck and my heartbeat surges. I freeze, wanting more, but unable to ask. My face falls as he slips his finger under my necklace.

He tugs it gently and I feel it slide up my stomach and between my breasts till it appears on my chest to reveal a key.

He smiles wickedly. "I assume *this* key, fits in *this* lock." He gives the journal a little shake.

His attention shifts again and he drops the journal into my lap.

He sits beside me and leans closer and I'm lost again in a deluge of his scent.

My heart skips a too-long beat in my chest as his lips pass so close to mine. Anticipation and want dizzy my head as he plucks a letter from my nightstand.

"You're—" I try to swallow the tremble in my voice. "You're in rare form. Are *all* my private papers your personal expedition?"

He smiles. "You don't reveal much. So I'm conducting research. I'm not often privy to the cave of the reclusive genius."

He's clutching father's letter. I don't care. I'm almost bloody unconscious.

His eyes scan the perfect penmanship and he looks up. His smile is crooked. "Digger? He calls you digger?"

I snatch the paper from his hands. "Yes. What of it?"

"May I call you it, too?" His lips are trembling as he tries not to laugh. He stands.

I spring.

He leaps out of the way, running around my bed.

I chase him and grab hold of his sleeve. I hang on as he tries to throw me off and manage to off a punch at his chest.

"You are a brute. An awful, sophomoric little boy in a

man's body."

Newton's bark is sharp, his hackles rising in my defense. He bears his teeth.

I point at the door. "Go, you imbecile! You shouldn't be in here in the first place. We'll both be let go!"

Henry runs out the door, but turns to look through the crack. "Good night, Digger."

I throw my shoe and he slams the door shut.

Chapter Eight

JUDGMENT DAY

Racing down Mutter Hallway
Henry

I flip my hair from my eyes and hurry down the Mutter hallway, checking my watch. My boot-falls echo wildly off the high ceilings.

I grit my teeth as a curse slips out; I am going to miss the meeting about Arabella.

"Blast."

A nightmarish blur of images fly past me on either side—a plaster cast of a fifteen foot colon, my wax specimens of syphilis and smallpox. I avert my eyes, breaking into an all-out dash.

I skid to a halt outside the boardroom door and make a last, futile attempt to smooth down my hair.

Father sits at the massive circular table, his hands folded

calmly before him. They itch to strangle me for my tardiness, I know.

Dr. Jeremy Montgomery sits at the one end, looking even younger than I. Father informed me he was three years my senior, but his smooth, clean-shaven face reminds me of my pupils back home.

Dr. Earnest sits at the table's head. His watery eyes crinkle with delight when I enter. "Henry! Welcome. We are very excited to have you join the Mutter. Your father's reputation precedes him—so I have no doubt we'll see some wondrous things from you!"

My smile feels like a cringe. "I shall certainly do my best, sir."

My eyes flick to father. I bristle at the grin playing at the twitching sides of his mouth.

I slide in between father and Jeremy, while Earnest prattles on to a secretary about the excursion.

Jeremy shoots his hand in mock-introduction, and I give him mine. He gives it a vigorous pump, as if we've never met.

"Glad to have you, Henry." He leans in, whispering conspiratorially, "I can't tell you how relieved I am to have someone of my own species on board. It's been a lonely three months."

"You're new to the Mutter, as well then?"

"Yes. I am a Philadelphia native, born and bred. I've heard rumors about you from the staff."

My eyebrows rise. "Such as?"

"Your reputation with the ladies. I could use some help with one particularly recalcitrant female. Perhaps you might scribble some of that infamous poetry of yours—"

The door opens and Jeremy breaks off and sits utterly still like a naughty schoolboy caught cheating.

Stygian enters.

The temperature in the room drops a degree and the hairs rise on the nape of my neck.

He sits and all eyes around the table fly to his attention. Except father. His eyes tick up in polite regard, but quickly return to scanning the document before him.

Stygian inhales, his barrel-chest protruding. "Gentlemen. I shall not waste your time with small talk; we all know the purpose of this council meeting. There has been a motion to add Arabella Holmes to the expedition team. We are gathered to present arguments both for and against this appointment."

Earnest clears his throat. "I will begin. I will admit, when Mr. Holmes wrote, requesting we appoint his daughter to the staff, I was more than a little reluctant. But knowing his reputation as I have the past twenty odd years—I knew he would never let his personal feelings override his judgment."

My eyes lock with father's in silent agreement. *Feelings? What feelings?*

Father looks away before a smile erupts.

"I have not been disappointed. Her education is impeccable. She is competent in two languages, anatomy and basic physiology."

"Don't forget fingerprinting, ballistics and is an expert chemist," father says, adding an ingratiating smile.

Stygian looks murderous; a vein throbs in his forehead, cutting a path across his pallid skin, reminding me of a blood-trail through snow.

He stands, leaning forward, his long fingers splayed on the tabletop. "I have come to terms with Miss Holmes as a curator. My concern for the acquisition team is obvious. Arabella is female. Our archeological expeditions are often quite dangerous. I need every man to be able to pull his weight—not have to be coddling a woman."

"Sir, respectfully." I sit up straight and wait till his black eyes challenge mine.

"Arabella is like no woman I've ever met. I've known her all my life. I've seen her scale trees, swim more proficiently than I, and ride like a champion equestrian. She will not be a burden."

Stygian's dark eyebrows bunch. His fingers twitch and I get the distinct impression they're itching to throttle me.

Capital. Put superior number two against me straight away. Well done.

"Thank you for that glowing testament, Mr. Watson, but I have another concern. Whatever her mind, she is utterly... female. I'm worried her presence will distract the team, or worse, put her in more lascivious dangers."

You mean, from others, not just you.

Jeremy snickers. I give him a glare.

He shrugs, murmuring, "Sorry. He has a point, Henry. Walking icicle or no, the girl is an eyeful."

Father raises his hand, but doesn't wait for permission. "Arabella is quite capable of protecting herself, I assure you. I was involved in planning her education. She is as well rounded as my sons."

Stygian drops his head. "Enough. Let us vote. Those in

favor of letting Miss Holmes join the expedition."

I raise my hand. Jeremy slowly raises his own, but only after watching mine.

"Opposed?"

My heart pounds and I feel a light sheen of sweat on my forehead. I force my hands not to wipe it.

Earnest raises his hand, avoiding father's glare.

Stygian smiles triumphantly. "Well, it seems we are at an impasse. I move to stay this loggerhead and reconsider at a future date. She shall not embark on this first expedition—"

Father cuts across him, eyes blazing. "Dr. Earnest? Have you had word from Mr. Holmes in regards to your grant for the museum's new hothouse?"

Stygian's face flickers with surprise. "What?"

The portion of Earnest's face not covered by mutton-side chops turns puce. "Yes, Fredrick. We *are* running low on funds. I petitioned Mr. Holmes about a new hothouse, where we might experiment with exotic breeds of plants, to draw a more genteel clientele into the Mutter."

Father's eyes are shrewd. "Yes, and I am sure Mr. Holmes will be even *more* disposed to produce such funds when he finds his one and only daughter was barred from the expedition on the basis of prejudice."

Earnest sighs and clears his throat, his thick hand rising. "I am sorry Fredrick. I change my vote. The motion passes."

Stygian's face is livid-red. "Fine. Three to one." His eyes shift to father. "If Miss Holmes meets some bitter end, I am very glad you were here to bear witness, Dr. Watson, and I hope you shall convey my opposition to Mr. Holmes."

Father nods, unruffled. "Of course."

Stygian storms out of the room, his black cape flung over his arm.

Father shakes everyone's hands, flashing a genuine smile. "Arabella will be so pleased."

My stomach tightens. *I* am so pleased.

Jacoby Manor

He knocked, again and again, breathing heavily; his exhalations ghosting up and away in the cold air like the specters in the night.

The butler's eyes narrowed as he opened the door a crack, "It is a most ungodly hour—" His chastisement died on his lips as his eyes widened in frightened recognition. "Sir, do excuse me—"

The man shoved him aside, striding in the foyer as if the manor were his own.

"Jacoby!" he called up the stairs.

The butler hurried past him, taking the steps two-at-an-undignified-time. "I shall rouse him, sir."

In mere moments, the portly man waddled down the stairs, white tufts of hair flying as fast as his feet. "Fredrick, what on earth has happened?"

He reached the bottom of the staircase, huffing.

"Miss Holmes has been approved for departure." He shoved an envelope into Jacoby's pudgy palm. "Here is what is to be done. Read it. Memorize it. Destroy it."

He whirled toward the door, his black cape swirling about him like a bat in flight. "I obviously must take charge of her situation, as disappointingly, not a one of you seem to have the stomach for it."

He stepped out into the night, not bothering to shut the door.

Henry's cottage
Henry

I glance out the window at the dimming light, fading to pink streaks on the horizon.

It's almost dark, we're almost late for the fund-raising ball.

I stride to my chest of drawers and whip out a tie.

"Father, I thought we agreed I'd *meet* Priscilla, not pledge my immediate, undying love on first sight." I rip the black tie off and begin again, eyeing him in the mirror.

One dark eyebrow arches. "Really, Henry? Pray tell, what is not to like? She is utterly gorgeous and well-connected to the museum. She is the perfect prospect."

"You court her, then." I wrestle with my tie, roughly slipping the knot up to my neck. I sigh, and spin to face him. "What're you up to, then? The truth?"

Father's chest and eyebrows rise simultaneously as he sucks in a breath and then exhales dramatically between his gritted teeth. "You are…"

"Difficult?"

"Yes, but not relevant to this part of the conversation."

"Brilliant?" I interject.

He half-smiles, as he does when I infuriate him. "Yes, also not relevant. Might I find my own word?"

I turn back to the mirror. "I'm growing old waiting for it."

"Unsettled. Unfocused. A rogue. Have too many interests—"

"I'm nothing like James, you mean."

His eyes flare at the mention of my older brother. "I said nothing of the sort, Henry."

"But you were thinking it."

"No, I wasn't."

"And so marrying would cure me of my many shortcomings?" I turn back to him and give my lapels a rough tug to busy my hands. So I don't poke him in the chest.

"The *right* woman, yes."

"And Priscilla, is that woman?"

He bends, picking up his hat and cane. "You've only just met her, give the girl a bloody chance. Henry—" he stops dead, revelation lighting his features. "You've already someone in mind, don't you?"

I will my hands to stay still.

His eyes immediately snap down. "Your hands are limp as dead fish. This is as much a giveaway as if they were fidgeting."

"You are impossible." I give up and permit my fingers free reign and crack my knuckles.

"Likewise." Father's lips purse as he considers. Comprehension and horror dawn as his mouth twitches beneath the mustache. He jams his eyes shut, shaking his head once. "Not Arabella? I thought we were past all that."

They fly open, waiting.

I shrug, and slide my hands over my already slicked hair. I walk towards the door.

Escape. Flee. Freedom.

"For the love of all that's holy, Henry. That's almost like being married to Holmes." He gives a little shudder.

"I daresay you're one to talk. For years, you chose a life with Holmes over matrimony, so that argument is full of holes. Do as I say, not as I do?"

Father's face softens, and he lifts a placating hand. "I love Arabella too, you know that. But, be reasonable. She... doesn't fit into polite society."

"Neither does Holmes and he's almost legendary now."

"She is unruly, headstrong, and will never, ever listen."

"I know. She fascinates me."

Both his hands shoot palm-up into the air, and then fly to cover his mouth in a prayer position.

I capitalize on his frustration to make my escape; walking swiftly for the door.

"We are going to be late for the gathering. Don't want to keep your pet, Priscilla, waiting. Really, father, Violet might be jealous at your obvious attachment."

"Love is too young to know what conscience is..."

A game from childhood, started by my mother. A perpetual contest between James and me—the most Shakespearean quotes meant the most sweets.

His stare burns a hole in my back. I whirl, and glare back and grind my teeth. I always won.

"Let every eye negotiate *for itself*, and trust no agent."

Father's mouth pops open. I shut the door before it closes.

Faculty Ball

"Remember your manners, Henry," Father warns and proceeds to dive into the sea of well-dressed science. Within minutes I hear his warm, resonant laugh and smile to myself. Father doesn't hold a grudge. Which is precisely why he and Holmes got on so well.

A ball of tension is lodged firmly in my throat, and my stomach clenches spasmodically. Nervous. *She actually makes me nervous.*

My eyes scan the room, from one gaggle of women to the next. Priscilla catches my stare, and beckons me over.

"Pardon me," I say, slipping past a portly scientist, whose name has completely vacated my obsessed brain. I weave through the finery till I finally arrive at Priscilla's side.

I nod. "Might I have this dance, if you aren't otherwise engaged?"

"Of course, Henry." She boldly thrusts her dance card into my hand. "Pencil as many as you like."

Very few spaces are filed, which is unheard of for a woman of her beauty.

She smiles, and her teeth are impossibly white, her lips a perfect shade of crimson. "And for whom else would I be waiting? I've been impatient for your arrival."

I try to smile, feeling like it's some odd, warped wince of my lips. I take her smooth hand in mind, twirling her into the fray.

My mind contrasts it. Bella's hands are so rough. Worn and calloused. I shake my head. *Focus, man.*

"So, Priscilla, do you share your father's interests in science?"

"Oh, no. I'm afraid not. I do love languages, though. I take after my mother…"

"My father's told me you speak three languages. And paint, and play the violin. You are quite accomplished."

The waltz tempo slows, and with it our revolutions. Priscilla spins away, while I keep hold of her hand. She twirls back in to touch my chest, and whispers, "I love children. I so desire a house full of children, Henry. How do you feel about them?"

Her perfume wafts into my nostrils, flowery and light.

I spin her away; my head spinning along with the sight of her. This dance needs to end.

She's clearly looking to wed.

She presses up against me again.

Or at least, bed?

I'm afraid I'm not available for either.

Something has happened. I have no desire for her. It used to be anything in a skirt could garner any and all of my attention. My mind drifts to the late nights with my lads back home. It no longer seems appealing.

Priscilla shifts, demanding my attention.

She permits no space between us, making sure I feel her every curve. I struggle to ignore the press of her.

I survey the crowd, and irrationally feel as if we are a magnified, glowing spectacle on the dance floor; our words broadcasted through a bull-horn so everyone is privy to our secret conversation.

Her fingers squeeze my shoulder, trying to re-orient me. "I love society—living in the city. I find the country exceedingly dull and uncivilized. What about you—I've heard rumors about you Henry, but you're so quiet I scarcely believe them."

"Hmm. What rumors?" I stare over the top of her head, still searching the crowd.

"That you are quite the ladies man."

I drop my eyes, risking a glance.

Priscilla smiles provocatively. "Prove it."

I swallow. *Time must've halted; for this is the longest dance I've ever endured.*

Irritation prickles.

My eyes finally tick down to regard her sky-blue ones, upturned and unfortunately hopeful. "I'm afraid I love the country. And it's the nature of my job to get dirty. I am often gone for long periods of time on expeditions. Which would affect the odds of a load of children."

"It only takes once." She stares. No trace of a blush. She means business.

She shrugs and smiles when it's clear I'm not scandalized nor tantalized by her forwardness.

"Oh, the traveling doesn't bother me. It would just make for sweeter homecomings."

I hear a bawdy laugh and I wrench my eyes away from her earnest gaze, scanning the dance hall. They flash over the myriad of colors and gowns and faces and finally, I see her. My heartbeat bombards my ribcage. My hands are sweating. While they are in Priscilla's hands.

This is not normal. Not for me, anyway.

I am dumbstruck. Arabella is so lovely I can scarcely breathe. She stands, hesitating at the top of the stairs, undoubtedly searching the crowd for familiar faces.

My mind races back in time to my childhood and my parent's parties.

Bella could never, ever tolerate crowds. I would often find her perched in a tree, party-dress and all, or playing fetch with our dogs in the garden.

She was better than Holmes, however, who would beg off each and every social function to which he was invited. If the gathering did not include science, crime or deduction—there was no amount of father's cajoling that would convince him.

I track her as she weaves in and out, finally appearing, hovering on the dance floor's edge. Arabella had worn trousers, in secret, for as long as I could recall.

But tonight. Tonight, is an Arabella even I have never been able to conjure in my wildest imagination.

The ivory silk dress is pulled tight around her tiny waist, and a green velveteen sash hangs to the side. A tassel drops provocatively at the bottom of the V in her décolletage. Her auburn hair flows around her shoulders in waves, unadorned.

Priscilla is talking. I can't make out the words.

Mercifully, the music stops. I almost forget manners and Priscilla's presence; I dip my head and quickly murmur, "Thank you."

She grabs my arm, demanding my attention. "Another dance tonight?"

"Most likely. It was delightful."

I walk in a straight line for Bella; my vision narrows as if I'm staring out a spyglass, and she is the horizon.

She's leaning against the wall, clutching a glass to her chest. Her eyes are pinched in distress, as if she's enduring a flogging.

Before, she was talking animatedly to father, about work, no doubt. But now that he's gone, she looks terrified and out of place once again. Her eyes jump like the staccato beats of the music behind me.

I reach her, and smile. Her eyes immediately quiet. Because of my presence?

Am I being arrogant? Or hopeful...

She extends her hand, which is covered in an elegant, ivory glove which reaches to her elbow.

I take it, grateful she can't detect the sweat.

"Lovely gloves."

She shrugs. "You know, the black stains on my fingers— they won't come off."

We share a very loud laugh and for a moment, we are the only people in the room.

Next to us a woman and her husband glare at our lack of decorum.

"I'm so very glad you're here, but I must admit I am shocked." I lean in so she may hear me above the band.

"I didn't wish to come. But knew if I want to be considered permanently for the expedition team, I must learn to do what is politely expected."

I notice the light sheen on her chest and her discomfort is my own; I yearn to alleviate her awkwardness.

I step closer. Closer than society allows. "Dance with me."

My mind explodes with forbidden images. My mouth and body on hers. My hands tracing the line of her legs.

I'm close enough to feel her breath. Her blue eyes widen, her mouth forming a perfect, pink O.

She shakes her head. "Please, Henry. I don't dance. I can't. Your father and mine, they tried to teach me, tried for hours on end, actually."

I smile. "Why don't I remember this?"

"Loads happened while you were away at boarding school. Please, I'll embarrass myself. I'm trying to keep my dignity."

"I will teach you."

"I can't be taught. I'm an orangutan in high heels."

I laugh so loud, my father shoots me a *death-by-dismemberment* look from across the room. He eyeballs his cane, whose insides conceal a short sword.

I try not to laugh harder.

Arabella presses her lips together, but a small sound slips out.

"I didn't know your father's wife was here."

"Yes." I turn to stare at them, now on the dance floor. "Miss Violet Hunter. I mean Watson."

"Does it bother you? That he remarried after Mary, I mean, your mother passed?"

I shake my head, considering. "No, he's happier. She's actually quite wonderful."

"I know. She has always been so kind to me." Arabella looks wistful. "Such attention, for your father to dance with his wife so many times. Defying convention in his older years, is he?"

"As if he ever obeyed convention. As if either of our fathers is even capable of it."

I turn to face her, and wait, unmoving till she meets my gaze. For a moment, all fades to nothing.

The crowd, the music, my purpose here.

Yearning clenches my chest. She resurrects the feelings of an awkward man-child.

New women, new travels have not managed to loosen her grip. I find the distance I so carefully created ripping away, edging me ever closer with every bat of those eyelashes and I swallow as the banished feelings return.

She doesn't break the stare. "Henry…"

A tap on my shoulder breaks the trance. Dr. Stygian.

"Sir."

He gives a curt nod, his eyes full of suspicion. "Watson.

You and Miss Holmes should turn in early and prepare for departure. We will see you tomorrow on the steamship. Seven sharp."

I nod. And fight the urge to break his jaw.

I push the images of his advances from my mind.

"Henry?" I hear Priscilla's call from across the room.

Something flares in Arabella's eyes.

"Blast. I promised her another dance. I'm sorry. I will see you tomorrow morning. I'll stop by your room to see if you need help with your steamer trunk."

Her expression is unreadable. "Have a wonderful evening."

I return to the gaggle of skirts and Priscilla's face is puckered as if she's just tasted a lemon. "Who is *she?*"

"Arabella Holmes. She is one of the scientists."

"She doesn't look like any scientist I've ever seen."

"You met her the other day, in the lab."

"That looks nothing like the girl I met. Will she be going on your expedition?" She scowls.

I nod, and can't stop the grin. "Yes, she will."

Chapter Nine

BEHAVIORS MOST INAPPROPRIATE

Mutter Ballroom
Henry

I give my pocket watch a surreptitious glance. Almost midnight. Five dances with Priscilla and my father was grinning like the bloody Cheshire Cat.

Arabella vacated the premises as soon as was socially acceptable. I watched her deny no less than seven requests to dance. I grin, wondering if their interest would wane once she opened her mouth. Men aren't used to the weaker vessels spouting physics equations and talking about corpses as if it's polite dinner conversation.

It took every shred of self-restraint I had not to follow as I watched that lovely ivory dress ghost out the door and into the night.

"Priscilla, I must be on my way. Our expedition leaves

early in the morning, and I have much to prepare."

Father steps beside me, Violet on his arm. She gives me a clandestine wink.

"Perhaps we might all meet, somewhere up the Hudson. Surely you'll get a day off now and then," father says helpfully.

"Oh, yes. That would be grand!" Pricilla claps her hands and turns to look at Dr. Earnest for approval.

I shoot father a look I hope conveys the string of profanities bursting to escape my mouth.

He smiles. Even. Wider.

Priscilla is back to staring at me, doe-eyes awaiting a response.

"I-I will see what I can do. I'm new; I don't want to take any liberties." My grin is so sheepish I may bleat at any moment.

"Oh, Henry. We'll see you get a few days off anyway," Dr. Earnest chimes in helpfully, sealing my fate.

I tip my hat. "Good evening. Violet, Priscilla. Father—I will *see you* tomorrow."

"Can't wait, son."

I tilt my head and grimace when only he can see, and head out into the darkness.

The streets are quiet and misty. I arrive at my door and stop, staring up at the cottage. Anxiety squeezes my chest and I resist the compulsion to pace. I am not at all tired. My head is bursting with questions.

I continue on, staring at Arabella's cottage. All the lights are dark. She's either asleep...or out.

Intuition sparks in my chest and I continue down the street.

My footfalls echo, slapping on the damp sidewalks. I squint as the foggy air wets my face.

Questions pop in and out of my consciousness, each more perplexing than the one before.

Neanderthals or Nephilim?

Priscilla and paternal approval or...Arabella?

What has Stygian to do with the sausage plant?

When I think of life with Priscilla, I see a Sunday-best suit, buttoned to the collar, starched and proper.

And when I picture a life with Arabella, my mind conjures a half-buttoned shirt, sweat, dirt and adventure.

Nothing ordinary. That girl is anything but ordinary.

"You forgot lust," I whisper. I take a deep breath and walk toward the park, which is situated on the opposite side of her dwelling.

"This is madness. Sheer madness. Highly inappropriate."

I stop dead.

Alongside the building stands a copse of trees and a small lawn. *I was right*. A solitary woman flits back and forth in the night.

Arabella bends down, picks up a ball and proceeds to hurl it across the lawn. She's still in her ivory ball gown, the green sash swinging madly with her every move.

Newton yips and barrels with glee across the lawn. He leaps, snatching the ball in his jaws and then bounds back to her feet, waggling all over.

"She's mad. In her dress, at this hour. It's not safe."

I instantly search the streets, looking for danger.

She hasn't noticed me yet. Suddenly her ivory form

crumples to the cement stairs of a monument, her face buried in her hands.

The dog wiggles its way between her bent arms and its pink tongue licks her face.

Her hands slowly drag down the length of her face, which is crumpled with pain.

Her white gloved fingers lace into the dog's fur. She hugs him, squeezing her eyes closed.

I feel awkward, like I'm a voyeur on an emotional exchange I have no business watching.

Her face rises as if hearing my thought, and our eyes lock.

She weakly lifts her gloved hand in greeting.

I walk swiftly to her side and sit down beside her on the steps. I notice her parasol beside her.

A parasol?

It's nighttime? I add it to my list of Arabella-questions with no answers.

"Arabella…" My tone chastises. I cannot help it.

She stares straight forward. Her words sounding rehearsed. "I know. It isn't safe. I'm still in my dress. And ladies don't play with dogs in the dark."

I imagine she's heard this and so much more about her improper behavior.

"Yes." I stare at the side of her face, but she won't meet my eyes.

Suddenly her head swivels and her eyes narrow. "Calling on a lady at midnight is highly out of decorum, Henry Watson."

I smile. "I know. I—just wanted to be sure you were

alright. At least you weren't crying."

"I don't cry."

"What do you mean, you don't cry?" But I do a quick search of my childhood memories.

A litany of images of a tiny Bella, and then an older, shapelier Bella.

Arabella angry, Arabella joyous. I have no recollection of ever seeing her weep.

"I. Don't think I can."

"Why? That's not natural."

"Oh, I'm fully aware. It…wasn't encouraged in my household."

I try to picture Holmes comforting a screaming child, and end up with chills.

This is very close. Very personal. She never lets me in this far.

All our lives, our conversations danced around her pain. It seemed saying it outright might destroy her. I feel privileged— she's lifting the curtain—which will drop on my head with the slightest wrong word.

I don't know if I should say it.

I scrutinize her face. Her bottom lip is trembling, like the prelude to tears. But her blue eyes are dry and are tight, as if she is in pain.

I take the leap. "What would happen when you cried?" I'm holding my breath.

Arabella's eyes widen at my forwardness, her mouth works, but no sounds come forth.

"I'm so sorry, you don't have to answer. I'm quite sure

this isn't helping."

Her fingers wrap about my elbow and she carefully lays her head against my arm. Her musky perfume intoxicates me. At complete odds to Priscilla's flowery one.

Steady, man.

She stares ahead. "He would get angry. And so I learned other ways to deal with sadness. We got along best—"

"When he is teaching you." I finish her sentence. "Sharing his obsessions."

Her red head pops up, her dark eyes alarmed. "Please don't misunderstand. He does love me. I know that. He just doesn't show love the way other people do."

I nod. "Yes, I imagine that's so."

"If I called for him right now—he would appear as quickly as he was humanly able."

"I believe that, too."

She stares at the dog and her lips press together.

Her voice is low, "I have inherited his mind, but also his inability to...*relate* to others. To humans, anyway."

I cock my head. Bella is a natural with any animal. I picture the nine-year-old version, standing in the backyard, walking toward a snarling mongrel. My mother's vehement warning's flying from the porch. In moments, the dog was curled in her lap like a harmless pup.

I keep silent, unsure how to respond to this. I...always understood her. She was not the stern, cold exterior that she portrayed to the world.

She clears her throat. "I just. I am having trouble leaving him." She ruffles Newton's fur.

"Father will take him; watch over him till we return."
I smile with pleasure as I think of Newton's drool all over his
spotless waistcoat

I cannot wait to see his face.

"Really? Henry that would be wonderful. Thank you so
much."

I stare at her hand, the way it caresses the dog's fur and
ask a rhetorical question.

"I remember your attachment to animals. So that
continued after I left for school?"

"Oh, yes. Newton came with me from England. Dogs
are another of my hobbies. I have three at home." Her eyes blaze
with what I recognize as Holmesian obsession.

She drops her voice, as if sharing a secret. "Would you
like to see something I'm quite proud of?"

I smile, relieved at the shift in her expression. "Of
course."

She snatches the bowler from my head, and flings it into
the air. "What? What're you doing?"

It catches the breeze, and sails up into the dark sky,
landing twenty feet away.

"Shh. Watch." She shakes the dog, getting his attention.
"Newton. Find. Hat."

Newton cocks his furry head for a split-second and
bounds across the grass. His teeth barely touch the brim. He
heads back toward us, tail wagging and drops it into Arabella's
lap.

"Good boy. Good dog," she croons. She smiles proudly.
"He has a vocabulary."

My eyes narrow. "Really? Whatever do you mean?"

She shrugs. "I've worked with him for five years. He knows sit, stay, come, find...and more interesting commands."

"Such as?"

"Growl."

A vehement growl rips from his throat.

Newton's hackles rise and his gums retract, exposing gleaming white fangs. His growl intensifies, and I instinctually shift away.

"Desist."

He stops instantly. Tail wagging and tongue lolling once more.

"I'm astounded."

"There's more. B-i-t-e."

"B—" Arabella's hand shoots to cover my mouth. "Do not say it. I don't know if he will respond to someone else's command, but he might."

"Fascinating. What else can he do?"

Stones shuffle at the end of the little park. Our heads whip in tandem in the direction of the sound.

Footsteps retreat. The dog growls, low in his throat, and his hair shoots up in a furry line from his neck to his tail.

A tall, caped figure darts behind the building.

The dog lunges, barking madly and I lunge for his collar, restraining him.

"We should go investigate." Arabella grasps her parasol and stands. I quickly grab her hand, before she darts off.

"I don't have a weapon. It's late. Remember the expedition."

Her eyes flick from my face to the spot the figure vacated and she sighs. "It's cat and mouse. I follow him, he follows me."

"You don't know it was Stygian."

"Most likely not him, one of his lackeys, perhaps."

"Arabella, we depart in…" I check my pocket watch. "Less than six hours. We both need to be very careful. Stygian would like nothing better than to dismiss us. I will walk you to your cottage."

She glances to the spot where the figure disappeared and sighs. "Very well. But my life is getting more complicated every day."

We quickly walk to her cottage.

I check that we are not being watched and then usher her inside, sighing as I picture her tiny frame, stalking her stalker. Mad, she is.

I start to shut the door, but she places her foot in it, slowly re-opening it for my departure.

"Who do you think that was?"

"I have several ideas," she places her hand on my chest and eases me back onto the porch. "But we will discuss it tomorrow."

Next day
Bella

The steamship is anchored and sailors scuttle up and down the gangplank like sea-crabs, loading trunks and equipment.

Stygian and Earnest chose well; they hand-picked the vessel because of her size and ability to house the entire team, our equipment, and...the hand. A chugging, steaming home base, capable of a quick departure should the situation degrade.

Another ship glides past, garnering my attention. The river was always full of ships as its mouth culminated in New York, and the ocean.

I search for Henry, my eyes picking through the crowd lining the ship's railing.

Violet and Dr. Watson arrive, instantly veering toward me.

My mind replays childhood days with Mary, John's first wife, and then my recent teener years with Violet. The time with them was never enough. It felt stolen. I always wanted more.

I see Violet's arms open, and steel myself for the hug.

I'm quite sure I've never had so much affection. I'm trying to grow accustomed to it.

I hand her Newton's leash. "You're sure you don't mind, Violet? He's a rather active dog?"

"No, not at all. I love animals, my dear." She smiles slyly. "I married John, didn't I?"

John laughs. "My dear. I will miss you so. At least you'll have the dog to keep you company."

I give his ears one last scratch. I hate to leave him.

Animals, only love you. They never disappoint, never judge.

"I will miss him so."

"We'll be back before he realizes you've gone." John

says bracingly. I search his face, thankful for him. To John, my concerns have always been valid.

A familiar laugh echoes behind me and I experience a brief falling sensation. Henry has arrived.

His voice simultaneously thrills and terrifies me.

Father said our years apart were for our own good. And yet here he is, back by my side.

I turn toward his voice and murmur, "Sherlock Holmes, thwarted." And I smile.

I almost hear one bolt on the heart-box throw open. I may have to add him to my list of obsessions.

Henry eyes the leash in Violet's hands.

"So this means…" He gives his father a meaningful look.

"I'm coming, my boy. Don't try to hide your excitement— let it run free."

Henry briefly closes his eyes and swipes a hand across his face. However, in seconds, he's recovered.

"Wonderful."

I hear a tinny, forced laugh behind me. Priscilla. Perfect time to make my exit. "Excuse me."

I pick through the people on the deck and linger at the railing.

I watch their exchange. Henry's strained expression, and Priscilla's rapturous joy, just to bask in his presence.

Her eyes find me for the briefest of seconds, and she scowls. She leans in forwardly and pecks Henry on the cheek. His face goes instantly scarlet.

I turn away, fighting the nausea.

A flutter catches my eye. Across the river, on a tree limb.

My heart trips.

A whole line of them; their wings beating in a synchronous tandem. A cluster of black butterflies form an eerie congregation.

"*Why* must you vex me?" I square my shoulders, but goose bumps explode on my arms, just the same.

My perpetual mystery. Driving me mad to solve it.

They flit through my past; silent observers running alongside my childhood memories.

Following me down to the river.

Landing on my knee while I was swinging.

Almost *watching* Henry and I, while we climbed trees, playing pirates.

Henry arrives beside me, and follows my stare.

"That's very odd, Arabella. Their formation."

"Yes, I know. They follow me."

Henry's eyes cloud, his face explicitly worrying for my sanity. "Could you explain that in more scientific terms? Lest I recommend a visit to my father? Or perhaps a physician more focused on the mind?"

I grin. "Oh, I know how that sounds. They are the perpetual thorn in my side. The singular puzzle I cannot solve. I actually told father about it."

Henry's eyes light with familiar excitement. He loves deciphering and deduction. "What did he say? He didn't think you mad?"

I nod. "At first, yes. Then he began to watch, and saw them too. We conducted many experiments about them over the years."

"And the conclusion?" Henry stare returns to the flock.

They lift from the limb in tandem, exploding in a black cloud, and then dispersing across the Hudson.

"We never solved it completely. Father's hypothesis is that I exude a certain chemical that attracts them—like specific flowers do."

Henry rubs his face, nodding. "Fascinating. You're a butterfly magnet."

I roll my eyes.

"Arabella. Henry. It's time to go inside. A meeting is assembling." Dr. Watson strides inside, not waiting for a response.

Stygian and a burly man are shuffling up the deck, lugging a colossal black chest between them. The hand must be inside.

Henry notices, too and grabs my elbow. "Let's go."

I glance behind me one last time. A singular black butterfly sits on the exact spot my hand vacated.

Slowly beating its wings.

Chapter Ten

THE FIRST PARTY'S FATE

The Ship's Bowels
Bella

My stomach lurches with the rolling of the steamship. I stare out the window, searching for the horizon. My inner ear adjusts, and with it, my breathing. I still fear I may vomit all over Henry's boots.

His fingers drum lightly on my chair as he fidgets. John sits beside him, one leg draped lazily over the other. His cane rests languidly across his lap.

I know better. That cane, in the hands of John Watson, is a deadly weapon.

Something is making him nervous.

Henry notices, too. I watch his eyes dart to his father's cane, and then around the room, searching for the source of danger.

"Welcome." Stygian spreads his long arms dramatically. "We are headed up the Hudson, where last month's storm has unearthed more possibilities."

With considerable effort, Earnest stands, and shuffles to his side. "We know there is heated scientific debate as to the skeleton's origins, but for now—our primary objective is to recover it, and get it back to the Mutter."

Stygian continues, "We will divide into teams. Dr. Watson, Arabella and Henry shall form one, and myself and Dr. Montgomery on the other. You may be curious why we've asked Dr. Watson to join us...as his specialty is not antiquities, but crime."

"And medicine," Earnest adds.

"Yes. The previous team, Marston and Klink, Sully and Archival; who unearthed the hand...never returned. A portion... of Marston's body surfaced in the Hudson only yesterday."

A murmur of horror ripples through the scientists drowning out the waves lapping against the boat. The voice of the Hudson. Which silenced our predecessors.

A picture is being passed back through the rows. I track its approach by the 'its-a-shame' head shakes of acquaintances' and horrified expressions of the team's closer colleagues.

It arrives at Henry and he grasps it, holding it still for John and I to see.

Marston's bespectacled, somber stare catches my eye first. His hair streaked with gray, the oldest and undoubtedly the team's leader.

Sully's arm is draped around Archival's shoulders in an obvious friendship. They make an unlikely pair: Sully's unfashionable long hair, tied in a leather strap, in stark contrast to Archival's clean-cut altar-boy looks.

And Klink rounds out the team—smiling so wide his gold tooth showed.

"Were you well acquainted?" Henry asks quietly.

"Only in passing. They were in and out on expeditions since my arrival."

People begin speaking out of turn.

"What happened to them?"

"How did they deliver the hand?"

Stygian raises his hands for calm. "Quiet, please. We cannot explain over the ruckus."

Earnest's bushy eyebrows waggle up and down like wooly caterpillars. "They shipped back the hand by courier, and never returned."

"How long ago? How many days?" Henry asks, not raising his hand.

"Is his body available for examination?" I eye John, his mouth half-open. I know I've beaten him to the question. He hides his half-smile and shakes his head.

"Already buried," Ernest answers.

"That's convenient," John murmurs.

"Like you've never exhumed a body," Henry quietly retorts.

"I can tell you that the wounds were clean, perhaps a knife or axe." Stygian's black eyes scan the audience.

I shiver as déjà vu takes over.

The ghost of his hot breath tickles my ear. His insistent hand on the back of my corset. The flush spreads down my chest and I bite my lip.

The meeting has disintegrated into chaos; men gather into small groups, lamenting and gesticulating their frustrations at their colleagues' demise.

John and Henry are whispering, oblivious to me.

While the chaos continues, Stygian finds my face in the crowd. His stare is not cold or hard, but *dead*.

And wicked and lustful. Still.

His eyes are inanimate, like a puppet.

I do not think he is done with me. There is much more to his obsession.

I flick my thumbs as Shakespeare pops into my head. "Something wicked this way comes," I whisper. The words slip out.

"What did you say, Arabella?" Henry has turned back to me.

Stygian smiles; an ugly, twisted curling of lips. It reminds me of my old cat—a big wooly Tom who would torture his prey, paralyze them, play with them, before finally devouring them.

Stygian breaks the staring contest, his face reanimating to its professional façade.

"Meeting adjourned for this evening. We wanted to keep you abreast of the turn of events, to have your guard up, and keep your staterooms locked."

Sailors milling outside the door murmur amongst themselves. One of them looks skeptically toward Stygian.

I overhear one say, "Nice of him to tell us this *after* we've left port."

We walk back down the hall, toward the stateroom.

Henry and I are alone in the hallway, and an inky blackness gathers outside the porthole now.

"Why, fancy that. My room is right next to yours," he smiles mischievously.

"How did you manage that?"

"Father traded with me."

"Really? I'm very shocked at his allowing temptation."

He half-smiles and bites the inside of his mouth before teasing, "You think you're a temptation, Miss Holmes?"

"I. I don't know. Am I, Henry?"

I don't move. I've never, ever attempted to entice a man. Not one has ever held my interest. I hold perfectly still, willing him to me.

Henry steps very close. Too close for propriety. "I believe Father's more concerned for your safety than your chastity at this point." The grin fades from his face as something dark crosses his mind. "Do you want me to sleep with you?"

"Henry!"

"Don't be daft." He lowers his voice to a whisper. "It's Stygian. I don't like the way he regards you. He makes no effort to conceal his…lust."

I nod. I won't deny it.

His expression is black. "I. I'm afraid I want to *hurt* him. So—I will not be getting a wink of sleep, even next door to you."

I open my stateroom door and take one step inside. Henry places his hand on the door, long fingers splayed. "Bella, I am going to have to insist. For your safety, of course."

"No. I'm quite capable of taking care of myself. I escaped

his advances once, didn't I?"

"That gives me no solace."

I step inside, shutting the door till only an inch of his face is visible through the crack.

His blue eyes wrinkle in frustration, "Please, Arabella. I know I'm vexing you—but I am deadly worried. I *promise* to be the perfect gentleman."

"I don't know if you're capable of that, Henry. What if we're caught? Your presence alone would be enough for Stygian to dismiss the both of us. That my *feminine wiles* are distracting you into fornication."

"We will not get caught. On my honor. Open the door."

I sigh, trying to ignore his beautiful, pleading face. No wonder the silly girls fawn all over him.

"Fine, but only because you said please. Henry, I will never forgive you if we are dismissed."

I step aside for him to enter, and look out into the hallway to assure we are unseen.

He slides past me, his chest brushing mine in the tight space as he eases into the room.

He halts, our bodies blistering against one another. He stares down at me. "We won't get caught."

I shove him inside, close the door and throw the bolt.

He stoops and steals a kiss and my breath, and is on my bed before I've managed a word.

He folds a hand behind his head. "Shall you sleep with me, then?" He pats the covers beside him.

I snap my gaping-aghast mouth shut and pelt a pillow at his head. "Get on the floor."

###

Midnight
Henry

I wake as the boat lurches, assailing my stomach. I am momentarily disoriented and take deep breaths as I wait for my brain to categorize the most recent events.

I squint around the stateroom, which is utterly black, as is the porthole on the wall.

"Arabella?" I whisper.

Nothing. Complete graveyard silence, except for the rush of the waves past the bow.

I pat the top of the bed, my hand searching for her warm body. As I've been doing every hour on the hour since my head touched the pillow. The bed is smooth.

"Oh, please." I hurry to stand and light the lamp. Her bed is empty. "She is a lunatic and is going to take me down with her."

I reach inside my bag, extract a tiny pistol and jam it in the top of my trousers.

I crack open the door and immediately hear the ruckus.

I see the flash of her auburn hair as she rounds the corner. "Blast."

I bolt down the corridor, pistol drawn.

She's made it outside and is walking in tight circles

with a smallish man. He lunges, swiping within an inch of her forearm. I inhale sharply. The knife flashes; he charges her.

Volcanic anger erupts, incinerating all other thoughts.

I bolt forward, my thighs burning.

She swipes a knife at his face. He blocks, grasping her forearm.

Her hand rotates forward, loosening his grip.

If I weren't so utterly terrified, his face would be comical; it screams, *A woman who can fight?*

Her boot juts skyward, connecting with his jaw.

I had no idea her body moved like that? Like a contortionist?

Almost there.

Bones crunch as his jaw snaps shut and blood trickles out the side of his mouth as his face turns murderous.

He lunges, and manages to grasp a handful of her hair.

"Ah!"

She screams and is still.

His face is triumphant. "That's right, lovey. My word, you're a petal." He licks his lips.

The whole scene flares to red as I burst onto the deck, panting.

His eyes dart to me.

Arabella seizes the distraction; her boot flashes up again to strike his gut and his breath exhales in a *whoosh.*

He releases her, but yanks, ripping out a handful of auburn hair.

"Ah!"

A droplet of blood falls to the ground as every movement

slows to a crawl in my horror.

I'm bolting toward them; he's moving her away, toward the railing.

No. No, not over the side.

She rushes him, her face contorted with pain and rage, her knee connecting with his crotch.

"Oof."

He doubles over.

Hatred twists his face into a leer. "That's it, missy."

He jabs right, into her shoulder, knocking her off balance. Her head snaps back with the force.

Arabella rights and her boot swings into the air.

I hear a catch snap and see another flash of silver as a knife pops from the toe of her boot.

She slashes, cutting up and across his thigh.

"Ahh—you little wench!"

His head swivels as he registers my footsteps.

He gives her one final shove, sending her sliding bottom-first, across the deck.

He limps for the railing.

I launch forward but he dives, down into the black waves, and disappears.

I reach down to haul her from the deck and we both rush to the rail, searching.

In a moment, his head breaks through the black water and he begins to swim for shore.

Chapter Eleven

Both Wonderful and Terrible

Steamship Mess Hall
Henry

My eyes skip across father's paper, strewn across the breakfast table. The headline reads, 'More hospital admissions from tainted sausage.'

My eyes narrow and I carefully fold it away and slip it into my pack for later-reading.

"Describe him again, Arabella." Father's notebook is in his hand, his face serious.

"Father, she's already told you. Please, she should be resting." My voice is more irritable than I intend.

Arabella's eyes flick to me and her stare manages to be both affronted and appreciative.

"Henry, I told you. All is well. John is merely doing his job. I am no wilting flower. This is necessary data collection, as you are well aware."

Petal. Her expression digs up the assailant's word and I grind my teeth together. I clutch and squeeze my hands together under the table, wanting to throttle someone. Anyone.

Get ahold of yourself.

The scent of morning coffee does nothing to ease me. She and father grasp their mugs and smile at one another as if it's bloody afternoon tea.

Arabella places her hand on my forearm, and I forcibly restrain myself from throwing her over my shoulder and running. I did not expect this. When I saw her hair dangling from his hand; something happened.

Both wonderful and terrible.

I stepped from a ledge of infatuation into an utter free-fall.

I want to *protect her* and stop all harm from touching her. I want her away from here, away from Stygian, away from the danger of the expedition.

Would he go to such lengths, just to remove her from the expedition? Or is something more sinister afoot...

Her lips purse as she ponders a question from my father, which I didn't hear. I should be hanging on every word, evaluating.

Stygian has barely uttered a word. His black eyes skip around the table, taking in people's expressions.

"Most unfortunate, Arabella," Dr. Earnest finally says. "Do you maintain your original wish, to stay on the expedition? No one would fault you, my dear, if you chose to return to the Mutter."

Just go, Arabella. Please.

Stygian cuts across the murmuring. "Yes, Miss Holmes, after this turn of events, surely you must be in need of rest?"

"Yes," I agree. Bella's eyes narrow and catch fire.

I amend, "Perhaps just for a few days, to catch your breath?"

"I am fine, sir. As I assured you, I am not like other girls. It is my firm desire to find that skeleton."

This will not do. Arabella will never sit at home, by a hearth, out of harm's way.

Nor would I have ever wanted that of her, when I was just her friend. It's who she is, she breathes for adventure.

My hand drags down my face. *How am I to reconcile the two?*

Her need for danger and my new, mind-numbing fear for her safety?

One of her hands drops below the table; her speech never falters—she delivers the blow by blow in a fluid river of words. "He was most definitely English, not American."

"However could you tell?" Montgomery asks with genuine interest. "His accent?"

"Accents can be faked, but no. The cut of his jacket, the shape of his boots, were decidedly European. He'd ripped out a handful of my hair, and that's when Henry arrived."

I am astounded by her Holmesian details, though I shouldn't be. It's completely Arabella.

"Black hat, brown boots covered in a reddish mud. Small frame, white, thick scar from the left side of his lip down to his throat."

However.

However, Arabella's eyelids have drifted half-closed.

She is lying. Or withholding information.

My mind erupts in Bella-memories.

Sherlock Holmes's incinerating gaze and stern face. "Arabella? Did you and Henry remove the microscope from my laboratory?"

Bella, tiny, maybe ten. "No, Papa. Why ever do you ask?" Her eyelids drooping, half-closed, like now.

My foot taps out my impatience and her eyebrows rise with the sound.

Unexpectedly, I feel her fingers in my lap, under the table, searching for mine. I release my death-clenched hands, to allow her one. Her fingers rub the length of mine, in small, concentric patterns.

I *feel* the stare.

I slowly raise my head and see Stygian's gaze boring down. He raises one questioning eyebrow. It's most definitely rhetorical, however.

It's as if my entire inner monologue is laid bare on the table, and he's shifting through the words.

He knows. My heart has apparently left my sleeve and is now a sign hanging about my neck.

Arabella senses it too. I feel the muscles in her arms grow tense. Stygian turns toward Montgomery, who is murmuring in his ear.

Bella's eyes flick and return to father. It was no longer

than a single beat of my heart.

It was enough.

Stygian's normally-pristine clothing is rumpled, having been roused from bed at this ungodly hour.

A dark, black streak, an inch across, pokes out from his unbuttoned shirt sleeve.

A tattoo.

Bella

The steamship slows, easing its way into the first port. Henry stands at the rail, staring down the rickety dock with uncertainty.

This new Henry was reluctant to let me retire to my room without him, which is very much at odds to my memories of youthful Henry. If anything, he was always goading, always testing the limits of my courage—the bigger the risk, the better, really.

I picture myself, hanging upside down from a tree, skirts awry and oblivious, and cringe. As a girl, I had no idea what was appropriate. At times, I still don't.

He turns when he hears my footsteps. His eyes immediately soften. My heart stutters in my chest.

"Feeling better?"

"Much, thank you."

The boat shakes as it slides into port, and the sailors swarm the deck to begin the securing process.

Local fishermen dot the shore as well, manning a small fleet of canoes. All eye our boat with suspicious interest.

"How long are we scheduled to be here?"

My bag feels heavy, laden with picks and brushes and spades.

"As long as necessary." His forehead is wrinkled into a deep set of lines that match his downturned mouth.

I have only moments before Dr. Montgomery and the others arrive from below deck.

"Henry, are you cross with me?"

His lips pull to the side as he bites the inside of his cheek and he gives me one terse head-shake in the negative.

Bad liar, Henry. I hope you haven't inherited John's inkling for gambling. You will lose your shirt.

"You have everything you need, then?" Stygian arrives, dark as a murder of crows.

Black boots, black coat, black hair and eyes.

To match that black heart.

"Yes. We'll send word as to whether we'll stay at the farm, or will be back for the evening."

Stygian smiles. It takes me off guard, as it almost appears genuine. "Dr. Watson will be staying on board. He's examining the men's stateroom and the deck."

"We're off, then," Henry says.

I bite my lip. Henry doesn't shake his hand. An out-and-out rebuff.

He's either mad about me, or mad in general to cross Stygian.

My mind clicks into surveillance. Deciphering expressions

was never my forte, nor father's. He actually developed a chart, based on human observations for us to memorize.

Henry is cross, despite his assurances. His jaw is locked, his hands in fists and every rigid step screams his displeasure as he heads towards the tethered horses on shore.

Two sets: one for Stygian and Montgomery and the other for us. Two separate locations have been identified for potential burial grounds.

The hairs on my arms lift and I shiver. I discretely glance behind me. Stygian *was* watching. He is not now, but I absolutely felt it.

Gusts of wind push hard against my face like autumn water sprites skittering across the river's surface.

I hear the squawk of geese and turn to see their V flying south across the water.

The Hudson rushes by; a reassuring constant.

My eyes flick to it. There's something off about the color today. Its normally murky waters appear to have the slightest tint of color.

"Arabella. We're wasting daylight."

I smile. "Why what perfect impatience; you sound precisely like your father."

He grimaces as I swing into the saddle. "I have the directions. You have the map?"

"Of course."

He clucks his tongue, easing the mare up the hill. Her hooves shift through the blanket of downed leaves and the sound reminds me of a crackling fire.

I follow, rubbing the horse's neck beneath his mane.

We venture into upstate New York, winding down a main road until we reach the small goat-path leading to our destination.

It's been a lonely ride, save the traveling carnival we passed. Its bright colors looking distinctly out of place in the barren countryside.

The sky is dark and brooding, much like Henry.

He's barely uttered a sentence. He's contemplating, trying to work out what he wants to say. The weather seems to mimic his mood, as if the breeze holds its breath in similar anticipation.

I shiver as the wind whips across the road, pulling my hair from its Gibson-girl bun. I know the hairstyle to be fashionable, but truth be told, my mane of hair is merely more manageable piled on my head than fluttering about my face like those blasted butterflies.

A multi-colored shower of fall leaves spiral down and dance in circles as they're caught in the updraft.

"The farm is about two miles due north. You handled yourself remarkably well with the…attacker. Tell me the history of that boot. I've read of such contraptions, but never seen one first-hand."

I smile and resist the urge to finger the knife strapped to my thigh. "Father, you know. Before he would give his blessing, for my appointment at the Mutter—he insisted I undergo certain…trainings."

"Really. Why am I not surprised? Such as?"

Henry's eyes soften, but the rest of his face remains stubbornly rigid.

"He had a retired military friend tutor me…in cane fighting, and self-defense."

"Would that retired-military-friend be my father?"

I ignore the question. "Together, they created several contraptions, all to ease his mind. It doesn't seem to have worked. He still writes me constantly, and becomes incensed if I don't immediately respond. I am quick about it, as I don't fancy a visit until I am certain my position is secure."

Henry's eyes turn queer. An expression I cannot place. "As we are a scientific team, we must discuss our differing opinions. And it is best to do it now, before anyone can overhear our disagreement. We must be, or at least appear, united."

"Proceed."

Henry's eyes sharpen. "When my father finally gave his blessing that I could accept the position at the Mutter, I visited every museum and library in London … " His voice is cautionary as he attempts to sound diplomatic.

I feel the irritation burning around my collar. It's irrational, but I can't seem to stop it.

"What, pray tell did you find?"

"Have you read nothing? You are just accepting the assumption of Darwin's hypothesis of natural selection?"

"Yes." I turn my chin up in defiance and meet his gaze. "Darwin's theory is scientific. Not a bunch of voodoo, designed to temper the sting of death."

Henry's mouth spasms. He jerks back on the reins, halting the mare. A rare blaze of emotional comprehension flares.

His mother. He's thinking of his mother. I must sound so very cruel.

My mind flashes a memory of a crumpled little Henry. Three crumpled men, really.

John, cradling the boys to him, while father paced helplessly before them.

The telegram from my uncle Mycroft, wanting to visit. They argued viciously, then. I'd never seen John so angry.

"No, do not let him come," John told father. "Our lives are complicated enough right now."

"He is concerned..."

John's voice was fierce, "So am I. He lost his say about her, remember?"

Father nodded, and stared at me. *"Too True, Watson. I'm so very sorry for your loss."*

It took years till the Watsons were sound, once again.

I wondered for many years, why father stared *at me* that day. How did I figure in with Uncle Mycroft?

Henry flips his bag around to his front, returning my mind to the present. He reaches in and extracts a stack of parchments in his gloved hand.

He clears his throat. "I may not have a map with pins, nor a photographic memory—but I am perfectly capable of doing my own research. Apparently the United States has had many archaeological discoveries involving giants. In Minnesota, in 1888, seven skeletons were unearthed, each seven to eight feet tall. In West Virginia, in 1884, a skeleton measuring seven feet, six inches was found in a temple-like chamber. This was a report from the Smithsonian. I have a friend there. You think *The Smithsonian* is forging data?"

"No, of course not. Those skeletons are Neanderthal men. A race that developed prior to humans, from apes."

Henry shakes his head. "This isn't like you. The Arabella I knew would never-ever write a conclusion or form an opinion till that red-head was bursting with facts. You are thinking with your heart, not your mind. There's something deeper. What're you not telling me? As your scientific partner I demand your honesty."

Hot, searing anger floods my nose and cheeks. "I believe in *myself.* I've seen no evidence of a higher power in my score of years. There is only science and rules."

Henry glares back, nostrils flaring as he jams the papers back into his pack. "No evidence? You've never seen *anything* out of the ordinary?"

"Every day. There is always an answer."

He smirks and I want to slap it off.

He's staring behind me. Chills erupt. I know what is there. I don't want to turn.

"Really?"

His eyes dart over my head and lock. "Always an answer. What about them, Arabella?"

I finally relent, and turn.

The blasted butterflies.

The branch is cluttered with five hundred black and blue wings—wings beating in an ordered, beautiful, *taunting* synchrony.

Explain us. Explain us. Their little black bodies proclaim.

I bite down hard on my bottom lip and taste the blood as my chest heaves with anger.

Henry moves the horse closer, his eyes calm now. His voice drops. His tone is low and melodic, like a lover. For a brief second, I picture our bodies intertwined.

"How do we explain them, Arabella? Your scent notwithstanding—it's too late in the season, and their multitude? I'm beginning to see a pattern…"

Emotions battle in my heart; the Holmes side flares in anger at my inability to rationally explain away their wretched existence, the other, the missing side…makes me feel sad and hopeful and scared that I'm hopeful.

Another bolt is thrown on the heart-box. And I struggle not to wrench it open.

Just be done with it and give it to him.

I shake my head, releasing his gaze. "You win, Henry. I cannot explain them. They defy every hypothesis I've ever formed." I glare at them.

His gloved hand takes mine. "It isn't a contest Arabella. I just want to illustrate that science cannot explain *everything*, and at times, I abhor its arrogance. Amazing, unexplainable events happen every day. Let's just keep our minds open. To possibilities."

The flock of black lifts, darting and swooping across to the open field beside us.

My lips twitch in a small smile, and I nod. "To possibilities, then."

Chapter Twelve

Upstate New York
Henry

Our horses clop into a long, meandering lane shielded by a carriage path of gigantic oaks. At its end is a crooked, white farmhouse; it's chimney out of point and leaning.

Arabella shivers hard enough I hear her teeth rattle. The overhanging tree-tunnel is so thick and overgrown the sun's rays are almost completely blotted out. Our horses step over dappled spots of sunlight.

My mare shudders and with a violent shake of her head, halts and whinnies. I lurch sideways, grabbing the saddle horn as she stutter-steps.

"Whoa, girl."

Arabella's mount skitters, backing up. She pats its neck. "Shh. Shh. What's wrong?"

The horse rears and Bella grips the saddle horn as its front hooves slam back into the dirt.

The mare's ears flick flat against her head, twitching in panic.

"Shh, it's alright, it's alright," Arabella croons, leaning down onto its neck, unflustered despite almost being unseated.

The mare's ears tick up, one at a time. She reluctantly steps forward at Arabella's urging, still chomping her bit.

Gratefully, my own follows suit. I decidedly *do not* have Arabella's gift with animals.

"That's odd." I scan the fields, the trees, the house, looking for danger.

Arabella's eyes are sweeping, identical to mine. "Not really, Henry. Animals' senses are much more acute than our own. For instance, before an earthquake, dogs often act queerly."

I smile, but don't pull my eyes away from the house. "I hadn't heard that." She detects the hint of mirth in my tone.

"Nothing other-worldly. It has to do with gravity."

"Of course."

She meets my gaze, long enough to shoot me a dagger-eye.

My breath catches as we leave the tunnel. To the right of the house is a massive green cornfield. And to the left...

Arabella has halted the horse and stares. Pumpkins.

A sea of orange rolls out to the horizon.

"I've never seen so many."

Arabella smiles. "They're beautiful, aren't they?"

I ease my mount alongside hers. "Bella."

"Hmm?" She's still enthralled by the pumpkins.

"Are we a team?" I hesitate. "Like your father and mine?"

She ponders. "Better than your father and mine."

I smile but her eyes instantly narrow. "Speak plainly, Henry. What do you wish to ask?"

"This will be our last moment alone. You. Are not being honest with me."

Her eyelids sink. "Whatever do you mean?"

Anger threatens, but I strive to control it. It will not extract information, nay, a fight is what she wants—to distract me.

"True partners divulge any and all pertinent information."

"Well, that is debatable, father—"

I hold up a finger. "One. What is on that inventory list? And although I rather enjoyed the disguise, the contents were important enough to make you skulk about in the worst area of Philadelphia, and be almost raped by a lusty, pimpled teener. Really, I think you broke the poor lad's heart."

She stares, red lips pursed, obviously contemplating.

I forge on. "Two. The morning after the attack. I saw."

"You saw what?" Her face flushes scarlet.

"You staring. Stygian has a tattoo. I caught you looking at it."

"I confess myself impressed, Mr. Watson."

"Bella, *bloody-well what is it?*"

So much for not letting her bait you.

"Giurio di vendicarmi."

Latin. I've always hated Latin.

I force my mind to recollect. She doesn't wait.

"I swear to avenge myself." Her eyes sharpen. That photographic data machine behind them turning on.

"That is what the tattoo says?"

"Yes. Stygian has one. As did the man who attacked me on the steamer."

Worry hardens like a musket-ball in my stomach. "Do you know what it means?"

"I think so."

"Mr. Watson? Is that you?" A decrepit voice calls from the farmhouse.

Blast.

I do not know if I can behave normally. I must know. How much danger is she truly in?

I raise my hand in acknowledgement to the wizened man on the front porch and grind my teeth together.

"This conversation is not over. Merely postponed."

She shrugs and gives me a maddening smile. "Whatever you say, Henry."

She sets the horse to a trot and I grit my teeth and reluctantly follow.

The caretaker is as crooked and out of point as his dwelling.

"Good day, Sir. I assume you are Mister Abner?"

He nods. It manages to look like an effort. "Yes."

"I am, indeed, Mr. Watson, and this is Miss Holmes. We will be in charge of the dig."

He eyes Arabella as if she's sprouted horns. "And by *we*, you mean *you*, correct?"

Arabella goes instantly rigid.

"No, sir. Miss Holmes is the osteologist."

His ancient eyebrows furrow in confusion.

"The bone expert. And she is here as a fully competent antiquarian."

Not that it is any of your business.

He harrumphs. "You can give your horses to the stable hand and follow me inside. I've made up rooms in case you choose to stay on."

In a few minutes we're inside. We follow him into a simple kitchen. "This is the way."

He shuffles us through a sitting room filled with shabby furniture most likely older than he.

Arabella's gaze drifts over the pictures on the wall. It stops and holds.

I see what she's fixated on. In the center of the paintings is a faded, circular oval, as if a long-hung painting was recently removed.

"Your fields are astounding," I offer.

Abner nods. "Yes, they are quite…fertile."

Arabella draws close and whispers, "And you are quite creepy."

Henry

"Arabella, this is madness. It shall soon be dark and the dig is acres away."

After unpacking, and a quick visit to the writing desk,

Abner insisted we eat. I watched Arabella pick at her food and tap her fingers on the table, her eyes flicking outside every ten seconds. She'd nearly flown out the door once it was remotely polite.

"I *said* it's too late, wait till tomorrow morn."

Her horse is tethered to the white fence. Bella's eyes shoot to the barn, the sky, and then to the main house as she contemplates.

As she throws her pack over her shoulder, more auburn hair escapes the half-bun at her crown. A trickle of auburn slides across her back, clear down to her buttocks. I stop dead and stare. At both.

She whirls in exasperation. "Henry, you mean you will be able to sleep—or even *sit* with the dig so close?"

Her shapely leg flips over the saddle.

Focus, man.

I shake my head. I cannot believe Stygian was right. Arabella is the *definition* of distraction. I'm missing details left and right.

I relent, gritting my teeth. "Fine."

I call to the stable boy and hastily scribble a note. "Could you be sure this is sent—to let our party know we'll be staying the night?"

The young man nods, and takes off toward the main house. And another thought occurs to me. "Wait—two more, if you please?" I hastily pull more letters from my overcoat. One of them Arabella's—addressed to none other than Sherlock Holmes.

The boy looks irritated but takes them just the same.

My smile feels smug as I anticipate my Smithsonian friend's response, how I will gain the upper hand, how—

She's already cantering across the field.

"Blast."

She urges the horse into a full-gallop and gives him his head.

I launch myself into the saddle.

"Ha!" I gently kick my horse into action. I'll never catch her; she's had too much of a head start.

Thunder rumbles overhead. "Perfect."

I feel the birth of panic, squirming to life in my gut.

She keeps ducking in and out of my sight. The rain will only decrease the visibility.

A little voice chastises, *keep her safe, keep her safe.*

The forest rushes past on either side, the barely visible path becoming *in*visible as the brambles thicken.

"Arabella!"

Stupid. I shouldn't call to her. What if someone *is* watching, following? I just revealed our exact location.

A flash of black darts in and out of my peripheral vision. My head jerks to the side and front, trying to catch a glimpse. To find the smattering of black within the green forest.

I weave the horse faster like a barrel racer in and out of the thick trees.

Thunder groans into a cracking, sharp bark, in time with a white flash of lightning.

"For the love of …."

My breath shudders out. She's mercifully stopped, waiting for me at the cave's yawning black mouth.

Chapter Thirteen

DARK MANIFESTATIONS

Bella

Henry pulls the lantern off my saddle and lights it.

His dark blue eyes turn heavenward; his face illuminated in the lightning flash.

"Honestly Bella. Could you have picked a worse night?" Henry's eyes are weary and for once, he is unable to disguise his frustration with me. I shrug. "I know, you're probably right, but we're here now." I sling my pack across my chest. "Ready?"

"No," but he follows me into the dark. "From what Jeremy tells me, Stygian usually sends a few laborers out with the staff. He must be desperate to keep this dig quiet."

"I expect he is. He won't want the Smithsonian or any other institution, beating him to the dirt. Assuming you aren't giving away any of our state-secrets to your friend there. What's his name?"

"Oliver. Oliver Goodwin, if you must know."

"I have a friend named Oliver as well."

"Is that so?" His face appears disgruntled somehow. "What is that strange look?"

I shrug, feeling the heat to my collar, and thankful for once, for the dark.

"Is this Oliver sweet on you, then?"

I pick up my pace, weaving through the rubble as best I can with the dim light.

Henry prompts apparently giving up the fight. "I also wrote to my old professor."

Henry then passes me and stomps forward to take the lead. Stalagmites and stalactites surround us like stony teeth jutting from the cave's mouth.

We carefully pick our way through them. "How far did Mr. Abner say it was?"

"He said we'd come to an underground pool. That was where they found the hand."

The sound of dripping water intensifies with every step. I take deep breaths as my chest tightens.

It's nothing. It's your imagination. Be sensible.

The black before us and the black behind press in like a suffocating cloth against my mouth. Only the lantern holds my panic at bay. I feel the sweat pop on my brow.

"Henry?"

The dark is a slipknot; tightening, tightening on my windpipe, choking me.

"I hear the water. It isn't far now." Henry turns, highlighting my face with the lantern. "Bella! Are you ill?"

I jam my eyes together and the panic blossoms; the hair framing my face goes damp. "I—I."

"What? What is it? We need to go back. We'll go see father."

"I'm fine."

His voice turns steely. "You are not *fine*. Unless you consider wax-corpse to be a normal color. At least tell me your symptoms. I am not going a step further until you do. I can be just as immovable as you." The lantern dims.

The light flickers and my heart pumps madly in time with its guttering flame. "Oh laws, Henry. Do. Not. Let it go out."

"Claustrophobia," he diagnoses, his blue-green eyes searching my face. "Yes."

"You didn't foresee this as a problem?"

"The other digs I visited were not in caves."

"Ah." He shakes his head. "Dance with me."

"What? Are you mad?" My hands are shaking.

Henry's arms wrap around me, pulling me flush against his hard body. I revel in every glorious inch of him. The panic lessens the tiniest degree.

I shake my head. "I'm so sorry, Henry. I—I am hindering the dig, just as Stygian said I would."

"Drowning."

"What? What're you talking about?"

"I'm afraid of drowning. Have nightmares about it."

My voice cracks, "Claustrophobia *feels* like drowning. On dry land."

His hand balls the back of my shirt into a taut knot. The motion somehow feels desperate.

Something is rising inside me. Something I've always been able to control. Desire warms every inch of my body and I'm sweating, for a different reason. It blossoms as a hot-house flower in my mind, wrapping and deliciously warming every inch of my body.

I am so very grateful for the dark; my face is so hot I fear I shall combust.

I step on his foot. "I told you. I'm hopeless."

"There is no such word in my vernacular." He eases our bodies together in a slow, tight circle. Our boots crunch against the stones on the cave floor.

It's the closest I've ever come to a dance. My brain is recoiling. I never allow anyone too close—permit them this power over me.

The pain of rebuffs...is intolerable. Better to avoid attachment altogether.

The metallic taste of fear floods my mouth, which I'm certain is from the heart-box melting and back flowing up my throat in a last-ditch warning.

Henry bows his head; his fine, straight lips inches from mine. "Do you remember when you commented on father's particular attention to Violet at the ball?"

My mind flicks to the pages of my etiquette rule book, which father insisted I memorize. "Yes. It's considered excessively attentive for a man to dance with his wife more than once at a social outing."

His lips part. "I, would dance, each and every dance, with you—if you would have me."

"I—" The panic is gone. The claustrophobia is gone. All

that remains is Henry. His breath blows warm against my lips.

I feel something rough on my back, and realize I am flush against the cave wall.

His lips brush mine, softly, waiting.

They're soft and hard and irresistible.

I press back harder. His lips part mine. My breath comes in quick, harsh gasps as I open my mouth, searching, exploring the velvet of his tongue.

His breath is as loud as mine, and somewhere my analytical mind worries we'll use up all the air with our panting. I laugh against his lips.

"What?" He doesn't remove his kisses; they just trail down my neck, toward my collarbone.

"Nothing."

"Don't think."

I take his face in my hands and every stroke of his lips sends the hot sting of longing from my neck, down my back to my core.

His tongue traces my lower lip and I see the word *self-control* ignite and catch fire. Burning the rules.

My hands race down the front of his shirt. *I want him.* It's dangerous and wrong *and*…and my heart pounds against my ribcage, silencing my protests.

Now, I understand how it happened. How I happened. How my mother made her grave, selfish mistake.

To bed a Holmes, out of wedlock—this resulted in me in her belly and the loss of her most precious commodity…her chastity.

And to her leaving me, alone.

I must find the will to stop. History shall not repeat with me.

"Arabella—I—" Henry whispers.

The lantern goes out. Footsteps and shouts are everywhere. I feel a club strike my hand, then Henry's back slide through my fingers as he crumples away from me in the dark.

Chapter Fourteen

A Stable of Choices

"Henry!"

He doesn't answer. Hands seize my shoulders, jamming my back into the rock, trying to bash my skull.

The man's whiskey-laden breath is on my forehead; my mind estimates the height of his crotch.

My knee shoots up, connecting with soft flesh.

The body halves, his hair brushing my hand on the way down.

My mind whirrs. *You are no match for him. Use a weapon.*

My hands slips down to the knife anchored at my heel. I whip it out, flip it upside down, and grasp his hair with my left. I crash the knife's butt down, smashing it against his head. His hair drops away as he hits the stone.

"Ah!"

"Get off!" Henry.

My mind estimates the lantern's last location. If it hasn't been kicked.

I drop to my knees, hand on the wall for perspective, and crawl along the stone floor. Keeping my left hand anchored to the wall, my right hand scrabbles in the dark, searching.

My stomach contracts. The dark. The dark.

Henry. I no longer hear him.

I will away the invisible fingers squeezing the air from my lungs and suck in deep breaths.

My fingers finally brush metal, and I pull the light to me. I strike a match and the room illuminates. I sigh in relief at its yellow glow.

My attacker lies sprawled on the floor.

The second man straddles Henry, pinning his chest. The assailant's eyes shoot to me.

Mistake. Always focus on the opponent.

Henry's fist collides with the man's jaw with a sickening crunch. I spring forward and kick, my boot connecting with the man's kidney at the same instant Henry clocks his other side. Unhinging his jaw.

He howls in pain and crumples off Henry, scurrying backward.

Henry leaps up, and flings himself after him.

The man pulls a gun, halting Henry in mid-lunge.

"Just give me 'im, and no one will get 'urt." He gestures to the man on the cave floor.

I'm searching, searching.

Black ink tattoo? Large ring?

My attacker struggles to his feet, woozily walking to his partner, steadying himself on the wall.

"Now you two—"

My eyes tighten. I aim and launch the knife. A yawning gash spews red as the blade slashes the man's forearm but doesn't imbed.

He gasps as the pistol and knife clatter onto the rocks.

His fingers splay and shudder and I spy the heavy, circular ring, now covered in blood.

The ring is emblazoned with an **R-**.

Henry dives, sliding for the pistol.

Both men dart into the tunnel, and are instantly swallowed by the dark.

Henry looks up from the floor, cocking his head.

"Next time—we listen *to me*. Next time I say it is too dangerous. It is too bloody dangerous!!"

###

The Hudson Shoreline
Henry

The steamship is just over the hill; we decided not to dig at first light—feeling the need to report the attack. We debated returning last night, but the trek through the dark woods seemed unadvisable.

Arabella has been quiet since waking. I know this might

start trouble. She's anxious. But I must have this information.

I stare at her hands; her digits are white, clutching the saddle horn.

"Bella. Please tell me the contents of the inventory sheet."

She stares straight ahead. "A fortnight prior, Newton brought me a bone."

I laugh. "Normal behavior for any dog. I expect he was quite proud of himself."

Her fingers turn bluish-white as she winds the reins tighter. "I believe it to be a portion of a long bone. Of a human. It was broken at one end. The epiphysis was slanted."

I swallow. A human. "Where did he get it?"

"I told him, 'Find', and...he led me to the sausage plant."

"What has this to do with Stygian?"

"I was called to his office, and quite innocently saw a paper with the sausage company's letterhead."

"Conjecture, at best." But that didn't stop the tingle on my scalp.

"I am aware. Stygian has made at least two trips to the plant that I am aware of." She shivers, biting her lip. "The inventory list contained orders for 375 pounds of potash and 50 pounds of arsenic."

My mind searches the chemistry. "I'm sorry. I'm not following. Perhaps I should..."

She grimaces. "My memory fails me. I suspect those two ingredients could dissolve bone, Henry."

Revelation presses heavy on my chest. "You think he's boiling evidence in the sausage vats? You think he was involved with the first party's disappearance somehow?"

"Possibly. I need more proof. And I need to confirm my assumption. I'm not going to bloody get it here. But I didn't dare turn down this assignment."

"Does father know any of this?"

"No, and he must not. Henry, he would never allow me in such danger."

The all-consuming fear returns making my mouth dry. "And I should, Bella?"

"Henry… I cannot be with you."

Pain like a sucker-punch contracts my gut, followed by a flare of anger. "Who said I wanted you to?"

Her voice is caustic. "Yes, I know you have a veritable stable of choices. So why choose me, Henry?"

My teeth grind together. I should be reasonable, I should not speak. Everything about her makes me lose my reserve. Decorum commits suicide within five feet of her.

"I—I don't want a stable. I don't know whether to throttle you or hold you down till you kiss me again. I won't tell him Bella. You have my word."

My insides ache. Like withdrawal from an addiction.

A picture of Holmes in one of his cocaine-ravaged periods pops to my mind. My mind draws perfect recall of the leather case where he kept the syringe, '*in a seven percent solution*' father used to say, with a face full of disapproval.

What did Arabella do as a child, when his mind went on holiday?

I see the girl from my childhood, in her room, dogs all over her bed. Alone.

A lump rises in my throat along with my father's voice in my head, "She doesn't know how to love properly."

Fine, then I shall teach her.

I turn to look at her. Her stare is cold, but there's a vulnerable quiver in her lips.

We've reached the embankment. Below, the docked steamer awaits.

"Henry! Come quickly!" Father bellows.

Father is on the shore, arms waving madly above his head. Shipmen swarm the riverbanks, their torches bobbing like a congregation of fireflies. Disembodied shouts ring through the morning mist.

"What's happening?" Bella whispers breathlessly.

"Coming!" I scream toward the shore. Then turn to her, "Hurry, Arabella."

A streak of sunlight cuts through the mist—and then I see it.

The Hudson—is red. A large circle is growing and growing, ten feet from shore. Not precisely red, but most definitely not the Hudson's murky brown.

"Don't even mention the word *Nile*."

I shake my head, too stunned for debate.

We arrive, and instantly dismount.

"What's happened?" we both ask father in unison.

"One of the crewman claims he saw a body." Father's eyes narrow and scan the water.

A passing sailor halts, interrupting, "Begging your pardon, Dr. Watson, but I's known Tivaldi since we was lads. He's no excitable fellow. If he says he saw a body. He saw a body."

The man drags his hand across his lined face and plunges back into the fray of moving bodies.

Stygian and Montgomery bark commands to search the surrounding woods for signs of foul play.

Arabella moves toward the water and I follow.

I call into the crowd. "Fishing nets, do you have any?"

"Aye, sir." A young, fresh-faced boy scurries up the decks and returns within a minute with a long, thick net.

Father, Arabella, and I need no words. I pick up one end, father at the other, Bella in the middle.

I open my mouth to ask her to stay on shore, and shut it. She's going in, no matter how I plead.

My heart throbs. My preoccupation is distracting me again.

The water is cold against my thighs as we wade into the shallows. In moments, we've reached the circle. The crimson is as thick as the dread filling my mouth.

I glance quickly at Arabella and shudder. Her white shirt is saturated with bright red blotches. She looks as if she's the murderer. Her eyes are serious, but unafraid.

A few more steps and the water is licking our necks.

"There's a drop-off, do not step any further," Father warns.

Stygian and Montgomery are on shore, watching carefully. "Nothing, Dr. Watson?" Montgomery calls. He's pacing.

"Not yet."

Father inhales in preparation to dive.

"Don't. Father—I know you're a soldier, but I have twenty years on you."

I plunge beneath, not waiting for his argument. The river is black and murky and I am essentially blind. I breaststroke through the water in large, exaggerated movements—my hands searching for anything resembling a body.

My head shoots up and out of the surface, and I search up and down the river. No ship.

"Anything?" she asks.

"Not yet. Throw me the net."

Father quickly casts, and I catch the end. I swim toward them, the net dragging the water between us. Arabella looks over my shoulder, biting her lip. "Hurry, Henry."

I reach her, and under the water she gives my arm a quick squeeze. Our eyes lock, and for the moment, all is forgotten.

We drag the net to shore, the water slowly inching down from my waist, my thighs. When it's at my knees, Arabella gasps.

"What?"

"Hurry, pull it closer." She abandons the middle of the net, sloshing around to the front.

We raise the net from beneath the shallows.

One dead-white hand. Red, ripped strings of flesh dangle down from it like jellyfish tentacles. Around its wrist, a leather strap.

And an arm, severed at the shoulder.

Bella stares at it. Others, I know, think her horrified. I know her to be thinking—our eyes lock and I recognize the Holmesian manic glint.

"The strap."

That is all she needs say. My mind flashes to the photograph of the four lost antiquarians. Sully's hair in the photo—tied back with a leather strap. And one extra around his wrist.

"It's Sully," I reply.

Father stiffens and walks forward, stooping to examine the body parts.

I hear Montgomery on the shore. "God help us all."

Chapter Fifteen

The next day
Bella

My mind is whirling. The dead man, the red river. I glance over. *My now-complicated relationship with my once-best-friend.*

Henry is angry. His body is statue-rigid atop the mare. A muscle bulges from his angled jaw as he grinds his teeth.

He turns onto the road leading to the excavation farm without a glance in my direction.

I open my mouth and close it. What do I say?

I cannot love you? I'm not sure I can love anyone?

My stomach knots behind the saddle horn and I squeeze it till my knuckles whiten.

The scowl on Henry's face is identical to John's.

I flip through the pictures of my life.

The very same scowl on a younger John's face. On one of my many summertime visits, I snuck down the staircase, eavesdropping on their conversations. They were so foreign to me as father and I never had small-talk. Foreign, but lovely.

I always found emotions vexing. Any word for which there was no picture was difficult to define for my tender, young brain.

Love, for instance. What was it?

I learned about love from the Watson's.

When I watched John's face, the way he spoke to Mary, it was better than any word, thesaurus or an entire collection of dictionaries.

Love was illustrated in living, breathing color on John's face; in the playful upturn of his lips as he laughed at her horrid jokes or the serious crinkle of his eyes when she spoke in hushed tones.

"John, did you see what Arabella did to the doll I gave her?"

John's brow furrowed. "She...dissected it."

"Yes. John, I know it was not done in malice."

"Yes, she wants to know how everything works inside. Everything. Dolls included."

Mary's eyes sparkled with unshed tears. "It did not bother me, but one of the maids found it—"

"I know. My dear, Arabella is like Holmes in miniature. Parts of her mind are developed far beyond what you or I will ever reach. But others..."

"Are in scarce supply," Mary finished his sentence. "She must be taught what is acceptable and not-almost a rulebook for behavior, if you will. We shall not always be there to protect her. And forgive me darling, but her father isn't much help. He encourages her."

"Yes, I am well aware. It will be a balancing act; to teach her to behave within the realms of society, yet to not suffocate those unique traits, which really, you and I may never comprehend."

I realized then I was not cut from the same cloth as Mary. As a wife or mother. I was never mothered, or even parented.

Father treated me like a tiny adult from the time I could speak.

A ray of sun breaks through the gloom, warming my cheek. I turn my face up, allowing it to sink in.

The sun never ceases to produce déjà vu, reminding me of warm summer days and picnics and lemonade when John and his first wife Mary, would visit.

They are my most precious childhood memories—both showered me with attention. Mary would brush and arrange my hair and never once complained as I endlessly fidgeted beneath her hands.

And John would hug me to him, over and over. Perhaps because he was just happy to spoil a little girl, as he had two rowdy, mischievous sons. I saw the looks he shot at father, if he disagreed with my punishment or a scolding.

My time with the Watson's was like summer holidays—too fast, too wonderful and never enough.

During the winter, there were long periods of Watson-less existence, which left me melancholy.

It affected father, too. As if John was his catalyst to

connect with mankind. Father and I would attract and repel, wandering about the house like opposite-poled magnets, wanting to connect, but not quite knowing how.

We were too similar.

Returning to my daily life after summer break was like re-entering an austere classroom.

Ever interesting, but aloof and calculating. Father loved, but not in the same, all-encompassing way as the Watsons.

Holidays and boarding school breaks would roll around, just in time to save father and I from each other.

And Henry. When Henry came home, all was right with the world.

My face prickles with a different kind of heat, the intuitive kind. I open my eyes.

Am I truly able to endure another Henry-less existence? He is offering himself to me.

I think of his years away at boarding school. I was overly-driven, obsessed with obtaining my Mutter appointment. There was no balance.

Henry is the balance. My mind rebels, trying to deny it. Repulsed at the thought I may not be complete as I am. Alone.

Fear and self-loathing collect in my chest.

Henry has halted his horse, and is staring, his blue-green eyes fixated upon me.

We're surrounded by a field of wildflowers, slowly withering and dying in the autumn air.

Like my heart, without Henry.

I grit my teeth, struggling to accept these realizations. "Henry?"

His lips falter, but he gives me a sad smile. "I'm sorry I kissed you. We're working together… it would be more than difficult."

A glut of contradiction sickens my heart.

I want you to kiss me. Don't stop Henry. Make me love you. Leave me no choice.

My stomach cartwheels and heat flushes my face. Anger surges at these resurrected feelings; feelings I cannot control. Feelings that *control me.*

His presence ruins every plan I've ever made.

Love was never in the equation. Work, my obsessions. To control my own destiny.

His eyes skip over me, cataloging every minute expression. Henry knows people; and he's reading me like one of his books.

"Bella. Could you please answer me? Don't lie. You're a horrid liar."

"Henry." I drop my eyes as they burn. The unfamiliar sting of tears prickle beneath my lids.

Best to be honest, not play the ridiculous games of those fan-wielding females.

"I—I cannot fashion myself into the woman you want. You'll want a wife, children. I don't know if I can be either of those. I cannot change what's inside my head, inside me? Even if I tried, *if* I loved you—I'd end up hating you. And you, me. Because I'd be playing a role, pretending to be normal. *I.* Am. Not. Normal."

He urges the horse closer. Our lower legs are touching. My heart hammers and the reins go slick in my palms.

You are to be thinking of skeletons. Of Nephilim. Of finding answers.

I search for the analytical side of my brain, which urges me to think, not feel; but it's lost, drowning beneath the pressing flood of unfamiliar emotions.

"What if?" He leans closer. "What if, I needed none of those things? Well, except marriage. I could never make you a harlot. I've never much cared for normal."

But my face is stone. I've never let anyone near my heart, let alone seize it, beating in my chest.

My heart flutters against its box, aching for release.

Terror spreads across my ribcage.

Henry's eyes tick anxiously, watching for my reaction; in a blink he's off his horse.

His hands slide me off the saddle. His arms are hard around my waist, and his eyes have a matching, steely glint. His mouth sets, as if preparing for verbal battle.

"Do you remember our one kiss? I was eighteen, I believe?"

I nod. My voice has vacated my throat.

"I've been to many places. Kissed many, many girls."

"So I've heard."

"But you. I've never been able to forget you. And believe me I've tried, Arabella. Please, just…consider it. Consider *me*. Who knows you better?"

No one, my traitorous heart whispers.

His head dips, our lips barely touching. A new, all-consuming bonfire scorches a trail to my core. I shove my lips against his, hard enough to hurt.

A low moan escapes his mouth. I shudder and push against him. My tongue darts out, tracing his thin lips.

My soul opens, incinerating my doubt in a pyre of want. My mind is full of him.

Lingering mental images float around, equations and flashes of the mystery enveloping us. I block them with a solid, black curtain.

We fall into the dying flowers, between the horses. My mare stands between us and the road, blocking the view. Not that I care.

Nothing else exists in this moment. Except him. And the way he makes me forget who I am.

His body slides onto the length of mine, his hands slip behind my neck.

He kisses my cheeks, my neck, my collarbone.

"Tell me."

I find his lips and kiss him back, not answering. Not committing.

He pulls his face away. "No. Say the words."

Every inch of his lithe body sears me. Hoof beats shatter this perfect bit of suspended reality.

This will end.

I try to shift him off. He doesn't budge.

"Don't you hear them?"

"I don't care. Tell me."

He kisses me again—sending a surge of heat coursing through my veins. He abruptly breaks the kiss, leaving me breathless, panting.

Our eyes lock and my stomach contracts. "Fine. I'll

consider it. Don't get your hopes up."

"Too late," he whispers in my ear.

His body is up in a blink, hauling me to my feet, picking dead flowers out of my hair—all in what seems one movement to my lust-addled wits.

I smooth out my expression as I see Montgomery and Stygian approaching through the field.

"Is everything alright?" Montgomery asks and smirks. He knows. I want to leave a boot print on his cheek.

"Miss Holmes felt a little ill, so we were just waiting till it passed."

Stygian scowls. "If Miss Holmes's *delicate constitution* is restored, we should press on. Science is waiting."

Henry

Stygian and Montgomery halt their horses, waiting at the cave's mouth. "You have the *Very* pistol, Mr. Watson?"

"Yes. We will be sure to fire the flare if we run into trouble again. I will wait for Miss Holmes. We will report back at day's end."

What is keeping her?

Stygian nods and he and Montgomery canter across the field to the other suspected excavation site. I slide off and tether the horse to a tree. She whinnies, her ears flat against her head.

I remember Bella's comment about animals and danger and pull my father's old service revolver.

I'm not taking chances this time.

My gaze shoots south toward the sound of crunching underbrush.

A muscled hulk of a man, with flaming auburn hair, is lumbering toward me, through the forest. He's large. Large as the skeletons we search for.

I glance at the pistol. I'm not sure a shot would halt him. Maybe if I unloaded every shot—it would slow him.

He stops, ten feet away, black eyes scrutinizing me under bushy red eyebrows.

"You should not be here. These lands are sacred."

"Says who?"

"Says many generations—older and wiser than you, boy. Who walked the earth before you were even a gleam in your father's eye."

"I'm an antiquary—"

"I know who you are." He lumbers closer. I don't want to shoot him. He looks mentally deficient. His cheek is scarred. I squint, trying to make it out. It almost looks like a letter.

"You and the girl...tread lightly."

Hoof beats break the forest silence, approaching fast.

Arabella is driving the mare through the woods, her eyes fixed on the giant. She hoists the riding crop menacingly above her head.

I nod, telling her to ease off, and she lowers it.

The massive man shuffles into the trees. "Heed my words."

"Who are you?"

He waves his hand. I turn to look at Arabella. Make sure she's not going to attack. She slows the mare to a trot.

I glance back, and he is gone.

Gone?

Arabella vaults off the horse and we both rush to the left, mouths ridiculously agape.

She snaps hers shut. "How?"

I sigh. "Amazing consequences happen every day. Many without reasonable explanation."

She huffs, crossing her arms. "Preposterous."

She stamps toward the last footprint. They disappear into nothing. Bending down, she pulls a measuring string out of her pack and bites her lip as it reaches the toe tip.

"How large?"

She huffs again scribbling it into her tiny notebook. "Seventeen inches."

I walk over, and place my size 12 boot into the impression. A chill scurries up my neck.

It looks like a child standing in his father's print.

"So he was around—" My mind starts the math. I pull out my own notebook, starting a graph. I walk backwards, measuring and recording the length of his strides.

Arabella mutters under her breath, staring past me as if I've disappeared with the footprints. "The average length of the foot from toe to heel is the exact length of the forearm from elbow to wrist."

She stands, extending her measuring tape with a flourish. She wrenches my hand away from the notebook, straightening my arm. Starting at my elbow, she measures it to my wrist. I shiver.

The tape runs far past the ends of my fingertips.

I feel curiosity's burn in my chest. He was huge. Not as huge as the giant we seek to unearth, but a mountain of mankind, just the same.

"This measurement is more accurate—the other is—"

"Just an estimation of his height. What, 7 feet?"

She nods. "More or less."

A high-pitched caw makes me start. I turn and notice the birdcage tied to her saddle. A small, black crow peers out from behind the bars.

"Is that what was keeping you?"

She smiles and walks to the horse, reaching inside her saddlebag to extract a tome.

"Is that—?"

"Your father's chemistry volume?" She smiles wickedly. "I stole it from his stateroom whilst we were back at the ship."

"You clever, rotten girl." I smile back. "Have you looked up the ingredients, then?"

She ignores me, lifting the cawing crow and walks towards me.

I am perplexed, my eyes narrowing on the bird for a half a minute. Arabella follows my gaze.

She smiles, clearly thrilled to be winning the mental match-up. "It's for—"

"Detecting poisonous gases. Elementary, my dear Holmes."

She glares at me. "Let's go, genius."

Chapter Sixteen

LOVE WAS NEVER IN THE EQUATION

Bella

Time seems to halt in this wretched tunnel. Henry's endless joking is beginning to wear on my already thin nerves. So far, our trek has been uneventful. I take deep breaths and keep reminding myself. *The hand.* Its match may be buried just ahead, or with any luck, it's entire skeleton.

"Henry, wait."

My eyes flit to the bird. Is it my imagination—or does it seem woozy?

Henry turns toward me, holding the lantern closer to the map. His eyes flick to my face, and drop to my chest—monitoring for hyperventilation.

"How are you managing?"

I swallow—trying to ignore the suffocating press of the cave against my lungs.

"Fine," I lie.

He smiles, raising a disbelieving eyebrow. "And our little friend?"

"Alright for now. How much further?"

We've been walking for a quarter hour, which feels more like a fortnight.

Anxiety tightens my chest at letting Henry have total control—of my steps, of the excursion. I cannot even attempt to lead however, as it takes every bit of my willpower to beat down the claustrophobia.

Anxiety dulls my senses, like the night I had too much port. Once was enough. I abhor this weakness and my inattentive, sluggish wits.

"Not far." Henry turns, squinting into the dark. He holds up the lantern.

"Help me attach this rope to the stalagmite. It feels like the path is veering down."

I set down the bird and help him secure the rope. He hands it to me. "Don't let go."

I pick the bird up in the other hand, and we slide along the rope as the floor descends. I follow behind Henry as he grasps the lantern in one hand, and the rope in his other. The lantern illuminates a tiny circle of yellow, keeping the cave's utter blackness at bay.

The sound of rushing water fills my ears.

"An underground river?"

"Hmm?" Henry turns, mid-stride to look at me, and loses his balance.

The rope between us jerks and I fight to stay upright. The

floor tilts with a sudden lurch. My boots slip on the loose rock, and my feet fly into the air.

My bottom connects with the hard ground. "Ow!"

We slide like a coal shuttle, faster and faster. My pace speeds because of my lesser weight and my boots slam into Henry's back.

The rope burns a line into my palm as it slides madly through my fingers.

"Don't let go!" I scream to him.

Henry looks ridiculous as he tries to hold the lantern aloft, sliding like a boy on a snow sled. Dread closes my throat.

If the light extinguishes…the dark.

The suffocation.

The bird. I won't know if the bird is still alive.

The cage is crashing off the ground despite my efforts to keep it up. The crow's squawking raises the hairs on my neck.

The cawing is no more.

We finally slide to a stop. Henry has managed to keep the light safe. His face is covered in black dust and if I weren't so mind-numbingly terrified, I'd laugh.

My breath sucks in. "Henry!" I point. The words won't come.

He follows my gaze. Bony fingers stick out of the dirt, submerged to the metacarpals.

"That's odd."

They shouldn't be exposed. It's as if someone started and quit midway through the extraction. I fly to them, pulling the spade out of my pack. I thrust it into the dirt, but hit hard rock. "You'll need your pick." I suck at the air, wheezing like I've contracted consumption.

I fling the bag open, searching for it.

"Arabella."

My fingers find it. I whip it out and begin peck, peck, pecking around the bones with specific force and care.

"Arabella!" Henry's tone startles me.

"The bloody bird!"

The crow is sprawled, lifeless, on the bottom of the cage.

"NO! No, no, no!"

"Stop shrieking. You're breathing in more of whatever's down here. Get up. We must go."

I hesitate. My mind does feel thick.

His fingers are instantly on my shoulders, tugging roughly. I resist, pecking harder. "Just one more piece, Henry."

I'm in the air. My head flipped over his shoulder and down to his back as he hauls me to the rope.

He flips me to my feet again.

"Now, please." He shoves the rope in my hands.

I comply, my rational mind taking over. The incline is approximately forty-five degrees. I start; hand over hand, step by step, scaling toward the surface.

"Bella, remain calm. We must be quick. I need both my hands. I'm going to have to leave the light." He slurs the final word.

Panic explodes in my head, radiating flashes of pyrotechnics to my vision; fear fireworks behind my eyes.

"Keep moving. I'm putting it out now." I nod. "Of course. The gas may be flammable." My voice breaks on the last word.

Utter blackness.

My breath shudders out. I remember being frozen to my bed in the darkness, unable to go to my father's room for help. The suffocation paralyzed me.

Like now. I stop climbing.

Henry bumps into me on the rope. "Arabella, stay calm. You *must* move."

"I—cant. Henry, go without me. Pass me, save yourself. Henry, I looked up the ingredients. The combination would dissolve bone. If I die, you must find the truth."

His voice is calm, but I hear the quiver beneath. "Don't be ridiculous. You are not going to die." He coughs.

"Henry! Go!" My thoughts pitch with a jerky panic—like a Ferris Wheel. With every revolution I'm further away. Darkness presses, inside my head.

Henry whispers in my ear. "Darling. Darling you must move."

His voice pushes back the dark panic, just a sliver of calm. I shuffle a step. "Henry?"

"I'm right here, love. Right behind you." "I can't." But I take another step.

He exhales against the back of my neck, relief coloring his voice. "That's it."

Something wails below, in the dark.

Henry stiffens.

"What in the name of—"

"Keep talking, please. Talk about anything." My feet are moving again, one in front of the other.

"I'm going to keep calling you darling. Do you understand? You're lying. About everything. I see it in your eyes. You do want me. But you push it away, again and again. I will not have it."

I struggle to keep my breathing even, my fingers inching up the rope a fragment at a time.

Step. Step. Shuffle. Step.

"I don't care if you blow things up, have ink permanently tattooed on your fingers, or even do not want children. I want you, Arabella. And all of your glorious...differences."

I smile. And for a brief flash, I'm glad for the dark.

"What about your bachelorhood? Such a carefully-crafted reputation, going to waste," I manage.

He laughs. "I told you. I'll never touch another."

"Henry, there are more skeletons here. A burial ground, perhaps? And they've been moved, it's obvious."

"Bella. Stop sucking in the air."

Mercifully, the floor begins to flatten. A speck of light glows in the distance. I feel Henry beside me.

He shoves a handkerchief into my hand.

"Run."

Henry

I sit on my bed, staring out at the night, my hands fidgeting in my lap like restless toddlers.

Stygian and Montgomery have retired after peppering us

with questions for what felt a fortnight. With our discovery of the hand, they've all but abandoned the other dig site.

I should be exhausted. I can't sleep. Arabella is down the hall. One or two hands also live on the second floor.

Stygian and Montgomery are also restless on the third floor; their boots clomp from one end of the room to the other, wearing a hole in the ceiling above me.

Finally, I hear the bed groan above as one retires.

My mind shifts through the past week, examining clues, data.

The large man...who disappeared.

Surely, the giant wasn't...a Nephilim. While I believe in a higher power, I find the idea of one still walking the earth impossible. I think back to my boarding-school bible studies, thrown in with every other subject under the muted London sun, to produce a well-rounded graduate.

The flood was to have destroyed them all.

The pins. The states. The hands. The dead bird. Stygian's tattoo.

"Giurio di vendicarmi." Something about the phrase prickles the inside of my skull like déjà vu. And I remember.

I open my belongings to extract a London paper. I'd requested our butler forward The Times to me, so that I might remain abreast of all that I was missing in London.

I shuffle through the pages, searching right and left.

It was a story from a few months prior about the murder of an heiress.

'Giurio di vendicarmi' was scrawled on the victim's wall and is thought to be connected to the vigilante group L'uomo

Deliquente, who are suspected of the murder. Sherlock Holmes assisted Scotland Yard in bringing most of the organization to justice, but several fled prior to trial.'

I wonder if Bella has made this connection.

I shove the paper back in my bag and bite my lip.

My hands press against my temples and I squeeze my eyes closed.

A worm of unease wriggles in my gut.

I must know if she's safe. I do not trust her.

My legs walk me toward the door before my brain can restrain them.

I've never, ever pursued a woman.

They pursue me. Hang on my every word and letter. No woman has ever rebuffed me. Arabella puts me off every day, ever-increasing my insatiable idée fixe, as my French friends call obsession.

She's *my* seven percent solution.

A pang of fear sparks.

Is that why I want her so badly? If she finally returns my affections, will this longing cease?

I pray not. The thought of hurting Bella is utterly repulsive. Her intellect may be like few others, but in many ways she is childlike.

I'm almost at the end of the hallway, barely noticing the doors flying past on either side in time with my strides.

The fourth door is cracked an inch. I stop short.

Out of my periphery, I swear I see an eye peeping out.

I look again, cocking my head, but…nothing. Just a faint yellow column of light, cutting across the dark hallway.

I lean on her door and rap lightly with one knuckle. "Arabella? Are you awake?"

Silence.

My heart skips then thrums against my ribs.

I sneak a look behind me, then try the door knob.

It's unlocked. I curse.

I hesitate a moment, thinking of my pistol, useless in my pack in the room, but decide to act. I slide inside, hearing the door click quietly behind me.

I sigh.

She's in bed, facing toward the window.

I rush to the bedside, bending so my face almost touches her chest, listening for breathing.

Her perfect ivory flesh rises and falls in deep slumber.

I exhale and sit and drink in her face.

She's so rarely still.

I gently slide the hair from her cheek and over her shoulder. It reaches her bottom like a red-headed Rapunzel. Her fringe of hair brushes her thick eyelashes, which twitch as she dreams.

I take a curl, and loop it around my finger. Decorum says I should go. I cannot.

Her eyes flutter open, and I drop the curl.

Her eyes pop wide and I shoot to stand.

In a flash, she rolls, swipes a parasol from beside the bed, thrusting it at my throat.

"Arabella! Shh!"

Her eyes squint in the gloom. "Henry? You daft fool. I could've killed you."

I smile. "Death by parasol?"

Bella jams the handle in. A long, sharp blade pops from the end, inches from my jugular. It glints in the moonlight.

"You were saying?"

"Unbelievable. Another contraption? How many are there?"

"I don't have to tell you all my secrets." She pops it back in and shrugs. "Plus I didn't know if we'd be forced into some society function while here."

I laugh. "May I?" I gesture to the bed.

"You should go." But she bites her bottom lip.

My heartbeat surges, heat flying to every inch of me.

Do I imagine the wanting in her stare?

"Fine. Only a moment."

I sit, feeling her warm stomach against my hip.

"Henry?"

I snap to attention the uncharacteristic, fragile tone of her voice. "Yes?"

Her hand reaches up, pausing above my cheek.

I wait, holding my breath. Wanting to lean into it, but I hold firm.

"You." She swallows, licking her lips, letting her hand drop.

I may go mad.

Her face contracts as if the admission causes physical pain. "Henry, you make me feel...safe. I never feel safe. I'm always careful, waiting for a loud sound or a painful jibe or..."

"Shh." I press my finger to her lips. The honesty spills out, "You are safe. I know who you are, Bella. How you hide your other side. Your non-Holmes, vulnerable side. The little girl who brought home and mended every fallen bird."

Her eyes widen. "How—"

"And splinted cat's paws." My smile is wide. "I know your heart. The icy exterior doesn't fool me."

My hand slides over her heart. Her breath catches and she sits up, crushing her lips to mine and her tongue darts out, licking and biting my bottom lip.

Our breathing is a synchronous heaving symphony that fills the room.

My scalp tingles as her fingers wind into my hair and ball.

I break the kiss.

"I. Must. Go."

"No, Henry. Stay. If you meant all you said. Stay."

Her maddeningly soft lips trail up my neck to my ear.

I growl, "Arabella. I'm a gentleman, but I'm a man. I am not that noble."

I stand, chest heaving, staring down at her.

Her face falls like I've wounded her. "Go. I'll see you tomorrow."

I swallow, checking my desire. To be sure I am controlling it, and not the other way 'round.

I kneel, taking her small hand in mine. I kiss it.

"It is because I want you too much. I told you. I want... *everything* from you." My face burns with the utter truth of it.

My hateful analytical side whispers, playing devil's advocate.

Fear waters my mouth. *Do I mean it?* I will crush her soul.

My mind fills with images. Arabella, in her trousers, dig after dig, year after year; with every scene her face more lined, her auburn hair lighter.

Desire and devotion vibrate every inch of me. *Yes. I do mean it.*

Profound relief washes over me as weakness floods my knees.

Her eyes are huge and electric, weighing my every word. Watching every emotion cross my face.

"If you cannot give me your hand, I'll wait. But your heart. May I have it?"

I extend my hand palm up, waiting.

She smiles, and tears threaten, but do not fall.

She nods. "Yes, Henry. You already do." And slides her other hand into mine. "You always have."

Chapter Seventeen

DON'T TREAT ME LIKE A NORMAL WOMAN

Abner Farmhouse
Bella

I'm shivering. Opening my eyes feels like prying open a nailed coffin. I squint and wait as they adjust to the dim light of my room.

The pink fingers of dawn are just stretching across the horizon.

My mind whirrs awake and I picture a clock's gears as the data flows before me in a steady, visual stream.

Stygian's ring. The tattoo. The giant and the skeleton. *How do they all fit?* I flip the images round in my mind like a giant puzzle, trying to organize them.

Henry was supposed to wake me. Perhaps he overslept?

I fight my way out of the coverlets and quickly dress. I turn to pick up my chisel, my pistol and my bravery.

I'm not frightened of the dig or claustrophobia or even Stygian. I'm afraid of Henry. And his capacity to destroy me.

Work is safe. Work is logical. Working out puzzles is calming; matters of the heart…are none of those things.

I shake my head, banishing the thoughts and sneak into the hall. Downstairs there are signs of life. The smell of eggs frying amidst some low murmurs.

I reach Henry's room and turn the knob.

I step in and freeze. His bed is empty.

Anger and fear battle in my chest.

What if something happened to him?

My mind whispers, *you mean, what if Stygian happened to him.*

My eyes flash around the room. His pack is gone. He's left without me.

Anger wins, incinerating fear. Henry has a bizarre preoccupation with my safety. Father had it too, but he never stopped me from learning, doing. Would he have left me out of the dig, just to protect me?

I grind my teeth together and head down the servant's staircase which will allow me to sneak past the prying eyes of the kitchen staff.

I pass through the door, undetected, into the weak morning light.

The early morning air is frigid. The sun's crept higher, and I can walk without fear now as I reach the stables.

In minutes, I'm galloping across the pumpkin patch, orange orbs rushing past like a strange scene plucked from the pages of my beloved Wonderland.

I hear Henry's voice in my head. Counting off our extraordinary circumstances. Fear flutters my heart, and I look for them.

They are near, my little black sentries; the hair rises on the back of my neck as if I'm being watched.

The butterflies stay with me till the first snowflake falls. Long after their normal counterparts have fled for the southern hemisphere.

A little croak escapes my lips. They are here; an undulating black mass, which hovers from tree to tree like a flock of migrating birds. Following me.

I swallow. How can I deny them? They defy explanation.

Is Henry correct? That some events cannot be explained away?

"Ha!" I kick the horse's sides and put my head down against the wind till I reach the line of trees.

My mind ruminates. One scientist perished in the Hudson, or at least that is where his body was deposited. One possibly melted away, dissolved in a sausage vat.

I shiver. Two to go. *Where are you gentlemen?*

I reach the trees and slow my mare to a trot.

Three packs lie open on the forest floor.

My heart free-falls.

Henry, Montgomery and Stygian's, alongside a yawning hole in the earth. A mineshaft?

I am stunned. I slide off the horse and quickly flick his reins around a tree and slide the pistol into my pants.

I skulk forward and freeze. Laughter wafts up from the shaft below.

I peer down, over the edge and three faces turn up to meet mine.

Montgomery, oblivious and joyous. Stygian sporting a one-sided smile that screams *you are not needed, woman.*

And Henry with trepidation. "You're up and about. One of the hands told me you were ill last night. So we let you sleep."

"What? I'm quite well."

Stygian interjects, "How perfectly odd. Well, you're here now. Miss Holmes, we've found another way to extract the other hand. Would you be a dear and throw down our packs?"

His smile is sickening.

"Fine."

I squint and discern the outline of the long skeletal fingers jutting out, half-buried in the dirt. My eyes dart to the hole in the rock wall behind them, large enough for a man to pass.

It must be a series of connected tunnels. How many? How far do they go?

I look up, and the butterflies alight. "You're a load of help, whatever you are."

I throw their pack down. "Another skeleton? You've found another? This *is* a burial ground, then?"

Henry is digging and carefully tapping around a metacarpal with his chisel. He shrugs. "I expect so?"

Stygian's black eyes flick to me. "Only time will tell, Miss Holmes."

Henry continues to shoot me furtive looks till they're finally out of the hole, hand, in hand.

In another hour, the hand is secured for transport and we're back at the farmhouse, packing.

Henry tries once again to explain, attempts to distract my foul countenance with the case at hand.

His eyes darken. "I reviewed my London papers. A man with Stygian's description is wanted...for murder and still at large. A tattoo was mentioned but not its exact description. And his brother...was sent to the gallows by none other than Sherlock Holmes." He pauses, letting it sink in.

"L'uomo Deliquente was functioning as a vigilante group—performing executions, and it's rumored they engineered a few rapes for women they deemed to be harlots. It all fell apart when they targeted a barrister's daughter. He made it his personal mission to bring them down. L'uomo Deliquente headquarters was raided and its members dispersed about two years prior."

I stand and begin to pace. "Or defected. Around the time Stygian arrived for his post at the Mutter."

Henry nods. He must see my response as an opening in my mood because he says, "I still don't understand why you're so angry. I was merely trying to be a gentleman."

I whirl on him. "How many times must I tell you? I do not *think* like other women, Henry." I tap my temple roughly. "Don't be the gentleman. *Ask me what I want.* Not what convention dictates you do."

Henry's face reddens with anger. He nods. "I'm sorry. I'm sure you were disappointed not to be present."

I pace, throwing clothes haphazardly into a bag. "I don't understand why *we* must take the hand to the Mutter? Shouldn't Stygian? We should stay and dig."

Henry's hand massages his stubbled cheeks. He's forgotten to shave; his face looks years older with the growth hiding his boyish features.

"It is odd, I agree. Unless Stygian is just determined he and Montgomery should get all the fame."

My eyes narrow. "Or unless he has something to hide here. But he has something to hide in Philadelphia as well. Do you remember the paper's headline, about the tainted sausage sickening patrons? The morning you noticed Stygian's tattoo."

Henry's eyebrows pull together and his face drains to paper-white.

"Oh my word! The ingredient list! You are thinking of the sausage factory. Could a man be such a monster? To grind up a human and fashion him into sausage? One of the lost four? You think there is a connection with the tainted sausages." I nod. "But without proof, it is all conjecture. We know he has ties to someone at the factory. Tight ties, for the person to take such a risk for him. The proprietor's name is William Bane."

"Time will tell. There is never enough of it. Speaking of time," he snaps his pocket watch closed, "we have to hurry."

In an hour, Henry, John and I are on a train, speeding toward the Mutter. The mysterious hand is under our seat, locked safely in a box.

Oddly, the unearthed hand matched our hand. Why was the skeleton in pieces, in different locations?

"Henry, why would the hands be so far apart?"

Henry shrugs. "Could it have been dismembered? Animal degradation?"

John beats me to it. "The skeleton shows no signs of trauma. Just ancient decay."

I nod in agreement. "Someone moved them. Perhaps

they were interrupted, and moved it piece-meal."

My foot taps. I cannot wait to return; hoping and praying Stygian doesn't further tamper with the burial ground.

I stare out the window, still irritated at Henry as he and his father exchange endless jibes.

"If you wouldn't of touched it, Henry, we could of analyzed—"

"The body was *on* me, father. I'm sorry if I panicked. I was bloody fourteen."

They both laugh, and turn to me when I'm silent.

Watson touches my arm, his tone placating. "Arabella. It's a few days. You'll be back in the dirt in no time."

I don't answer. As we pull away from the station, I see a black cluster of wings depart, up and over the train. I shiver.

John clears his throat. This means he's changing subjects; I'm not surprised that his face, which was full of mirth moments ago is suddenly deadly serious.

I roll my eyes. "Yes Dr. Watson?"

I try not to be amused as their identical lips curl into wry smiles at my retort.

"Be careful of Stygian," John's voice drops an octave.

Henry interrupts, "You worked that out on your own then? That he's dangerous? I must admit, I've haven't been giving you enough credit." Henry laughs.

John shoots him a death-look. "I…found one of his papers in his office. He believes in L'uomo Delinquente."

"Which is?" Henry and I ask in unison, playing innocent.

"It means he believes people's physical traits can predict a person's personality. It's similar to phrenology, but instead of the skull alone, it's applied to the entire person. One can imagine the potential problems of that premise."

I nod. "Yes. Skeletons change for so many reasons. Trauma, birth, wear and tear. It may all affect a person's appearance. A hunched back, a twisted spine—on and on."

Henry nods ascension. "It seems very unpredictable. Too many variables to be called a real science."

"You mean like phrenology?" I jab.

Henry shrugs. "I never said I believed it to be true science. It's a lot of show."

"A sideshow," I mutter.

"Bella, really—"

John cuts him off. "Children, do pay attention."

John leans in. "Take that chap over there." He nods discretely. "According to L'uomo, his protruded, sloping forehead and cauliflower ears indicate he's a biological throwback. A savage."

Henry's eyes tick over the gent. "Ridiculous. He's reading the Philadelphia paper." His eyebrows push together as he squints. "His shoes are polished to perfection and expensive. His hands and nails are smooth and impeccable. He has money and servants. The heading on the paper poking from his attaché would indicate he's a barrister. If he's a savage—then he's a very well-educated one."

I clap appreciatively. A flash of text appears in my mind and I bite my lip. Perhaps it is time to confess.

"I do remember reading of it in England. I've heard nothing of it here?" I prompt, fishing.

"Yes, it hasn't caught on in the states," John says.

"That would indicate Stygian has colleagues in Europe. His American accent rings false, somehow. I cannot place it."

Henry nods. "Yes. It's an odd mix of sounds. Neither Northern nor Southern."

John's eyes narrow. "Their society was not purely academic—as they portrayed to the public at large. There were murmurs of vigilantism in the halls of Scotland Yard."

"I thought they merely wished to educate the public on the theories of Darwin?" Henry says.

John continues, "They were radical atheists with a leaning toward eugenics. Their members sought to maneuver political leanings toward their cause. They saw a new world of influence here, and plan to insert their candidates into the judicial system, to force change from within."

"Better for the public to believe in *them*, in their version of government, than in a creator?" I offer.

Henry's eyes flick to mine and away. "Yes, here men's rights are endowed by the creator, as per their constitution. It would be necessary to undermine self-reliance, replacing it with government. Ultimate control, really."

John seems confounded by our complete comprehension.

"Ah, my two youthful sleuths." John gives Henry a wide paternal smile. "It couldn't help but rub off, I suppose."

Henry puffs, disgusted. "Hmm. Holmes may have the upper hand to me—but you, father. I'd say we're evenly matched."

John opens his mouth to protest.

"Boys. Save the spitting match for later."

Henry meets my gaze. I now have no excuse for excluding

John from our information. He suspects him of belonging to L'uomo Deliquente and hasn't chastised me or insisted I return to the Mutter.

Our eyes hold a silent conversation. He nods.

My eyes flick away from Henry's to his face. "John."

"Yes, darling?" The sparkle in his blue eyes dims at my expression. "What is it?"

"Henry and I...have much to tell you."

Chapter Eighteen

MEMORIES, RESURRECTED

The Music Hall
Henry

"So the hand is safe, father?" My eyes dart around the music hall. I can't shake the sensation we're being watched. "Yes. I delivered it myself this morning whilst you and the princess slept."

Father's eyes keep leaving mine. I know what he's looking for. I raise an eyebrow. "Calm yourself old man. You'll have a seizure. She'll be along before the orchestra plays."

Father's head shoots back. "You little insolent—"

"John!"

Violet is rushing across the marble floor, a vision of color and lace. She moves with the grace of a much younger woman.

Father grasps both her hands, and leans in to kiss her cheek. I look around awkwardly.

"Henry? Is that you?"

I cannot believe I am actually relieved to hear Priscilla's voice, but even speaking to her is better than watching my father and Violet *get reacquainted.*

I walk over to her. She is lovely, there's no denying that. Her long blond hair adorns her head in a crown of curls.

I don't *feel* anything, though. Admiring her beauty is simply like appreciating a glorious painting.

"I wasn't sure you'd be here. Father said you'd delivered another specimen to the Mutter."

"Yes, just this morning. We're only here till tomorrow, then it's back to the dig."

Her face puckers. "Where's your *partner?*"

A stab of irritation heats my face. "*Bella,* should be along shortly. Why do you ask?"

Priscilla steps in, so close. Too close. I avert my eyes. Her hand trails down my chest. "I was hoping to have you to myself. Not that she's really a rival or anything. I mean, look at her."

"Pardon me?" I firmly grasp her wrist and and return it to her side.

Priscilla takes one step backward. "Really, Henry. She's fine for the museum, but who would have her? The girl has no idea what is proper, what is ladylike—"

I hold up a hand, grind my teeth and spit, "Arabella has more integrity than anyone I know, and more honesty. You're right—she's not proper; but that is only because she is incapable of pretense."

Her expression turns quizzical. "How do you mean?"

"She cannot lie, or pretend. Whatever is in her mind

usually shoots directly out her mouth."

Priscilla smiles. "Exactly. Who could want such a woman as a wife, yes? I do hope you've been thinking about our conversation. I've told father about it and I—"

"Priscilla. I should sugarcoat it. Convention tells me to do so, but I have not the time. You and I—*we* will not be venturing any further."

Her mouth widens in a huge O. I'm quite certain by her look of horror that she's never been spurned.

"You prefer her? That odd, unfashionable—"

Anger surges. "That's quite enough. And yes, I prefer her to you. To anyone really, male or female."

"What?" Her foot stamps beneath her ivory dress, sending shimmery undulations down the train.

"Did I stammer?"

A picture of white Foxglove pops to my head. Beautiful, deadly flowers. Like her.

I spin and tug at the collar of my shirt, knowing I've made a terrible enemy.

Bella

"Where is Henry?"

I smooth the dress and fidget with the vanilla gloves.

I duck into an alcove and close my eyes, sucking in deep,

calming breaths.

I detest crowds. The opera house is sold out. Every seat filled with whining, fan-fluttering ladies and pompous men. I detest feigning interest, especially with women.

Their tedious tendency to tell too much makes me want to rip my carefully arranged hair out. My hand strays to finger it. It feels heavy and foreign and I resist the urge to tug at the pins.

After the hand was safely delivered, Henry and John insisted we do one night of entertainment before returning to the dig. I would've rather just departed.

A gilded mirror catches the light, sending sparkles and artificial rainbows as it catches glimpses of the ladies gowns as they pass the alcove.

I stare across at my reflection. My cheeks are high with color which shines brightly against the stark-white skin of my décolletage.

Violet chose the dress and had it sent to me. It's perfect, naturally. Its vibrant cornflower-blue accents my auburn hair. Or so she told me.

"You can't hide forever."

I start and bang my foot off the wall. "One can try."

Henry's head pokes round the corner. He breaks into a smile and I lose my breath. He's so lovely. Every feminine heart will break just looking at him tonight.

"Couldn't I just stay here? Most of the music will filter to me, the acoustics are—"

Henry has rounded the corner, and swept me into his arms. My heart sings. So completely inappropriate. We will be a complete scandal if caught.

"Kiss me."

"Here? Are you mad?" My heart throbs its wild-song, its rushing beat in my ears. Drowning out the crowd.

He leans in, and I smell him. Musk and pine. I breathe deeper, memorizing his scent. My lips part.

His lips brush mine, and then interlock in the space between. My fingers entwine in his coarse hair and I press myself flush against him; leg to leg, stomach to stomach.

His eyes flutter shut and his nostrils flair and he moans quietly against my lips. My breath hitches hard and fast. I forget my fear of crowds. My itchy gown. Nothing remains except Henry.

My mental equations and chemistry scatter around his image, letters and numbers fall like snowflakes, hovering and fading in and out. As if perturbed at no longer having my mind's center stage.

My leg slides up, wraps around his. He moans again. But I feel his warm hand spread across my knee and press it back to stand. He breaks the kiss, breathing hard, and leans his forehead against mine.

He swallows. "Why is it I cannot convince you, but once you start…"

"I cannot stop. It's like." I close my eyes, searching for the right words. "Like a sea-swell of emotions batter a barricade in my mind. And when you're here. When you touch me. I drown."

Henry grinds his teeth. "You. Do not know what you do to me. This is madness. Just—be mine. Now. This waiting is intolerable. I cannot concentrate on the dig, on anything but you.

Bella, can you not alleviate this infernal suffering?"

My lips open to say yes. Does he mean marry him?

The heart box inside slams shut like an iron guillotine.

I stare at him. His eyes twitch with anticipation. And I realize we're both holding our breath.

"I cannot. I. I don't know. My feelings for you are so very confusing."

A flicker of pain pinches the corner of his eyes, but then an expressive curtain falls, leaving his face smooth and unreadable.

He puts his hands on my shoulders, putting distance between us, which I immediately want to close again. My body already aching to be next to his.

"Come, the others will be waiting for us."

We step out of the alcove, into the overwhelming fray of satin, cigar smoke and buzz of loud voices.

I lace my arm through his, and only then notice it's shaking. Henry's eyes stray to mine and they soften as he pats my arm in reassurance.

"Arabella!" Violet's warm voice rises over the crowd. She rushes toward me, shimmering and resplendent in a deep jade gown.

She claps her hands together, smiling. "My dove, you look perfect. Henry, have you been keeping her from us?"

Henry blushes. "Of course not. Have you located our seats?"

I see John's eyes narrow in response to Henry's blush. They quickly flick to mine. And I quickly look away.

Looking in John's eyes is like a reflecting pool. I might

as well give him the blow by blow of the past half hour.

He clears his throat.

"Our seats, Vi?" I wrap my arm in hers. Unhappy about relinquishing Henry, but more concerned about putting distance between John and my guilty face.

When Violet leads me into our box I let loose a sigh. The isolated seats are a temporary reprieve from endless female prattling and weighing my every word.

The four of us slide in just as the chandeliers flicker and dim. Violet squeezes my hand and turns her lovely face toward the stage.

The orchestra begins; a low thrum which vibrates to my core. I'm unprepared. It's been years since I've attended a live performance.

Aside from father and his insomnia-induced, midnight violin sonatas, that is.

The maestro raises his wand and the orchestra erupts to life.

The music washes over me. Layers of soothing sounds, licking at my skin. Filling in damaged crevasses in my mind, my heart.

The violins call, and my heart tugs and aches with every stroke of the strings. Emotion clenches my stomach, raising the hair on my arms. The music brings *pain*. Pain that I so carefully box and wrap in metal in my mind.

The violins wrench it off, piece by steely piece till I see my heart beating in the center of the box, exposed and vulnerable.

Henry is staring, I can feel him.

But the music. All I see, hear and feel, is the music.

My chest rises and falls in time with the emotion embedded in the notes.

Tears. They fill my eyes and stream down my cheeks, instantly dripping off my chin. I feel them splash against my collarbone, and slide into my dress.

"Bella?" Henry whispers.

Fear floods my mouth. A hot mortification blazes the side of my face.

Crying. I am crying. In public, no less.

I hear father's voice, caustic. "Scientists *do not cry* Arabella. Logic and tears are oil and water."

I cannot recall the last time. Henry's face is horrorstruck, his fingers fidget with mine.

The cello pleads, interrupting the violin, and the tones weave in and out. My head swims, vertigo *pressing and fading, pressing and fading,* with every weave of the bow between the strings. Every melodic adjustment of the musician's fingers along the instrument's neck feels like a stranglehold on my windpipe.

A whimper leaks out.

All three heads whip to my face. Henry's hands become vice-like.

"Arabella? What is it?"

I shake my head. I'm mute. I hear their voices. Far off sounds, like murmurs through cotton.

The tones tip my heart, up and down, in and out. Images fill my head. Like someone else's memory.

The pictures are misted and indistinct, like a dream remembered.

A beautiful woman. Sitting on a stool, the cello propped

between her shapely legs. She smiles at me, but doesn't really see me. *Momma?*

My analytical side curls up and dies. Trampled beneath feeling and conviction so strong, I feel my head expanding with the desire. With the abandonment.

"Father, what's wrong with her?" Henry's voice, almost hysterical. I've never heard it so.

But I can't come back.

I'm lost in this memory of the beautiful woman. My mother. Have no memory of her.

The strings have jarred the images loose. I don't, no—I can't, let her go.

"John?" Violet, her voice high with concern.

"She looks almost catatonic. Violet, move aside."

I smell John's woodsy cologne as he slides beside me. His hand grips the one not clutched by Henry. "Arabella, my dear. Look at me."

His cool fingers slide to my wrist, checking my pulse.

Henry's fingers touch my cheeks, desperately wiping the river of tears sluicing down my face.

"Bella? Bella? Where are you?" True fear now in his voice. I've never heard that either. "Do something!" He shouts at John.

And I hear the voice. The apparition from my mind opens her mouth, and it comes from her—a throaty, deep alto, resonating to my core.

But it's too real. I cannot imagine something that incredible. I shake my head.

The sound is coming from the stage. From a breathtakingly

beautiful creature on the stage.

My hands grip the carved banister of the box. I fight back a blackness crouching at the edges of my sight.

Fire-red spirals wrap lovingly around the singer's curvy body. Her voice fills the auditorium to bursting, calling and bewitching every soul. Every eye stares at her face, enraptured by the personification of heaven falling from her lips.

Henry and John's hands are at my elbows. I've stood up at some point.

The tears won't stop. I choke out a sob.

Several people look up into the balcony, concerned.

I feel John's grip tighten around my elbow. "Of all the careless—"

Violet gasps. "John. I didn't know. The tickets were a gift—I didn't check—How could I have known she would remember? She was so tiny," Her voice breaks.

Henry, on the other side. "What? For the love of all, what?"

I hear them muttering, conferring behind me. John's voice rumbles, "The singer is an alto, like Arabella's mother. So alike, she once starred in the same production as her understudy."

"What? I don't understand?" Henry, frantic

"The music must've dislodged suppressed memories."

I hear her voice fill my head, crumpling my heart.

I lose sight of the stage, as pain spreads across the back of my head as it connects with the wooden floor.

"Oh my—"

"Arabella. Bella?"

"Don't touch her!"

Henry's hands, strangling my hands.

The light shrinks to a pinprick. Her heavenly voice fades.

###

The Grand Entryway of the Opera House
Bella

"Are you certain you're alright?" John continues to hover, checking my pulse. More like a father than a doctor.

The sounds of the auditorium are giving me vertigo, but I refuse to say so. Make another scene. I take deep breaths; only a few more minutes and I can drink in the night air.

Henry is as rigid as the marble statues behind him. The voices echoing around the cathedral ceilings raise the hair on my arms. His mouth is set in a grim line. He's barely said two words since I became lucid again.

"Dr. Watson, if you please?" Dr. Earnest calls from a few feet away. Priscilla stands beside him. She sneaks a glance from behind his considerable bulk.

"What now?" John's face contracts in irritation, but he quickly fashions it into an approachable expression. "Coming."

Violet's eyes dart between Henry and I, and dear that she is, turns to begin speaking with a nearby woman to permit us privacy.

"You see. Do you remember? I told you your other self was strong."

"Henry, don't." I feel the metal gate quiver around my heart. "Don't speak of it. Any of it. I cannot bear it."

He nods, but whispers in my ear. "I'll bet you can play. I'll bet it's like breathing."

Touching you, is like breathing. I cannot say it.

I feel fragile, like a brittle leaf, ready to crumble to a million, fragmented bits.

"Henry?" John's voice is sharp.

Henry, Violet and I snap to attention.

"Henry, if you please?" His father motions him over.

Henry walks toward the group and stops, cocking his head to hear over the opera-noise.

Voices roar to my right. I turn to look. The opera singer is fighting off the mob, signing programs and smiling.

My mind replays hazy flashes of what I know to be my mother; her auburn hair, backlit as she pulled the brush through the length of it.

The fear. I sensed, even as a child, she was leaving me.

My stomach clenches. *Please do not vomit.* I flush with the potential mortification. Fear and a dark, black pain and a pressing anxiety hit me like a battering ram.

Violet grasps my elbow.

Henry's voice, angry and raised, whips my attention back to the gathering.

"What? You cannot be serious!"

John's expression is tentative, his mouth working to find words.

Priscilla. My eyes fall to her hands. Hands which are cradled under a very small swell of a belly.

"No." Violet whispers.

The world tilts. I bite down hard on my lower lip, bloodying it. I welcome the pain.

The world rights. The metal heart-box slams shut, bolts are thrown, clicking and locking protectively around my soul.

My barrier erupts as a fiery wall in my mind as anger scorches my tears and incinerates my vulnerability.

My shoulders square and I set my jaw.

"If it's true, Henry, I'm afraid you'll have to wed quickly. To avoid the scandal. And to avoid losing your position at the Mutter," Dr. Earnest says, his mutton-chop sideburns working furiously.

"Of course it's true," Priscilla smiles sweetly. "Henry is such the charmer. I'm afraid I just can't tell him no. To anything."

A searing, white-hot anger burns away my reason. Hatred infects my heart. I feel it rotting in my chest, pounding its last goodbyes to Henry against my ribcage.

"Vi. I have to go."

Vi's face is pale and her hands are trembling. "Of course, my darling. I will be over shortly."

"Don't trouble. I'd rather be alone."

"I shall bring the dog."

I swish past Henry and the group, not seeing anything except the open doors, providing my escape.

I hear the familiar footsteps behind me on the steps, but speed up.

"Arabella!" Henry roars. "Stop this instant."

I whirl. My fist cocks and I punch, punch, punch his chest, feeling the tears threaten again.

Several people stop and stare. One woman gasps.

"Move along," Henry threatens. "Bella," he croons.

"Do not touch me!" I shriek. I hold up my hands in defense. Protecting my heart. My mind.

"I trusted you. *You* are the villain. You make me sick. All the while, playing dress-up with that doll of a girl."

Henry's face twists with rage. "All it takes is one accusation and you've convicted me? All that I've said, all that I've done? I asked you to marry me two hours ago."

"Bigamy is illegal in these United States."

Henry's hands clench and unclench and he looks around for something to strike. "I never touched her. I never kissed her. Just believe me. I…will never touch another woman again."

"Such a sacrifice. Do you think your roving hands will be able to honor your pledge?"

All at once the pleading's gone from his face as a sharp, black rage rumbles across his brow.

"Bella." The ice in his voice halts me mid-step. I turn and give a little shudder.

Henry's lips retract, exposing his teeth. It's a halting contradiction, the beauty of his face contracted with such utter hatred.

"Your heart." He swallows. "Your heart is algor mortis."

His voice rumbles like black thunderclouds.

"My heart is like *cold death?*"

"Yes. I thought I'd put it in terms you could understand."

I've wounded him deeply. Possibly beyond repair.

I vacillate. A tiny, younger part of me cries to never hurt Henry. But the jealousy and betrayal silence it.

Anger floods my nose.

He deceived me, he deserves the pain.

"You are right Bella. You aren't like other girls."

My stomach contracts like I've been punched as he throws my own words back at me.

Henry retreats, backwards up the steps.

"Other girls recognize love when they see it."

Chapter Nineteen

LIFE WITHOUT COLOR

Bellevue Stratford Hotel
Henry

The glass shatters into a million fragments, raining down and sliding across the polished floor. I seize another vase and hurl it at the wall. It disintegrates and Violet steps out of the way as a stray bit nearly slices her.

"Henry!" father erupts.

That sobers me. That fact it almost sliced her, not his screaming. He's been screaming for a quarter hour.

My chest still heaving, I manage, "I'm sorry Violet. Would you please give us a moment? I. I'd rather you not see me in such a state."

Violet nods, and is gone in a flash of green.

A vein bulges in father's forehead, pulsing and angry like his face. He sits, waiting, fingers steepled in front of his lips as if he's praying. *Perhaps he is? For the prodigal son, at it again.*

"Breaking every piece of furniture will not alter reality. Bring Bella to you. Remove your obligations."

I bury both hands in my hair, balling my fists, welcoming the pain. I pace in front of him. To sit would be like suffocation. I cannot catch my breath, or control my raging thoughts.

"Henry. Is it yours?"

My head whips to regard him, my lips pulled back from my teeth. My hand shoots out to destroy another vase—but I stay it. It shakes in mid-air. I jam my eyes and fists shut, and drop my head.

"Do you think so little of me?"

Father sighs, a sad sound. "I must ask. Henry, consider your history."

"You mean my near-expulsion. My carousing? My gambling?" My chest heaves faster and faster.

My eyes fly open, boring down on him. "How long has it been since I caused you shame? Years. Have I not redeemed myself?"

I grind my teeth together. Red rage consumes me, and I see nothing, only feel the urge to destroy something. Anything.

"Henry."

I keep pacing.

"Henry!" Father's hands are on my shoulders, stopping me. "Just say the word. I promise to take you at it."

I shake him off. "Forget that lying she-devil. Tell me; tell me about Arabella's mother. Please, I must know."

Arabella's twisted face tortures me, like a knife driven and embedded in my heart.

I stare at him, waiting.

"Fine. She kept Bella till she was three. She was very poor and frivolous, spent everything as fast as she earned it. Refused to marry a Holmes. It was a tryst—probably the only tryst ever had by a Holmes. Knowledge is their mistress."

"Forget Holmes. Continue."

"She couldn't take Arabella on the traveling circuit. She frankly couldn't afford her. I believe she loved her, in her way— but she's a selfish creature. Her own lifestyle, in the end, was more important than keeping Arabella."

It will kill her. Murder any remnant of the little girl, still fighting to stay alive under the cold exterior.

"And now me. What must she think of me?"

"Henry. Your future is at stake. Not only your reputation, but your employ. *Did you bed her?*" He blasts, his careful calm finally exploding.

I shake my head. "No. Priscilla has set her sights on me. Beneath those frills and lace is a conniving predator. Someone else has bedded her, but I must be the more likely husband. Perhaps she knew the job might force me into a false confession."

Father stares, his eyes searching my face. Apparently finding what he was looking for, he nods. "Then we must tell Dr. Earnest. He's an honest sort. But the chances are grave you keep the job."

I nod. "Arabella. Where is she?"

"She refused to see me. She said she will write to Violet."

My heart feels anesthetized. Numb and weightless. I look around the room. The reds and blues look washed and faded.

If I lose Bella, life will lose its color.

"Father. I know she appears cold, calculating. But under it. She's as innocent as a child. This will...undo her."

"I know. Have faith. We must first deal with Priscilla. Then hopefully we will see Arabella back at the steamer. Perhaps you should talk to Priscilla, attempt to dissuade her from her plans?"

I shake my head. "You are much too optimistic...but I shall try. I'll go tomorrow."

I nod, staring out at the moon. And try my best to send my thoughts across the night. To tell Bella to hold on.

Clark Park
Henry

The morning is unseasonably warm; the Indian summer sun sears Priscilla and I as we walk through the park, past the life-size statue of Charles Dickens. I open my mouth to remark on the girl at the statue's base, but quickly close it. The girl, Little Nell, was a character from Dicken's story, The Old Curiosity Shop.

If it were Bella draped on my arm, her eyes would light at the instruction. Though literature was not her love, her mind thrives on every sort of information.

In sharp contrast, I daresay if my conversation veered from the society gossip pages or Paris fashion, I would directly lose Priscilla's attention. Indeed, her arm is wrapped so tightly through mine that I imagine a Boa Constrictor strangling its prey. I grit my teeth to maintain civility.

We reach the open field, with very little talk. People cover every bit of the lawn, soaking up every ray of the remaining sunshine before winter descends on Philadelphia.

"Priscilla. I think you're a capitol girl. But we both know I have not touched you."

Her blue eyes turn up coyly. "Ah, Henry. In my mind, I've lived the act many, many times. I will be a magnificent wife and mother. We can have a brood of children, I don't mind. Of course we'll need a nanny, and how many servants—"

"Imagination does not put a child in your belly." I stop dead. Fury bubbles in my chest.

"Why, whatever do you mean, darling?" She shifts closer, her fingers playing on my chest. "I recall every glorious moment—"

"Stop!"

I step out of her grasp, terrified of losing my self-control.

A dog growls.

"Henry?"

Oh, no. Please, no.

Arabella stands frozen, Newton's leash wrapped around her hand. Her eyes leap between Priscilla and I like an animal in flight.

"Darling, why, look who it is? Your dirt-partner. Isn't that charming? You are welcome to come and visit Henry and I and the baby." Her eyes drop to Newton. "Please, though, leave that filthy creature at home."

Newton growls again, his hackles rising down his spine.

"I—I," Arabella stammers.

Priscilla's eyes shine with cold vengeance. "Darling, you don't know what you're missing. Henry is…" she cups her belly, "such a scoundrel. But what a beautiful one, yes? Between the two of us, the baby will be breath-taking."

Arabella is shaking all over. Her demeanor crushed. She reminds me of a flower trampled underfoot.

"Shut up!" I roar. "You are not fit to speak her name."

People turn to stare. A few nannies shuttle children out of earshot.

Priscilla laughs. "I am not fit? Look at her." She gestures toward the mud lining the bottom of Bella's dress. "Really, Henry. Your lust has saved you from a very embarrassing match."

I step away from her, putting distance between us.

I turn my back on Priscilla. Her words have forced Bella back; her face pinches in revulsion—reliving every taunt she's ever endured.

My confident, intelligent Bella stands mute.

Newton slides his head beneath her hands and she squares her shoulders, her eyes narrowing. "I hope you will be very happy together." She nods, "Henry."

She spins on her heel, leading Newton back into the fray.

I whirl on Priscilla's triumphant face. "I told my father you were incapable of reason."

Her voice drips honey, "Oh, Henry—"

I grasp her elbow as I would a viper, and spin her around in the direction of home. "Not a word. Do not speak another word."

Bella

I reach my cottage steps and hurry inside and barely manage to shut the door before the tears come.

Well, at least I now know I am capable of tears.

"Ha. Twice in a fortnight."

I release Newton from his leash, but he halts, nose raised in the air. He growls. I remove a letter from the mailbox.

"Stop. Honestly. Go outside." I open the door and shove him toward it; he locks his legs, whining.

I manage to force him onto the porch, but he turns, staring at me.

I shut the door on his face and his claws scratch a moment later.

My eyes close as Priscilla's words echo through my head. How I would embarrass Henry, were he to choose me.

My disheveled reflection stares at me from across the room. I hurry over to it.

My eyes flick across my hair, my complexion. I turn sideways, examining my body.

Even unadorned, I am more striking than Priscilla. I've always known this in an empirical way, but put little stock in it. Bettering *my mind* was always my concern, not my appearance.

I am a Holmes, after all.

I haven't the slightest idea how to beautify myself.

"Violet. Violet would teach me how."

"Teach you how to what?"

My blood turns to ice. I whirl, my heart hammering.

A man. His face concealed by an elaborate masquerade mask. But I know to my bones, it's Stygian.

In my cottage.

"How? I thought you were at the dig? And how did you get in here?"

Images and data flash like a strobe-light through my mind. Escape routes.

His weaknesses. In inclimate weather, he limps—his right knee. Target one.

His left hand does not make a full fist. Most likely broken. Target two.

His groin.

He shakes his head. "I don't know what you're on about. Why, I broke in—a common criminal." His voice feigns innocence.

My mind runs the scenarios. A kick to the groin. Hurl my knife.

Will anyone believe me?

I must not let him near me; I'm no match for his strength.

Newton begins barking in earnest, his paws frantically scratching the wooden door. He will alert anyone nearby on the Mutter Campus

Stygian steps closer.

My hand pulls up my skirt, fingering the knife. His eyes

light with the showing of my flesh.

My face burns, but my eyes tick from his face to his hands to his feet. Ready to launch forward at his slightest move.

"Our roadblock has been removed."

"Whatever do you mean?"

"Please, Arabella. I saw the way you looked at Henry. He is no match for you. I, however, am the perfect match for you."

"You know you shouldn't be here. I should scream."

"Who would they believe, Arabella? You? Although a Holmes, your eccentric reputation precedes you. At the very least, I can commit you to the asylum till your father arrives. Which would be weeks. I have friends at the asylum. Indeed I have friends everywhere."

His eyes are dark and hollow.

I swallow. He's right. John would fight, no doubt, but he *could* have me put there for a time. Till the facts were sorted in court.

"Why, she pulled a knife on me..." he says sweetly, ambling back and forth. "I was only inquiring after her health—hearing of her public drama at the opera house."

"She was quite distressed. Unhinged, really."

Newton claws the window, slobbering, barking and biting the glass.

"You know, patients *disappear*, all the time at the asylum. Poor wretched souls, they just wander off, never to be seen again...I would hate for that to happen to you. Such a terrible waste."

He lunges. I dodge out of the way. His fingers seize and

hold the bottom of my dress. His hands instantly muddied.

I yank and it rips.

I fly toward the door, fumbling for the handle.

Newton has left the window; his wild barks inches away behind the door.

I turn the handle and it opens a crack.

Stygian slams it shut.

He shoves me against the door with his body, my arms spread-eagled. Bash, bashing my wrist against the wood till the knife clatters to the floor.

I cannot move.

His breath is at my ear. "Perhaps the asylum is best for now. I see the kind you are—its written all over your features—but still I must have you. You're like a wicked-siren-call. I will see to my affairs, and we will depart. I care not if you marry me. You *will* be mine, Arabella."

The window shatters, a crystal implosion; shards of sparkling sunlight ride the glass across the floor.

Newton leaps in, barking madly. He lunges, his jaws clamp down on Stygian's leg, instantly drawing blood.

"Ah! Vile creature!" He whirls.

My knee connects with the soft flesh of his groin.

His legs buckle and he falls, retching. I kick again, my boot striking his once-broken hand and he shrieks.

I wrench open the door, falling onto the porch. I scramble down the stairs, into the sunlight.

"Newton, come!"

The dog barrels down the steps to my side, still snarling. I bolt toward the museum, and don't look back.

###

Earnest Estate

Next Morn

Henry

Priscilla sits at the table, primly holding her burgeoning belly. *Is it my imagination, or does it seem larger since just yesterday?*

I allow my eyes to take in their estate. Beautiful, but not ostentatious. Too bad Priscilla could not be more like her family home.

Dr. Earnest arrives, and eases his bulk into the Captain's chair at the head of the long table. He's done well. Except for his only daughter, heaven help him.

She smiles at me. My teeth grind together and I feel my jaw muscle ratchet and tighten so hard I hear it pop in my ear. I drop my eyes and stare at my hands, willing them still.

"Well, Dr. Holmes, Mister Holmes. How to begin?"

I slam my fist on the table. "It is not mine."

My father's eyes roll, and he exhales, protruding his bottom lip. His stare conveys, *yes, thanks for that bit of self-control.*

"Henry attests the child is not his, sir. My son has many faults, but lying is not one of them."

Our eyes meet. I nod. Grateful. He does believe me.

"Well, I'm afraid it's her word against yours, my boy."

"If you will not marry her, I'll be forced to let you go, son. The museum can ill afford such scandal. We depend on benefactors for donations. You understand."

My insides tremble. I bite back a scream. What is to be done? I cannot marry her. Perpetual eunuch would be more tolerable.

My gut somersaults in fear. Leaving Bella. I had almost gained her full trust. I suppress the rage and hear a ringing in my ear.

Steady, man. Priscilla rises, making a show as if her barely-there bulge hinders her motion. Her bottom lip juts out. Tears trickle down her face. I wonder if she's pinched herself. What a perfect actress. She belongs with Arabella's mother.

Her bottom lip trembles. "Henry? How can you be so cruel? Our coupling was...magical."

"Magical?" I roar. "If it was, you must have wholly enchanted me. As I have no memory of it!"

Earnest's face is puce with mortification.

Priscilla reaches me, her fingers playing in my hair. I bite down on my lip and taste the blood.

"Priscilla, my dear. Would you please give us a moment alone?"

Her father is aghast at her public affection.

Priscilla's eyes narrow and I almost hear the feline howl building behind those pouty lips.

"Only a moment, my dear."

She curtseys and huffs into the neighboring parlor.

Dr. Earnest's bushy white brows waggle like fishing lures above his deep set eyes. "I must say Dr. Watson, I'm very much disappointed. I was so certain of your family's tradition of honor—"

"Please, stay your tongue doctor." Red tints father's face from his neckline to his hairline. "I believe Henry."

"What?" Earnest roars.

Bang!

A gunshot. Then something large crashes in the parlor.

We all rush to the door. I see Father's hand readjust on his walking stick.

I fling open the door and stop short. My jaw drops.

"No, my pet! I vill not have it!"

A young man with dark, curly hair grips Priscilla's shoulders, a pistol hanging half-clutched in his fingers.

"Pierre. What are you doing?" Earnest bellows. "What is the meaning of this? Unhand my daughter!"

The handsome man is dressed in stable gear. A hand to their elaborate coach house?

His finger juts toward her belly. "Ze child is mine. I will not have zis...*person*, touching her. Raising my child. I will not stand for it."

Priscilla's eyes roll back in her head, and father lunges to catch her, easing her down to the floor.

I wonder if she's feigning. I squeeze my fists together, quivering with rage.

Dr. Earnest's face darkens from pink to purple, and he extracts a handkerchief to pat his forehead. His eyes dart back and forth from Pricilla to me like a metronome.

For a moment, I fear he too, will collapse. But he blinks rapidly, clearing his throat.

Relief weakens my legs and I step forward so not to give way. I spread my fingers on the doorframe, leaning on it for support.

"Dr. Watson, is she well?" Earnest and Pierre inquire at the same time.

"Just a fainting spell. She will be fine."

Earnest whirls on the young man, who, to his credit, doesn't flinch. "I will deal with you later."

Earnest turns back with a sheepish nod. "I expect you and Henry are discrete men."

My father stands. "Of the utmost."

"Henry. You shouldn't delay in getting back to the ship." He stares around the room, trying to skip over Pierre. "The museum recently acquired an automobile. Feel free to drive it back to the steamer and collect your thoughts. For your trouble."

Bella

I arrange the wig on my head and chance a glance behind me. The Philadelphia night is foul and my eyes water as I approach the sausage plant.

I finger the letter. I read it directly after securing lodging after my scuffle with Stygian.

It was brief and scribbled in a masculine hand.

I think I found something. I heard you're in town. Who didn't hear about the other night? Come when you can, scrapper.

Yours,

Jimmy

Jimmy has been a most useful spy these past few months, keeping me abreast of the comings and goings of the plant. I think of Henry's teasing, how he is sweet on me...

And banish the thought. No time for pain for even Henry at this moment.

The soot-covered façade somehow makes the building look old and sad. Thunder rumbles overhead and the first drops of rain strike the bowler hat I've donned.

I hurry to the side entrance and rap twice.

I struggle to stay still. To try to appear non-descript, but my heart is racing and sweat trickles down my nape from beneath the wig. I glance up and down the dirty alleyway.

Hurry, Jimmy.

Finally, his face appears through the filthy pane.

He looks past me, up and down the side street as well. "Come inside."

He walks to the door which leads into the factory and locks it. The room has an undefinable smell; acrid but somehow appetizing. My stomach lurches uneasily.

"What is it, Jim? I am to depart in just a few hours' time?"

"Well, I have two things—but I must admit our arrangement doesn't seem fair. I mean a few coins for all my trouble?"

"Jim, what happened to your face?"

The young man's right eye is a shiny bull's-eye of yellow and purple and black.

"Never mind that. Our negotiations?"

"What did you have in mind?"

He sidles closer and I smell the rum. "Just a kiss, Miss Arabella. One for each secret. I swears they be worth it."

Please, Jim. Be a man of your word. I do not wish to hurt you. "Alright. A kiss only."

He leans in gently placing his lips to mine—they are hard and urgent and I peck back and step back.

"Firstly?"

"I thought you might like to know my uncle's been spending a fair amount of time here. This here's his handiwork." He puts a careful finger to the shiner. "I think he's going to get my Da in trouble. He's living here under an assumed name."

My heart goes apoplectic and I fight my breath. "And the name is?"

"Styler? Stickler?"

"Stygian?"

He snaps his fingers. "Yes, that's it. Give the lady a coin."

My mind whirls. I was correct. About everything. He is a not only a would-be rapist ... but a murderer.

I swallow, thinking of L'uomo Deliquente. About how many men and women live up to his stringent requirements.

Four dead scientists.

He may well be a mass-murderer. But I do not have enough proof.

"He was going on, trying to get me Da to join some society. The Brotherhood of the Revolution, he called it. My Da refused and they argued. My Da kicked him out, threatened him not to return. But I know my uncle. I. I'm afraid for me Da."

I nod. "I will do whatever I can to help, Jim. What is the second item?"

He steps closer. I fight the urge to tap my toe. His kiss is hard, wanting, and his lips begin to open.

I step back again, every muscle poised for fight or flight. "Jim! What is it?"

He shoves an envelope into my hand. I open it, trying to keep my hands steady.

I upend it, and two small bones trickle into my palm. So small, I think of mustard seeds. Little bits of fascia or muscle still cling to them.

My scalp tingles. "Where did you get these?"

Jim's face is alabaster. "It was at the bottom of the vat. I grabbed it before anyone else saw."

I step backwards, feeling behind me for the door handle. "Thank you. This is most helpful. As soon as I have any information, I will be in touch." I turn to go but whisper through the crack in the door, "Jim, take care with your uncle."

He nods, already heading for the other door.

I walk swiftly, heading towards my hotel.

I twirl the bone over and over in my fingertips.

The sesamoid bone is unique to humans. It acts as a ball-bearing in the toe. I shiver so hard my teeth rattle.

Another of the lost four most definitely perished in that vat. And this tiny, tiny bone is my proof.

I reach the hotel lobby, and stare at the envelope, undecided. I glance around me, but no one notices I'm even there. Piano music filters out of the bar.

I scribble on the front of it,

Henry Watson c/o Abner Farms and hand it to the clerk to post.

Chapter Twenty

Monogamous Mammals

Locomotive, enroute to the Hudson
Arabella

I bite my lip, and wince. It's still bruised from the music hall. My mind replays my interaction with Dr. Earnest and the police after the attack in my cottage. I close my eyes, letting the clack-*clack,* clack-*clack* of the train on the tracks lull my frantic thoughts.

"You didn't recognize the attacker, Miss Holmes?" the chief inspector is not buying my story.

I shake my head. "No. It was as I have recounted it to you. He wore a mask."

His eyebrows rise. Earnest steps out of the room as Montgomery arrives.

Inspector Giamatti lowers his voice, "Miss Holmes. I am dispatching a locksmith. I will be sure you, and only you, are delivered a key. Do I make myself clear?"

"Yes, Inspector."

He nods, tucking away his pad. "Contact me when you return from the dig. I will assign an officer to watch over you. *Do not argue*, Arabella."

He turns and opens the door. I smile at him as he tips his hat to Earnest on the way out.

Earnest's watery eyes are pinched with worry. "Please, Arabella. You should stay and rest. I will tell Dr. Watson—"

"I beg of you, do not tell Dr. Watson anything. He will immediately wire my father. Which I will do. I will tell him myself."

Earnest's eyebrows rise. "If I grant you leave to return to the dig, you promise me, you will inform your father?"

I nod. "Yes."

I didn't say when...

I sigh. I will wire him. And for the first time, I want him here. I am beginning, for the first time, to feel I am in over my head.

I must finish the dig. We're very close, I can sense it.

Then I will decide what to do with the rest of my life. A niggling worry squirms in my gut; will Stygian's obsession with me bring an end to my position? What if they do not believe me when I tell of his attack?

Surely, Stygian isn't fool enough to try again at the dig, in a houseful of staff?

The thought of leaving The Mutter brings tears to my eyes. It's the only place I've ever fit. Felt at complete liberty to be myself.

I open my eyes again and try to take an interest in the beautiful fall scenery whizzing past the train window. I want to be back at the ship, not stuck here with my thoughts.

I'm heartsick. Like my soul's infected with a dark, marrow-rotting depression. I picture a yellow putrefaction wrapping around my heart.

This, this is why I fear love.

My foot taps. My skin crawls. I want to rip off my dress. My flesh feels as if it's been stretched on the rack; every poke and rub of the fabric is like a million, tiny pinpricks.

John's voice pops into my head. *It's anxiety, Arabella.*

I sigh and detest the tremble in my lips.

He couldn't of…Henry is mischievous, bold and daring. Sometimes sarcastic, sometimes bull-headed. But never cruel. Never disloyal.

The angelic half of my heart plucks its heartstrings in reassurance; the other plays devil's advocate, whispering, 'There's always a first time'.

My eyes sting as the tears threaten to spill over. For years my eyes were as dry as a desert and now with Henry's reappearance they are as wet as the mighty Hudson.

My mind replays Henry's contorted face as I stomped off, "How could you bloody believe her? Do you hear nothing I say to you, woman?"

A man across the aisle shoots me the fifth smile this hour. I've counted. I try to smile back, but I only manage a miscarriage of a smirk.

I haven't seen Henry since the park, John since the opera fiasco. John wired he would pick me up at the station. I hope *and fear* that Henry will be with him.

The train mercifully grinds to a halt. I feel I've been on its rails two lifetimes. I grab my bag, hurrying out the door.

I stand on the platform and squint through the steam, searching the crowd. I see John's bowler hat, and his grim expression beneath it.

My heart falls. I truly expected Henry to be with him.

"I have lost him," I whisper.

My chest contracts as if strangled and I'm wheezing like I have consumption as I weave my way across the platform toward him.

John takes my hand and squeezes it bracingly as he leads me to the driver. His eyes, so normally bright are dull with worry.

He opens the door to the carriage without a word.

I sit facing him, but he turns to the coachmen. "Drive on."

He finally meets my gaze. His face is ashen.

"Where's Henry?"

He taps his cane.

"John? Where is Henry?"

"He insisted on driving. The museum just purchased an automobile, and he assured me—he wanted no company, and that his mind would be righted once he arrived in Tarrytown."

"When was he to arrive?"

"This morning. I'm sure it's nothing. No reason to panic." He stares out at the receding city. "Yet."

My mind whirrs.

$D=RT$

Distance equals rate times time.

Distance from Philadelphia to Tarrytown approximately 121 miles.

Maximum speed of the Model T=45 miles per hour.

"He should've arrived in approximately two and one half hours of departing Philadelphia."

"Yes, I am aware. Think of the human factor, dear. Perhaps he was still upset, taking his time. Though he could've sent word."

I am struck mute. I cannot speak or I will scream or cry or possibly strike John. A man I so dearly love.

I sit on my hands, staring out the window. Every ten seconds or so he glances my way, but doesn't speak till the port comes into view.

His hand touches my knee and my head snaps toward him.

His face is flushed and he nods. "Honestly. I don't know how I imagined Henry with Priscilla. She was lying, dove. Her lover showed up—bursting into the meeting. Henry's position is once again secure. I will join you shortly my dear. I have a few issues to sort in town before we cast off."

I murmur a hurried, "Thank you," and rush out of the carriage, running flat-out toward the river, ignoring the condemnatory stares of every proper lady I pass.

The heat of the Indian summer breaks a sweat on my brow. I spy a crewman I recognize and bolt to his side.

He tips his hat. "Miss Holmes. What's all the bluster?"

My hand clutches my chest and I feel the burning stitch in my side. "Mr. Watson, have you seen him?"

He removes his hat to scratch his bald head. "Yes. He

arrived an hour ago. Said something about taking a swim."

A woman's scream ices my blood.

"Momma! Momma help me!"

A small girl, too far from shore, treads water with a look of terror set upon her chalky face. "There's something out here!" I rush from the boat deck, down to the shore, bolting pell-mell for the mother.

The woman paces on the gingham blanket, wringing her hands about the child's dress. "Somebody help her. I don't swim."

A blood-curdling shriek erupts from the water.

I squint and shake my head, disbelieving.

A white hand floats within inches of the girl's circling, treading arms.

The girl's eyes widen and she panics, shrieking as she splashes water as she tries to distance herself from the hand.

Her face dips below the waterline and a gurgling, choking sound bursts forth each time she bobs up.

Sailors now swarm the shore and out of the corner of my eye, I spy a dingy being lowered into the water.

Is it Henry? Oh my merciful father, please do not let it be Henry.

I pray. I pray to a God whose existence I have questioned, promising life and limb. *Just spare him.*

A lump rises in my throat as I think of his deep, booming laugh and that devilish, taunting smile.

Take me. Just spare Henry.

I dive into the water, cutting through the shallows as fast as I can.

The illusion of the world spinning too fast overwhelms me. Screaming, shouting, and gurgling hit my ears in offset tones and with each breath between the strokes I see the bobbing white hand on the water's surface.

As if it beckons me to come join its watery grave.

A horrible image of Henry, corpse-white, and tangled in the river-grass pumps my heart to bursting.

I swim faster.

Six feet. Four feet. Two feet.

The girl's pigtails disappear and do not resurface. I dive—pushing through the dark water, groping in desperation for her.

My hands find purchase on her dress and around her torso—and I feel...

I scream underwater and feel the choke of the water overcome my windpipe.

Other hands grip alongside mine.

I grip the girl's dress and drag her, battling frantically upward, stroking toward the mottled light of the surface.

I break through, gasping, choking and haul her head to the surface. She barks a loud, wet cough, then vomits a tiny spray, and mercifully begins to cry.

I hear the men in the boat approaching.

A spray of water shoots skyward as a head pops to the surface.

The head. I imagine Henry's head, separated from his body.

I cannot look.

I recoil and throw my arm across the girl's chest, hurriedly backstroking toward shore.

"Bella. Bella wait."

I turn my head, feeling time slow.

My eyes widen and the emotive wall in my mind crumbles to bits and I choke, "Henry. Oh dear merciful heaven, Henry."

He strokes toward me awkwardly, dragging what seems to be a very long snorkel.

The dingy sweeps alongside me.

"Miss Holmes, hand her 'ere!"

I ease the girl to its side and in one fell swoop she's aboard, wrapped in heavy blankets. On the shore, the mother goes to her knees.

He gestures to the snorkel. "I saw the hand. Was trying to get it."

Henry swims to me and I shove the snorkel out of the way as I clasp his face in my hands and kiss his eyes, his chin, his nose. And his lips. Laughter and catcalls erupt from the boat above, but I care not.

His fingers slide into my hair, balling into fists as he kisses me harder.

The captain breaks in with half a laugh.

"That's enough now. You'll both be catching the death in there."

Henry's lips leave mine and he pulls me to him, with a quick whisper in my ear, "I am forgiven? You believe me?"

I nod and meet his eyes. "I am so stupid. A stupid, daft, arrogant girl. Whose heart really *is* algor mortis."

He shakes his head. "I didn't mean that. I…just wanted to make you suffer…as I was."

"Henry, what's in the water?"

He calls up to the captain, who is already departing for shore, "We need something to carry the hand."

I see it before I am close enough to touch it, a glint of sunlight playing off its surface.

A silver ring...emblazoned with an **R**.

Next morn

Henry

Arabella's tiny form shakes despite the layers of coverlets. She collapsed the moment we made it to shore. Father reassures me it is mere exhaustion from the chaos of the past few days.

Who could blame her?

An attack on her life, my supposed infidelity and then the body in the river? Which she assumed to be mine?

I resist the urge to hold her and force myself to stay put beside her bed, my vigil for the past few hours. I snap open my watch; father will be re-appearing at any moment, making his rounds to check on her.

I fold my hands, struggling and detesting the feeling of helplessness. A newspaper lies on the table, along with my untouched breakfast of eggs.

The headline reads, 'Body found in Hudson.'

'A decaying corpse was found in the Hudson yesterday under a dubious set of circumstances.

The corpse's foot, chained to a cement block, had kept the body submerged for an indeterminate amount of time.

It is currently undergoing autopsy before the name of the deceased will be released.'

Our names have mercifully been left out due to the very helpful chief inspector.

Arabella stirs and I drop the paper.

I sit at her side and slide her cold hand into mine.

Her eyes flutter open. "Henry?"

"I'm here love, it's over. We're all safe."

She quickly sits; her eyes wide and wild.

"The body? Do we know which of the four it was?"

"It was badly decomposed, but from the size of the skeleton, we believe it to be Marston."

"And John, where is he? Why isn't he here?"

"The old sawbones is fine, too. He should be along any moment. He's been more surly than usual. I expect his anxiety is getting the better of him. He's off plotting with the chief inspector."

Arabella stares plainly at my face. There's something different in her eyes, as if a barrier has lifted.

Her face contracts; fear, relief, joy and then desire flit so fast I can scarcely keep up. Her bottom lip trembles as she fights for control, but no tears come.

She pulls me close, touching her lips to mine.

I pull back, "Please, you've been through such a shock. I

don't even know if you're well—"

Her lips devour mine, and I surrender.

Arabella's leg lifts to wrap around my waist, and I slide my shaking hand up her thigh. My fingertips trail upward, savoring the smoothness of her skin.

I've waited so long to touch her.

My breath is rattling in and out, hard and fast, my heart pounding in my ears.

My hands stroke higher onto her thigh. And then, in my fervor, ram into…something very hard.

Alarm kills my lust. I break the kiss.

"What is this?"

I don't want to ask, to break this tentative breech in her protective bubble. But it feels like—

"A knife-holder? What else Henry? You really think I would leave myself unprotected?"

I silence her by covering her mouth with mine. Her lips part, opening wider for my entry.

A shudder courses down my back. I caress her lips, the top, the bottom; years of suppressed want pour out, saturating every touch.

My tongue explores her mouth, and she gives a quiet whimper.

Not a fearful sound. A sound releasing the glut of raw emotion and passion—subdued and tethered for far too long.

Her breath rises. Her panting matches my own, her hand on my chest, rising and falling with the sharp intakes of my breath.

She breaks the kiss. I trail down her neck, her collarbone.

"Henry, I don't think humans are capable of fidelity."

I laugh. "Utter nonsense. I assure you John Watson never strayed—neither on my mother, nor on Violet."

I want her to stop talking. To reclaim her previous state of recklessness.

"We are just animals, Henry. Trying to continue our species. Trained to have more than one mate."

My hands wind in her thick hair. "Anseranaie Cygnini."

She stops, staring. "What?"

"Swans. Swan's mate for life, Bella."

Tears fill her eyes again and she smiles. The second time in two weeks. Miracles. Do. Occur.

I squeeze her hand. "I shall never stray, Bella. I've never wanted anyone or anything the way I want you. I cannot get you out of my head. Your smell. Your touch—please, Bella. Just say you'll be mine. I don't care if you marry me right now. I don't care if it's ten years."

Her eyes change, lit with a new, acute fervor. Her lips trail to my ear. I vaguely register the moan, barely realizing it is mine. I whisper between breaths, "Well, please not ten years."

She laughs quietly.

The door bursts open—slamming off the wall.

Father's eyes widen in revelation. "Henry. I can't leave the two of you alone for a moment." His head hangs in disapproval, his foot tapping. "For goodness sake, make her decent."

I right Arabella's skirt, and help her to stand beside me.

"Father, I'm sorry. I know Arabella is not your choice. But it's *not your* choice. I love her. It can't be helped and isn't something to be undone."

Bella's breathe sucks in with my confession.

Father's eyes leap back and forth between us, and he sighs. "Holmes and I, have a most peculiar relationship. I... *we*...just...see the potential for problems between you." His hands turn palm up, almost pleading.

"You hypocrite! How can you say that? You worked alongside him for years, foregoing marriage—"

"You are as close as a brother to him!" I insist. "Closer than his brother," Bella murmurs.

He nods. "Yes, I am. And trying to imagine our inner workings, our struggles...molded into a male, female relationship...." He shakes his head. "It just seems impossible."

Arabella steps away from me. Heat floods my face. She always obeys my father's wishes more so than I.

Arabella whispers, "When you have eliminated the impossible, whatever remains, however improbable, must be the truth."

Father's head jerks up. His mouth opens and closes. He bites his lip and nods, in ascension. He stares at her, unmoving. "John." Their eyes lock and hold, almost an embrace.

They stare with more familiarity than I've ever recognized.

He, with an empathy I didn't think possible. Her, with a longing? Perhaps for his approval?

"John, please." Arabella's voice breaks. "I love him. I know I have the Holmes disposition ... stubborn. Rigid."

"Immovable," my father corrects. "Like trying to re-route gravity."

She smiles and nods, her lips now trembling like her voice. "I want Henry more than any experiment, or calculation. Do you believe me?"

Father's eyes shoot around her room. To the black powder, her microscope, her inks and pens. The black stains on her delicate fingers.

"He makes me better than I am. Better than I ever thought I could be and I ... I love him."

Anger darkens his features. "Blast it. I told Holmes it was unnatural. To have him raise you. You belonged with other girls, in school. And not another female in the house, save a housekeeper."

Arabella pleads, "John, please...listen to me."

Pain shoots through my nose, followed by a detonation of anger. I clench my hands and pray for willpower.

Do not intervene. This is about more than you.

A singular tear slides down her cheek.

I shuffle, trying, trying not to touch her.

"I-I did my best to fit in at school. You know I did. I just ... couldn't. I have nothing in common with those girls. You know that. Uncle did the best he could."

"Uncle?" I interject.

"*Don't* call him that. You only say that when you're angry, Arabella."

"I don't understand?"

"Shh!" They both hiss in tandem.

She is Mycroft's daughter?

Images of Holmes's more brilliant, more stoic, even more self-absorbed brother blast in my head.

I feel as if I've fallen down the rabbit hole, and nothing in my world is as I thought.

My heart suddenly beats with unexpected warmth towards Sherlock Holmes.

A new appreciation of him; that he, who was once compared to Babbage's adding machine, was capable of selflessness after all.

"Arabella—he's made indelible marks on your personality. I don't know if they are compatible with matrimony. It surely wasn't for him."

Arabella's eyes harden. "Fine. I wanted your approval, but do not need it." She strides backward and firmly grasps my hand. "I am with Henry. You cannot stop us."

A vein pulses on father's forehead, and I tense, ready to step between them. I rise on the balls of my feet.

I nod, stepping closer to Bella. "I don't want to disappoint you either, but I'm not leaving her."

Father rolls his eyes, exhaling through his gritted teeth.

Bella's voice is bitter. "What would you have had him do? When both my father *and* mother abandoned me? Send me to the orphanage or perhaps the workhouse? How very noble, Dr. Watson."

I stare at father's face; my stomach plummets to my boots. My father's eyes glisten.

"No. I told him…to give you to *me*."

Chapter Twenty-One

Abner Farmhouse
Bella

Cymbals crash beside my head.

I shoot to sitting, my nightdress clinging to my skin from the sweat that bathes my heaving chest. I blink and shake my head as the strobe blinks through my open window.

"Thunder. It's a storm you fool." I rub the bleary from my eyes and slide to the window, stripping off the shift. I stare out across the barnyard toward the woods.

Toward the dig.

Something shifts near the barn—my heart thunders against my chest as if the storm has shifted from the sky to my soul.

I blink. "It cannot be," I whisper to the dark.

The giant lumbers from the barn into the woods.

I spin, flying to the armoire, wrestling on my only pair

of riding trousers. A blaze of intuition sparks as the magnifying monocle, across the room, fairly screams to be picked up.

I walk to the mantle and jam it into my pocket.

I grab my pack and a lantern and in moments I'm darting down the steps, out into the vertical wind.

My rational mind cautions, *You should wake Henry.*

"I shall never catch him then." I run faster, breaking the tree-line.

I see the outline of his large back lumbering steadily toward the dig. He picks up the pace.

My boots slip in the mud and I stumble, snapping a fallen tree limb. The crack echoes through the wood.

He turns. He sees me.

"Blast it."

The giant bolts, veering course, heading into an open pasture. I change direction, leaping fallen logs to give chase.

I am gaining on him.

He limps slightly. *Rheumatism? Possibly caused by his—*

My hair gusts up, my stomach plummets as I fall. The ground rushes up to meet my—

Pain. Darkness. My mind-pictures flicker and dim, flicker and dim, as I fight to pry my eyes open. Anger at my stupidity tries to surge but I wince as it escalates the pain in the back of my head.

I am in a pit. Surrounded by…something. The light of my lantern gutters.

Through the hole above, tiny bits of starlight twinkle through.

A face appears to block the light.

The stars disappear, and a blackness as dark as death surrounds me as the panic begins.

Henry

A knock on the door rouses me and I squint at the weak fingers of sunlight crawling up my bed. I rub my eyes with the heel of my hand and stumble to the door.

Abner's housekeeper glares, brandishing a small envelope. "This came for you yesterday, Mr. Watson."

"Thank you, ever so much."

Kill her with kindness, I will.

Her scowl deepens and I shut the door before I laugh.

I walk across the room to stare out the farmhouse window and begin pulling on my boots, my head full of Arabella. Dawn's weak light filters through the window, chasing away night's shadows.

I hurriedly throw on my shirt, I've overslept.

The trip back from the ship to the dig was uneventful and quiet, with she and I lost in our own thoughts. It was a similarly quiet eve for once, our goal being to rise at dawn and head back to the excavation site.

Father remained at the ship. He was keen to view the autopsy and promised to come when all was stable.

She said she loved me. Not to me, of course, to father.

But it's a start.

I'm filled with hope. Surely, the past few days' events have solidified my devotion in her mind?

It may be years till she'll marry me.

I take deep breaths as my eyes flit across the woods.

I find I don't care. No one else will do.

Hoof-beats cut through the early morning stillness, and I stride across the room to the opposite window overlooking the turnaround in front of the farmhouse.

Father.

My heart lurches and crawls into my throat.

Something is terribly wrong.

There is so much to hold my father at the steamer; only a desperate turn would bring him here.

I hear fortune's breathy chortle in my mind. It murmurs happiness is not my destiny.

I shake my head, beating back the dread and fly out into the hallway and grit my teeth as I pass Bella's open door and hurtle down the stairs, two at a time to the kitchen.

I don't hear her downstairs. Only the murmuring, anxious voices of a half-dozen men.

Father halts in the doorway. His blue eyes bore into me from beneath two grave brows.

Stygian stiffens and turns to face me. "Mr. Watson, Miss Holmes is missing."

"What? How?"

My hands ball, as rage courses through my veins.

My father gives an almost imperceptible, cautioning nod.

My thoughts clear and return, curtailing the rage. This

could mean her life. I must not let on I suspect him.

I address Stygian. "When was it discovered she was gone?"

"About one hour prior. Mr. Montgomery went up to rouse her, to avoid a repeat of her previous hysterics at being left behind. He found her bed empty."

Stygian steps forward, black eyes narrowed. "When was the last time you saw her, Mr. Watson?"

I swallow. "Last night. We both turned in early."

Stygian's smile is icy; his black eyes like a reptile.

"What time, last night?" Stygian's voice isn't threatening, it's almost cordial.

Which somehow makes him more frightening. He's truly unhinged, relishing the cat and mouse.

I don't answer, but don't drop my gaze.

"It seems a hand saw you enter Miss Holmes' room at a most inappropriate hour." He smiles.

My mind whirls. Lie? Truth? Lie?

I was only there for a moment, to check on her.

"I was concerned for her safety. I went to her room and found it foolishly unlocked."

"Is that so?"

Every eye in the room is adhered to my face. I think of father, and Holmes. I've seen them interrogated many times. I smooth my expression to what I hope is unreadable calm.

I nod. "Yes. I left her room around 3 a.m."

A vein pops in Stygian's forehead; the anger finally cracking through his carefully crafted façade.

"Then *you* are a suspect, Mr. Watson. I suggest you

remain at the farm till Miss Holmes whereabouts are confirmed."

I open my mouth to swear, but father shakes his head. I snap it shut and grind my teeth together.

Stygian motions to the men and six follow at a wave of his hand. He turns back before heading out into the morning air.

Stygian's voice lowers. "I do hope for your sake, Mr. Watson, you are telling the truth, and your visit was not merely to slake your own lust."

He steps outside. I lunge for the back of his jacket.

Father grabs my hands, pinning them at my sides. I struggle, but am astounded at his strength. He wrestles me into the parlor.

"Henry! Compose yourself. We must find Arabella." His face is corpselike.

My mind is running again, along with my feet. I pace before him. I fight the buzz of panic, but it grows louder.

Father jabs his cane in front of my chest, halting my pacing.

"Henry. Stop. Think. Where would she go?"

I close my eyes, block my feelings, summon the facts.

I bound up the stairs toward her room, hearing father's hurried, cane-step-step, behind me.

I wrench open her armoire as he arrives in the doorway.

For a moment, we're completely quiet, both our eyes darting in assessment. Déjà vu flashes. It's as if he's present.

Holmes in pursuit. I can almost see the amber of his pipe, the smell as he tugs on it. And for once, I fervently wish him here.

I picture him in his study. I wonder if he senses it, like some intuitive bloodhound…knows she's in danger?

I speak first, breaking the trance. "Her boots are gone."

I know Arabella would never leave volitionally without the armed boots and the parasol.

"Yes, but she still could've been taken. They could've unknowingly forced her to put them on," father suggests.

I duck my head inside the armoire, and bury my hands in Arabella's clothes; the smell of her wafts through the air, distracting me.

"She dressed. She wore her black riding pants." I sigh in almost relief.

"Here's her nightdress." Father lifts it with his cane. "If someone snatched her, they wouldn't have given her time to dress."

My eyes dart so quickly I'm dizzy; my hands rifling through the bottom of her closet.

"Her parasol is gone. That settles it. She left on her own accord."

"Pardon?" Father feigns ignorance.

"You know precisely the parasol."

He ignores my statement. "Where would she go, Henry?"

I fly past him, grasping his forearm as I pass.

"I think I know. Hurry, Father."

We fly out the back door, in the opposite direction of Stygian's search party.

###

We enter the wood's mouth. Father is bent over, scrutinizing, doing his best to follow Arabella's boot prints which occur every few feet in the mud.

Thunder rumbles overhead, and the tap, tap, tap of rain hits my hat. "Blast. We'll lose the trail."

"Hurry, Henry."

I jog ahead, keeping well off her footprints, and slip on the new mud. I stumble and my hand shoots out and I right myself into a half-crouch.

I stare down at my hand, half-hidden in the grass.

My heart trips, halting like a gasp. Then surging quickly, catching its breath, its beat pounding fiercely in my ears.

My foot is dwarfed by a massive footprint. The same as the day Arabella and I saw the giant in the woods.

"Father!"

He hurries to my side, our eyes snaking along Arabella's trail.

Father swallows. I squint my eyes, and see it too.

Her footprints becoming further apart. At the same time as the giant's appear.

"She's running."

Father's eyes leap over her prints and he nods.

I bolt along the trail, ruining half of it in my haste.

"Henry! Slow down." I know he means more than my pace. He means my mind. Think.

I cannot. My legs and panicking heart are in control.

I fly, my long legs quickly leaving father behind. I automatically sweep the area, searching for danger and draw the pistol. Will it stop such a mountain of flesh?

At least I sincerely hope he's flesh.

If a bullet doesn't halt him, hand to hand will be a quick death for me.

My boots slide to a halt, skidding into the trail, ruining the prints. Holmes would mortally cane me.

I suck in a breath.

They are gone. No Arabella prints.

I run ahead. *Nothing.* No giant prints, either. Vanished.

Henry

I close my eyes, trying to think, to reason.

I stare back at the trail in the muddy ground.

Veering to the right, I encircle the spot where Arabella's footprints disappear.

Further away, the giant's singular trail reappears, heading toward the woods.

"He must be carrying her. Father!"

He arrives, only slightly out of breath. "What is it?"

I point with the pistol, and don't need a word. He understands in a blink.

"I will head into the woods, after the giant's trail. I'll fire twice in the air if there's trouble."

Father hurries into the tree-line and disappears.

I begin to circle again, searching for anything that will

prove me wrong.

I see it. *A blot of red, halfway across the field.*

My legs pump, but the world has slowed, spinning awkwardly on its axis, making my dash feel a crawl.

Panic-induced images flood my brain. Arabella spread-eagle on the ground, blood trickling from the side of her mouth.

I groan and grit my teeth and dash faster.

I arrive at the red splotch.

It's her handkerchief. I bend and snatch it, turning it over in my hands.

No blood.

"Henry?"

My name on the wind congeals with a shriek.

A high pitched keen, like a woman in pain, sounds to my right. From the tree line.

I spin, my eyes squinting, trying to see into the woods. My legs tense to sprint as the otherworldly cry sounds again.

I cock my head and I see it.

It's a fox; my head whips back toward the trail. It sniffs the air and our eyes meet for a brief second before it disappears in a red-brown streak.

But a fox cannot speak my name. Was it my desperate imagination?

My lungs fill as I hold my breath, listening.

Foxes sound like women.

Like a woman being murdered when they're in distress.

The hair rises on my arms, lifting each hair like a wildfire, spreading to the back of my neck.

"Help."

It's muffled. The fox cries again from the woods and hair prickles up my neck.

I bolt back to the trail, turning in useless circles.

"Arabella?" I speak in a normal tone, not wanting to bring the giant or Stygian.

"Henry."

"Where are you?"

"Henry, look down."

The sound issues below me, seemingly under my feet?

I drop to my knees, placing my ear against the wet earth.

"Henry." It's louder now, directly under me.

My hands trace the grass, feeling and probing.

My fingertips feel the end of a large board, covered completely with grass and dirt. If not for the rain, I might've noticed it, but the mud slick hides it most effectively.

Tunnels. I think of the mine-shaft. Many tunnels and rooms like catacombs, all leading to the underground river.

My fingers slide beneath the edges and I heave back the board as my breath shudders out.

Bella's face stares up, meeting mine. The underground room is large, an old mine. Similar to the one which housed the hand.

My eyes trip over every inch of her, searching for injury. I exhale.

She's fine, just filthy. Her chest rapidly rising and falling.

"Are you alright?"

She closes her eyes and takes deep breaths, staring pointedly into the column of light illuminating her face. "Better. I can see the sky now."

She's surrounded by skeletons. Giant. Skeletons.

And mounds of ash?

Her voice shakes, "It *is* a burial ground. But these skeletons have been moved Henry. Someone is hiding them here. This mine was not their original resting place."

I smile. Her pick and brush and tape measure and her sifter are lit by her lantern. She has actually been examining the skeletons, while trapped. I shake my head.

"How did you get down here?"

"I fell in, actually. The board was not in place, and I was running."

"From the giant?"

"Yes. Actually in pursuit of the giant. He did the most curious thing. His huge head appeared in the hole, and he put his fingers to his lips to quiet me. And then replaced the board— effectively incapacitating me."

I catalogue the info, but shove it aside. "We have to get you out of there."

Arabella's tiny hand points toward the dark. "They're more tunnels, connected. There's a huge rock, half-blocking the exit. I'll bet one leads to the cavern where we found the hand."

"Then there might be gases. You need to get out." I whip open my pack and scrabble around inside, searching for a rope.

"Listen to me, Henry." The urgency of her voice makes me drop the rope and I meet her gaze.

"What do you remember about Dr. Klink?"

My mind searches for details about the first set of antiquarians…the ones who disappeared. The lost four.

"He was a smallish sort of man."

Arabella stamps impatiently. "His defining characteristic."

"A gold tooth."

Arabella opens her hand. In the center of her soot-stained palm, a golden incisor shines.

"What?"

My eyes dart around the mine in horror.

Two smaller skeletons lie alongside the giants. I assumed they were children.

I see now it's a trick of perspective. They are normal sized men, but appear childlike next to the giant skeletons. They are also in an earlier state of decay than their larger counterparts.

Arabella's open palm is shaking, the gold tooth reflecting little sparks of light into the dark.

"T-they burned his body. This ash pit broke my fall." She drops her eyes and shudders. "The dead broke my fall. I've been sifting through their remains for a quarter hour. They must've been interrupted, and just stashed it all here, till they could finish the job properly."

She paces, counting, "Marston and Sully in the river, Klink, burned and buried...and perhaps Archival left to dissolve in the vat."

A new fear dawns in my chest. We are in grave danger here. Completely exposed.

My head jerks up towards the tree line.

Dog barks ring through the wood. The search party is drawing near.

"I know Stygian is in on it." She swallows reflexively. Like she does when she's hiding something.

How?"

"His ring, Henry. I got a good look when he took it off at the phrenology lecture. It had an *R-* on it. I couldn't remember why it looked familiar. And then I dreamt about it. Last night."

"What? I don't understand?"

"The scar on the giant's face. It was half of Stygian's ring. Like he heated it and branded the poor fellow. But he must've fought back, resulting in only a half of the crest on his cheek."

My mind flashes to the giant's cheek. "Yes. You're bloody brilliant, Arabella."

"And what Jimmy told me."

"What? When did you see Jimmy?"

"Never mind. Listen. He said Stygian was an assumed name, and he was trying to get his father to join this 'Brotherhood of the Revolution'. I think Stygian's just moved L'uomo Deliquente here, and is recruiting under another name. He has been at the sausage factory. I think we have him. I would've told you yesterday, but since the river my mind isn't functioning properly. And it's even worse now."

"Arabella, you need to get out of that ruddy hole. And what do you mean it's worse now?"

"I believe all the first team had the ring Henry; they were part of the society. But they must've changed their minds. Perhaps they found something that would alter their belief."

A trickle of red snakes down her shoulder. "Bella, you're bleeding."

"I." She hesitates, swallowing, then pulls her hand from behind her back like a guilty child. "I am injured, Henry."

So much blood. Her hand is covered in crimson. My eyes

race over every inch of her. "Where is that coming from?"

She reluctantly turns and the fear *explodes*, pounding my heart like a war-drum.

The back of her head. Her hair is *matted* in blood.

"I struck my head. My pictures," she points to her temple, "inside my head. They've slowed and are blurry. I am not reasoning as I normally do. It's as if someone sawed open my cranium and poured in molasses."

"Arabella. Now, the rope."

She waves the comment away. "Listen! There's more."

I feel the cold sweat erupt. "Grab that rope!"

Her voice cracks. "Oh, Henry, too much more." She pockets the tooth and snatches up a long bone in her hand.

She brandishes it at me, like a shaman shaking his rattle. I notice the magnifying-monocle clutched in her other hand.

"This bone." Her hand rakes her face, focusing herself. "This bone. This bone is very important."

The crackle in the underbrush heightens. I hear Stygian's voice.

"You're stammering. They're coming."

"Quickly, focus Henry." She turns the bone so that I can see the center. "It is *one-eighth* full of compact bone. And it is the size of a giant."

My mind is stutter-stepping, distracted by the approaching search party.

My eyebrows pull together. "You said bone that was only one-eighth full was for birds."

She nods, shaking all over. "Yes, for *flight*. Perhaps these skeletons' fathers could...fly."

Angels. Angels fly. The revelation rocks my head, and my eyes widen. "Fallen angels?"

She nods. "Nephilim bones. They found Nephilim bones."

Chapter Twenty-Two

THE BRETHREN OF LARGE

The crunching sound of rock sends Arabella skittering to the far wall.

A large boulder shivers and scrapes, like fingernails on a chalkboard.

"What?"

"I don't know," she says, flattening herself against the rock.

The rock halts, and a huge man, the giant from the woods, slides out from behind the boulder, which must've been blocking a passageway.

"I will hide the bone."

The booming voice cuts through the dark. My boot slips in surprise and I cartwheel, trying to not fall into the hole.

Arabella starts and collapses into the pile of bones, which results in an odd clanking xylophone of the dead.

She holds the lantern aloft. The giant takes a step from

the shadows, the scar on his cheek still an angry red weal.

"Who-who are you?" Arabella stammers.

The dogs are barking in earnest. I now see the search party. Stygian, Montgomery and five other men are barreling through the woods, headed directly for me.

"Hurry, they are come."

"I am with the traveling circus. Stygian contacted me some months ago. He knew everything about me, somehow. I am a fugitive. He threatened to turn me in if I didn't help him."

They are going to find him, find Arabella with this evidence. I fight the fear twitching my face. Panic breathes on my neck.

The group is so close I can almost read their expressions.

"They're coming. Wait...."

My breath shudders in relief as I see him; father intercepting the group, his shrewd eyes calculating my expression, stalling them.

"Make haste," I spit. I pretend to ready the rope.

"I belong to a society. The Brethren of Large. We giants correspond, hoping to figure out a common bond, or ancestry. Stygian found me through the closest giant in the province."

"What did he want you to do?"

"To hide these bodies. To burn them." His huge eyes widen and he gestures to the pile of bones. "I did not kill them. I was to move these large skeletons ... "

"What else?"

"I was to frighten you, to make you believe I was a fallen angel." He sighs. "But he then wished you harm. But when I saw the small lady...I could not bear for her to end up as one of these." His shovel-sized hand gestures to the skeletons.

"Quickly. I will hide the bone and move these out of the chamber, so you are not suspected. He is very dangerous, Miss. There are tunnels—"

"How far do they go? Was that you in the cavern by the underground river?"

I pitch the rope before Arabella.

"Tie it around you, Bella."

The giant lumbers over, bending to gather a skeleton into his arms.

"Arabella."

Arabella is rooted; her face working, her hands outstretched and cautioning. She is afraid he will damage the skeletons.

"Arabella! Move!"

Her life is at risk, and she is worried about preserving the bloody specimens.

"You are mad, woman. Tie that rope about you *now*," I order.

Anger and fear congeal, the need to protect her, a raging beast of compulsion in my chest.

Arabella wraps the rope around her tiny waist, securing it. "How will we find you?"

The giant shuffles into the dark. "I will find you, Miss." He brandishes the bone. The bone meant for flight. "I will keep it safe. That man is pure evil and I would choose any side opposing him."

My hands grasp the rope and I pull, hand over hand, hearing Arabella's boots grind against the rock walls as she scales from the pit.

Finally her hands appear at the hole's top, grasping in the mud for a handhold.

I drop to my knees and grip her round the wrists, hauling her out of the hole.

The giant and I lock eyes for a final second. I spy a brass fastener on the underside of the plank.

Arabella strides toward the search party, and I quickly bend with my back to the group, securing the rope to the handle.

The giant can fasten the rope from inside, delaying discovery, buying him more time to move the skeletons.

Our eyes meet, and I slide the plank back into place, leaving his upturned face in the dark.

###

Sunset
Bella

The team is gathered around the large oak table, and a blazing fire roars behind me, warming my back and further dulling my already-addled wits.

Henry is on my right, John on my left. Neither will permit me out of their sight.

"So, Miss Holmes, I find it most peculiar that a woman so careful as you, found yourself at the bottom of a pit?" Stygian stares, his black eyes pinched.

I shiver, my mind superimposing a mask across his brow. This is the closest I've come to him since the attack.

"I saw a very large man, a giant himself, in the woods from my window. I was dashing flat out in pursuit, with the singular thought of catching him ... " I hope I sound convincing. I am a horrid liar.

Mr. Abner skulks in the background under the premise of tidying, but I'm certain it is closer to eavesdropping.

Stygian sneers. "It did not occur to you, Miss Holmes, that you are a woman? And to go after said creature alone might prove dangerous or fatal?"

"I—"

"I cannot have your blood on my hands. One more impulsive venture and you are off the expedition. Do I make myself clear?"

I nod. There's no point in argument. I want his attention off me, and back to the bones.

Henry drops his pocket watch and it rolls under my chair.

My sock-clad feet slide it toward me. I stretch my toes wide and grasp it, lifting it into Henry's outstretched hand.

"Your toes are as acrobatic as the rest of you." Henry chuckles. "I've never seen such a thing. You're a regular primate." He smiles widely.

The whole table goes tomb-quiet. John is staring at Stygian.

Stygian's face is flushed and sweating.

"Sir? Are you unwell?" Montgomery prompts.

He shakes his head, and his eyes refocus.

"Fine." Stygian bends down and extracts a box from

beneath the table. "Montgomery and I have unearthed another part of the skeleton. A foot. He and I will be delivering it back to the steamer for safekeeping. A storm is coming, which will complicate the dig. I suggest you all make the most of tomorrow."

I escort Bella to her room and she is in bed before I shut the door. But the sound of the housekeeper's voice beckons me back to the stairwell.

I hunker at the top and have a clear view into the parlor and kitchen. "Dr. Stygian, this came this morning, but with all the chaos I haven't had a chance till now..." The old housekeeper's prattling dies on her lips as Stygian stares. She hands him a well-weathered envelope.

"I will take the rest for the expedition and distribute them. No need for you to take time from your already hectic day." He smiles sarcastically.

The woman's smile falters and I swear she shudders.

She then gives a quick curtsy and high-tails it away from his formidable scowl.

Stygian nods as she bustles out of the kitchen to the pantry.

His thick fingers quickly slide beneath the seal. He upends the package and something small slides into his hand.

For a fraction of a second, his eyes widen and he's rigid. But then I see the practiced calm return to his features. He slides the contents into his pocket and strides toward the roaring fire, pitching the envelope over the grate.

Who was that for? What was in that envelope?

He strides toward the parlor sits at the writing desk, whipping open the parchment drawer, scribbling madly.

I slide away from the top of the stairs and slide back into Bella's room.

"Bella." She doesn't stir on her bed. I quietly walk over. She's sound asleep, her boots still on.

I carefully slide them off. My eyes drift to the back of her head, where the ghost of blood still haunts me. She needs her sleep. The blow to her head has greatly affected her thinking. The ghost of her words flutter in my mind, "I am forgetting something important."

Unease twists my gut, hoping it to be temporary.

I will tell her on the morrow.

Chapter Twenty-Three

Transformation and Revelation

Abner Farmhouse
Henry

Below me are giant skeletons with upturned arms waiting for my demise, above me, beautiful-terrible beings alighting through the air like celestial birds of prey.

The beats of their mighty wings ruffle my hair and batter my face like a hurricane wind.

Angels. Beatific, winged creatures with faces full of judgment have drawn close to the earth. Like the four horsemen of the apocalypse.

I wake. A gale-force wind blows against my face from the cracked-open window and I'm shivering all over.

I throw back the covers and stand at the window, and take deep steeling breaths as I search the night sky, almost certain I may see them riding the night wind.

My fingers draw in the condensation of their own accord.

I run a hand down my face, disoriented. Thunder cracks, deep and booming, opening the sky as a deluge rains down. I shiver more violently.

A deluge is what destroyed the Nephilim; I hope it won't mean the same for us.

Where is the giant this night? Where has he taken the bone?

Thunder cracks and I start so hard my forehead smacks the window. With the flicker of lightning the woods illuminate like Edison's new light. And I see them.

Outside, lined on a branch like soldiers, are black butterflies. Their wings bend against the raging storm as they struggle to hang on.

Are they looking for her? I shake my head and turn my eyes toward heaven, then close them. There is no rational explanation for them. Darkness and another flash.

My eyes fly open, and tick left and right.

The butterflies are gone.

A trickle of intuition courses my spine. More like a deduction. Is Arabella staying put?

I don't trust her. She's so bloody impulsive when compulsion grips her.

The farmhouse is quiet, save the storm sounds. Another thunderclap blasts above, close enough the window panes rattle. Outside, I see a small tree uproot.

This storm's more like a gale. The wind blows like God's fingers; plucking out mighty oaks, casting them aside like wispy saplings.

I snatch my boots, my pistol and pack. The taste of fear coats my tongue.

I skulk down the hall, avoiding the crickety floorboards I've now memorized. No doors open this time and I exhale in relief.

And suck it back in.

Bella's door is open. I cram my eyes shut for a brief moment. "Blast that woman."

Think, Henry.

My eyes whip to the long window above the staircase. *Surely, she would not venture out in this?*

I look in her room and my heart sinks. Her parasol lies propped by her bed. And the knife-boots are at the bedside.

Snatched? By Stygian? I am going to hobble that girl and condemn her to stitch-work till she promises to stay put.

A hot stab of anger pulses through me, and I ball my fists; the walls of Bella's room loom closer and quiver, as if ready to cave in. I bite down on my lip, reorienting my brain.

The desperate way he looks at her. Like he would do anything to have her.

Would he? Could he?

My anger floods my nose and with it the return of reason.

She's either in the house somewhere, my eyes flick outside, *or out in this deluge.*

I examine the door. No signs of forced entry. But Stygian could have a key. Which would mean Mr. Abner is party to the game.

I bolt downstairs to the fireplace, and shuffle through the ashes. A small corner of the envelope was not destroyed, fallen off to the side of the grate.

I extract it between my fingers, shaking off the ash. My eyes scan the fireplace. I see another bit of brown on the other side and pluck it up.

My head swirls.

Abner Farm

c/o Henry

It is writ in Arabella's hand. It was sent to me. He has intercepted something important. Since she struck her head after falling in the hole, Bella has been off. She failed to mention this letter. *I have forgotten something important.* Her words whisper in my ear.

I open the corner envelope and see it and my heart skips.

I tip the tiny bone from the envelope into the palm of my hand and try, try, try to focus.

I close my fist around it and stalk toward the sleeping rooms. I head to father's room and knock lightly.

He's behind it in two seconds, his voice rough with sleep. "Who's there?"

"Father. It's Bella again."

In two minutes, he's up to speed and we're skulking together through the night like a pair of common criminals.

I halt him as he's about to alight down the stairs. I drop the tiny bone into his hand.

"Bella sent me this, in the mail while we were at odds. She must've thought them very important—too important to keep on her person at the time. Stygian intercepted it. He was obviously flustered—it is so unlike him to leave loose ends."

Father's eyes narrow as he considers. "A Sesamoid

Bone. They act as a ball-bearing, to help the foot to bend. I don't understand."

It hits me like a bloody steam locomotive. It was in the vat. I know it to my marrow.

"No time. Let's go."

I explain in a hurried whisper about the sausage factory, the vat and its connection to our missing scientists.

We hurry downstairs, past the rooms, to the main floor. A flash of lightning illuminates the room for the space of a breath, then extinguishes.

I notice Mr. Abner's door is ajar.

Father and I exchange a knowing glance, and don't utter a word.

My heart throbs so hard, so fast, I wonder if ribs can bruise from the inside.

Father draws his pistol at the same moment I reach into my waistband to extract mine.

He stands, back to the door, ready to cover my entry.

I rush the room, pistol brandished, swinging wildly.

My eyes sweep. Low embers in the fireplace, a still-made bed, no boots, mud or anything to indicate Abner has visited his room in many hours.

Father steps in behind me. "Hurry, Henry. No idea how long we have."

Father drops to his knees, looking under Abner's bed.

I stride to his desk, to the mess of papers, and rifle through them. Nothing.

A locked box sits atop the desk. I pick it up and shake it. "This box?"

I turn to see father brandishing a key he's extracted from under the bed's frame.

He tosses it and I catch it one handed and proceed to jam it in the lock. It pops easily open and I wrench open the lid.

The thunder rumbles once again.

My heart stops. I inhale and it restarts.

A letter. In Stygian's unmistakable hand. It is dated over two years prior.

To: Joseph Abner

From: Brotherhood of the Revolution

Joseph. I am pleased you have accepted our offer and welcome you to the society. I knew of your father from L'uomo Deliquente, and he was a good and faithful servant to the cause. Our most sacred mission, to further the Darwinian revolution, can use every willing hand. The discovery of the giant skeletons on your property is most unfortunate. I've made it my personal quest to seek out and destroy any and all I suspect may truly be Nephilim remains.

Mankind are animals, barely able to contain their impulses. Belief in men, not some ethereal God, is how we should exist. I will arrive shortly, and do hope you are as willing as your father, to help by any means necessary to further the cause.

Yours,

FS

My hand shakes, rattling the letter as I thrust it into father's outstretched fingers.

I fling open Abner's armoire, pitching his clothes out to the floor and father's eyes race back and forth across the text.

"So much for discretion," father says behind me.

He too, wrenches open Abner's desk drawers, looking for further clues.

A tree limb smacks the window and it busts open, destroying the latch. Father hurries to secure it and quiet its banging. The wind is so strong; papers alight in the air, swirling in a white-parchment whirlwind. The fire flickers against its force.

"Henry, it may be a tornado."

I nod, fixated on the cabinet.

Nothing. But the intuition tickles. *Something. I am missing something.*

I knock along its outside. It rings hollow. I search every angle, but all appears normal.

I step inside it, tracing, feeling with my fingertips, knocking every few inches. My knuckles rap the back inner wall.

It echoes like a cave.

My fingers trace the smallest space in the wood. I push, and a catch releases.

It swings open.

Bones. An avalanche of bones clank out. Femurs, tibias, fibulas, hands and feet rush out in a soul-chilling jangle of remains. They fill the cabinet, burying me up to my thighs.

I pick up a sheared off long bone and peer inside.

"Father, your magnifying glass."

I hold my breath as he slides it into the cabinet and I squint.

One-eighth full. Bones for flight. Nephilim bones. Every last one.

A startling crash erupts in the farmhouse.

Father whirls at the sound. "Henry."

His face is the color of a corpse. We both say her name. "Arabella."

Buried in the pile of bones, in the back of the false-cabinet is a painting. I swallow.

I rip it out, sending a shower of fingers around me.

*It's an **R-**.*

Surrounded by snakes, like a family crest.

My brain clicks like a trigger. I recall the sun-faded circle on the entry wall. I step out of the cabinet, the painting in my hands. I flip it for him to see.

Father understands immediately. "The painting from the entry wall."

My hands are shaking. "Please, father." I gesture at the paper. "That is your evidence. Keep it safe. You must keep it safe."

"Henry, look at me."

His eyes are murderous as he steps closer and grabs hold of me.

He shakes my shoulders. I almost see the ghost of the soldier's uniform fit to his body as he stares me down.

"This is the moment—be constant, miss nothing. We must find her. There is no time to lose."

I nod, willing the anger again. I start as another limb hits the window.

"We are going to need help. Who knows how many

Stygian and Abner have in legion with them?"

"I will go wake Montgomery. I cannot imagine he is in their clutches. I will send him for help."

I think of Jeremy's slightly wonky smile and shake my head. "I don't think so."

Father spins to go but I catch his shoulder. "Father, you should go with him."

"Out of the question." Paternal protection flares in his eyes. Just like when I was a lad.

"*You think*, now. Jeremy is a scientist, not a soldier, not even a scrapper. If he is intercepted, any hope for help goes with him."

Father is frozen, his eyes ticking furiously as he works through my assertion, considering, I know, Montgomery's skinny frame, his spectacles.

Father's eyebrows ball together. He grasps both my shoulders, shaking roughly. "Henry."

He swallows. A million emotions tear across his face.

It says; this might be the end. And all our differences, our battles. They don't mean anything.

I nod, feeling the same. "I know. I'll be fine. You taught me everything I know. And so has that stoic task-master you call a best friend. You must let me go."

He nods reluctantly and releases me, eyes still anxious. "Find her Henry."

He strides for the door, but quickly turns back.

He tosses me his walking cane, which conceals a sword.

He begins, "Be not afraid of greatness...."

The window bursts back open. I hear the bones shift

behind me.

I finish it, "Some are born great, some achieve greatness, and some have greatness thrust upon them."

He nods. "Consider yourself thrusted." And disappears.

I freeze, and sniff. I smell smoke.

Chapter Twenty-Four

L'UOMO DELINQUENTE

In the dark
Bella

The ache in my head is exquisite and the taste of chloroform coats my tongue.

"Miss Holmes. Not so very clever now, are we? Now you are just a girl, like any other." Stygian bends closer, so his black eyes are visible through the gloom.

Where am I?

Two Stygian's leer at me as my vision doubles. His face undulates and overlaps on itself as the identical-twin images hover back and forth.

"I had suspicions after my phrenology reading, that you were more than you seemed. Always so coy and innocent, yet somehow a coquette."

I shake my head vigorously. It sends vertigo rolling

around my brain like children's marbles.

I see stars, multi-hued and multi-sized as my awareness fades, and flares again.

My hands and feet are bound and the chair rocks backwards as he shakes me.

I squint, trying to discern my surroundings without drawing his attention.

More skeletons surround me. Above me, barely perceptible slits of light cut across the length of the ceiling.

Behind him, is a tunnel. Most likely connecting to the mines.

We are beneath a floor. Is it the farmhouse?

Stygian's hands grip my shoulders and shake. "Pay attention when I speak to you Arabella."

I feel tears threaten. No. I will not give him such satisfaction.

"I saw the talent in your feet, Miss Holmes, how you picked up Mr. Watson's timepiece. It confirmed my suspicions."

"What suspicions?"

"That my deductions were correct, and you harlot, belong to me."

I stare back confused.

"Only harlots can use their feet as such. It is well documented in my circles. No wonder Holmes shipped you to the America's. The pompous detective was saving face; he was embarrassed by you."

I nod and feel the sadness in my smile. "L'uomo Deliquente?"

Stygian's mouth pops open. "Miss Holmes, you surprise

me? You are a student of the writings?"

"Only a critic. It's appalling that people could be so narrow minded to classify human beings solely by their physical attributes. How many have hung or been fired or carted off to the wrong marriage suitor based on these mad ramblings?"

Stygian's chest is heaving. His eyes narrow to slits. I've insulted his God. His rule of law.

"I am not a harlot. I am a virgin."

"Liar." His face is against mine, and I smell the whiskey.

"But I shall soon know. I have two tickets for the train, and then a steamship. We will return to Europe. Revenge has never tasted sweeter. You see, my little scarlet letter, your father sent my brother to prison."

He paces, his fingers twitching and face contorting, "A man so wholly pure in virtue. But now he shall be vindicated and you...rest assured, you'll never be seen again." He leans in and whispers, "And I will have you."

I shake my head, willing back the panic.

Think, think.

What would father do?

I vainly search the dark. Nothing to defend myself. All of my weapons still in my room.

Stygian eases forward, lifting my nightdress to expose my thighs, white in the dark. Gooseflesh erupts all over them.

A noise, like a pot breaking, sounds overhead.

We both freeze, staring upward. Stygian pulls a rifle and aims it at the ceiling.

"Be quiet Miss Holmes. If you do not wish to die."

###

Henry

Stygian? Did I hear Stygian?

I stop at the kitchen doorway, willing the broken pot to stop spinning. I don't move for a full two minutes, waiting, searching, listening; pistol drawn.

Father and Montgomery departed a quarter hour ago. I am on my own.

The smoke is getting thicker. I look upstairs and see flames licking the staircase. The farmhouse is on fire. They are destroying the evidence. All those bones.

Abner leaps out, bat raised, his old arms quivering.

I shove him away from the kitchen. *Stygian will hear us.*

We roll to the floor. Wrenching his arms behind his back, I easily secure them with the rope from my pack.

I gag him, and haul him over my shoulder, running outside to the nearest tree. Heaving him to the ground, I tie him to the trunk and dart back inside.

I slide to the edge of the kitchen, listening over the fire's crackle.

Shuffling below me. I look down, confused.

"I may bed you now, Miss Holmes. I'll admit you've kept me waiting longer than I am used to." He sniffs. "Or perhaps we should move into the tunnels a bit."

My heart free-falls to my feet and a blast of horror ripples down my arms. I drop to the floor, peering through the slats.

Arabella is tied to a chair, surrounded by skeletons.

Stygian is kneeling before her.

I cannot see. The rage blinds me.

I hear father's voice, cautioning in my head. 'This means her life.'

My breathing is ragged and I fight to control it.

Stygian eases in, kissing her neck.

She whimpers.

"I shall have you, now. When we leave—you are a mute, using sign language to communicate." His free hand caresses her hair. "And if you are not, I shall make it so." His knife touches her cheek, threatening. "You will have a new life, with me. I will teach you how to quell all those unnatural ideas. I shall gift you with so many children you shall not have time for your precious bones." His fingers lift her dress. "What, say, one a year for ten years?"

Her body shakes and I hear her teeth rattle.

The rage returns, coloring my world in a shocking red film.

I leap up, frantic, willing him not to violate her.

There must be an entrance.

I rush down the steps to the root cellar, the musty smell of rotting apples and potatoes making me cough.

My hands flutter wildly across the walls, searching, pleading with them to open. Nothing. Solid stone.

Smoke is trickling down the stairwell. I hear footsteps in the kitchen.

Someone is yelling, but I cannot make out the words.

I slip back up the steps; a man is kneeling as I was, staring down through the floor slats, listening and nodding. I instantly recognize him—it is Bella's attacker from the steamer.

I charge. My gun-butt smacks the back of his head and he collapses.

"Littlebee?" Stygian's voice, concerned beneath the floorboards. "Are you there? Quickly, you fool, we must depart."

My feet swipe from under me, my head crashes against the floorboards. Littlebee's awake. And fighting.

My eyes widen as he flips to his feet, grinning down at me.

"Help! Help me!" Arabella screams below my head.

I hear the unmistakable sound of a foot connecting with a gut.

And another. An all-out scuffle has erupted beneath the boards.

I roll right, scarcely avoiding a fireplace poker to the face. It strikes the floor, sizzling beside my head as a searing tendril of smoke wafts up.

He jabs again and I roll.

I kick out and my boot connects with his thigh, sending him sprawling across the kitchen.

I leap up, draw the pistol and point it at his head. "Don't do it."

He lunges, launching the poker.

I spin and it soars past. It misses and I hear it clatter and slide into the living area.

He's on me, gripping my shoulders.

I swing the gun, and bash him in the side of his head.

His eyes darken like a snuffed candle. He crumples to the kitchen floor with a 'whoomp'.

I must get her out. I feel the panic. He will move her soon, I know it.

How do I bloody well get in?

I fly across the room to retrieve an axe from beside the hearth. I swing down, delivering an almighty *craack* to the floorboards. I slam it down, again and again.

It's no use. They will flee before I can cut an entry large enough.

A small hole reveals Arabella's terrified face.

I drop the axe and reach behind, into my waistband for the pistol.

"He has a rifle!" Arabella screams, hysterical. "Watch out!"

A white hot pain sears my shoulder. Then a crushing pain on my skull.

And blackness.

Henry

My eyes fly open, tripping madly across the unfamiliar room. "Where are we? Where's Arabella?"

I can't stop coughing, and it feels as if the inside of my chest is stuffed with cotton. Every breath a struggle.

"Easy, Henry."

A pain in my shoulder sears as if the poker connected.

But I know it didn't. I clutch the spot, staring bewilderedly at father.

"We're at the closest Inn. You were shot. The house burned to rubble. We were lucky we found you, and that you didn't die of exposure."

"How did you make it back in time?"

"We happened on the law not five miles down the road. We found you outside, beside Abner, whom I'm assuming you tied to the tree. It was a miracle the fire continued. The storm abated, giving the flames a reprieve—which was all they needed."

"Who? Someone saved me? I collapsed in the kitchen. I should've died. The smoke…"

My mind reels. I wheeze and cough and my chest screams.

"You were surrounded by huge footprints."

I nod, and a wave of gratefulness spreads across my chest.

I cringe as I struggle to sit. "What time is it? We have to get to the train station. We may be too late."

I flip my legs out of bed and stagger and lean against the chest of drawers.

Father shakes his head. "The storm delayed much transportation. But yes, I've called a car, and we'll head to the station. We'll need a disguise."

He motions to clothes, wigs and even two false noses lying on the bed.

I sit and begin shrugging into the shirt. "How will we find her? No doubt he's completely changed her appearance."

"No doubt." Father massages his face. Which means he doesn't have an answer. Panic perforates a hole in my chest.

He holds up a key and a journal. "The key was around your neck, the journal in your coat."

I blanch. "The giant. Arabella *never* removes that key. It's to her journal."

Father nods. "He got them both somehow."

A light of revelation dawns and I laugh. It sounds mad.

Father looks concerned. "Perhaps I should go alone. The smoke may have addled—"

I hold my hand up, still laughing with relief. "No. No. *I know*. I know how to find her."

"Go on."

"Where's Violet?"

He checks his pocket watch. "She should be arriving. I cabled her while you were unconscious..." His face lights.

"The dog!"

I nod vigorously. "Yes. She's bringing him, yes?"

"Of course, they're bloody inseparable. I'm told he sleeps in my bed." He grimaces.

I nod. It should work. It should work.

I slide on the shirt, and the pain dries up the humor.

I stare at the key. "Should I open it?"

Father stares at it. "It's covered in soot."

"She left it in the tunnel, for someone to find." My mind whirls with worst-case scenarios.

They're already gone. I will never ever find her. He will bed her over and over, year after year, forcing children into her.

My heart feels leaden in my chest.

Father nods. "It's a desperate move."

"The giant must've been lurking, and retrieved it, along with her journal."

I shove the key inside as my hands shake. Her words.

If she dies...these pages will be the only remaining whispers of her voice.

I shake my head and grit my teeth. I flip the pages, secretly pleased as I see my name many, many times.

I leaf to the front, to find a subheading. Finally, the words: DOG COMMANDS, leap from the page.

I smile and shake the journal at him. She left it to give us a clue. "She was telling us to use her dog, too."

Father snatches the book, leafing through it as he simultaneously jams on the false nose. "Look at what she taught them. I've never seen the likes of it."

I grab the overcoat, taking a final look in the mirror. The false nose, bowler hat and wig make me almost unrecognizable. Except for my eyes. I grab a pair of dark glasses, and a white cane. I shall be blind.

"We have to go. Where are you meeting Violet?"

Bella

I whimper quietly as my head bounces off Stygian's back. I see the pain like a pick and anvil, tap-tap-tapping against every suture in my skull. I keep losing and regaining consciousness. The images in my head stop and start like a faulty reel at the moving picture show.

Stygian slides me off his back to stand and I feel his hands steadying my shoulders. "Stand up Bella."

"Don't call me that," I spit. I cringe, waiting for the slap.

He tugs at my hat. *My hat?*

My hands fly to my head, feeling. A hat, a wig.

I reach underneath to my hair. He's cut it, to above my shoulders—undoubtedly to fit it under the wig.

I stare down at a dress I do not recognize. He...undressed me. I analyze my body. I don't *feel* any different. I am mercifully intact, undoubtedly from a lack of time and fear of discovery than any moment of remorse.

My perception clears and I register dripping sounds and close, tight air. It seems to barely seep in and out of my lungs.

We are still in a tunnel. A very tight tunnel.

My breath halts. And restarts. I'm instantly panting.

Only Henry's reassuring presence was able to fight the phobia. It's crippling. I collapse to the stone floor, sickened by my own vulnerability.

Stygian halts, his eyes narrowing. "What is this?"

I stare up at him, his face blurring in and out of focus. His eyebrows rise and his face bursts into a sickening smile.

"Claustrophobia." He rubs his hands together, like it's the most delightful joke. "Ah, you see, the mighty Holmes's do have Achilles' heels. Yours...is claustrophobia. And I shall wager that I now may discern Sherlock Holmes' weakness as well. *You.*"

I'm ill. I might as well tilt my head and present him with my jugular as well. I picture my head on a chopping block, with Stygian holding the guillotine's rope.

He hauls me to stand. "Walk. We will be late for our honeymoon darling."

I half stumble for what feels like miles. And then I hear it. Voices. Loads of voices.

The tunnel splits, becoming more shabby and tighter and we are at the crossroads, perhaps in a drainage tunnel.

Far off, I see the tiniest speck of light in each direction. "To the right." He releases my arm, arranging our luggage. A bag I don't recognize will undoubtedly hold unfamiliar clothes, ready to alight me to a life of rape and torture.

Faces of whom I shall lose flip through my mind.

Violet, John, Father, my dogs…Henry.

I whisper, "Henry." Willing him to me.

Stygian bends over.

Anger surges as my heart rockets to life and I leap forward. With all my power, I kick out, clocking the side of his head.

He swears, buckling to one knee.

I run, swerving with my vertigo the left.

My chest is hitching as if an invisible hand clutches my lungs and my head wails with indescribable jags of pain as fits of light spark behind my eyes.

I whimper with every boot-strike.

Forty feet, thirty feet, ten feet.

I hear laughter. Rescue is just feet away.

With the force of a steam locomotive Stygian slams into

my back, driving me to the cave floor...

My face bashes against the stone as Stygian tackles me. I scream, and hear the voices overhead halt, listening.

Stygian's hand covers my mouth, and I bite down.

He yells and straddles my chest, pinning me.

I knee him in the back. He moves an inch. It's all I need.

I punch his groin and he flies off.

I crawl. Toward the light in the ceiling. A drain in a public house?

And then I feel it, something slipping over my head. I'm drowning, without water. The phobia reduces me to a child, begging for release.

Paralyzing, crushing fear erupts, "No, no please."

A maniacal cackle is his reply.

Blackness.

The phobia crushes me, immobilizing.

He has shoved me inside a sack. I feel my body hoist over his shoulders once again.

Chapter Twenty-Five

Man's Best Friend

Henry

"Stay close," Father says, loud enough to be heard over the crowd in the train station.

Father turns sideways, his profile altered by the bulbous false nose. I resist the urge to adjust my wig. I tap my white cane, playing my part of the blind man.

Father gestures to a bench. "Sit, Henry. Keep looking."

We deposit ourselves on a raised platform which provides a bird's eye view of the station. Father flicks open a newspaper, glancing over top.

Beside me, Newton growls and shifts uneasily. "Easy boy."

I speak low, so only father may hear. "This is maddening. I don't even know what I'm looking for. What color hair, what clothes."

"That's why we have Newton. Sheer genius, my boy. Keep him still."

"Sit, Newton." He sits, but reluctantly.

I stroke the dog from his neck to his tail, but his coarse black and white hackles refuse to lie down; his hair's as vigilant as his mind in his quest to find his missing master.

After a quarter hour, Newton stands, quivering all over. A whine of longing rips from his throat.

Father folds his paper, anticipating.

My heart hammers as my eyes tear through the crowd and frustration heats my cheeks.

The station seems in order; I see nothing abnormal. People hugging, departing, coming and going. Children screaming, porter's lugging suitcases.

My eyes tick from person to person, checking facial features and expressions. Finally, a movement catches my eye.

A woman rips her arm out of a man's grasp. His fingers close around her forearm and her lips quiver in an unmistakable grimace of pain.

"I see them."

Arabella's red locks are poorly stuffed beneath a black wig while Stygian sports a false moustache and an unconvincing limp.

Newton wriggles and whines, straining against his lead.

Father's hand shoots under his overcoat and I know he's drawing his weapon.

I extract Arabella's handkerchief from my pocket, shoving it beneath Newton's snout.

He whines pitifully, and then his ears perk as he sniffs

in earnest, nostrils flaring as he inhales his master's scent. He dances skittishly, nails clicking against the floor.

I stare straight ahead, eyes never leaving the pair. Afraid I will lose them in the masses.

"Ready?"

Father nods.

"Find Arabella, Newton." I release his collar.

The dog *leaps* from the platform, growling and snapping, barreling into the crowd.

"A dog is loosed!"

"Somebody catch him!"

Women and children scream and a path appears through the thick crowd as patrons leap out of his way.

Father and I hurry behind, bolting to keep pace with him.

Stygian has caught on, his limp discarded. I see the top of his hat swerve and head for an exit.

"Blast! He's making a run for it!"

"Keep moving, Henry."

I cannot see him. His hat's disappeared.

"Hey, you! Catch your wretched dog! You aren't blind!" An irritated fop gives me a rough shoulder.

I ignore him and weave quickly. I see the tail end of Newton's leash disappear again and bolt forward.

But he's too fast. His barks echo through the station, but I cannot see him. The path he cut has filled back in.

Somewhere I hear a bobby's whistle. The crowd will slow him.

"Excuse me. Excuse me." I push my way to a statue, and scramble up onto its feet, searching.

Father's face peers up, along with twenty other perplexed faces.

"I see them. Head for two o'clock!"

Father is gone, instantaneously swallowed by the multitude.

The bobby spy's me, his whistle bleating in earnest.

I meet his fiery gaze and bellow, "Call Inspector Giamatti. Hurry!"

He hesitates, but seems to choose to believe me and scurries toward the exit.

Stygian jerks Bella and her head snaps with the force, pushing her toward the door.

Bella slides to a stop, Stygian colliding into her back.

A man blocks the exit.

A huge man. A giant.

He places his hands on his hips, and spreads his legs wide, blocking their escape. I see him mouth the words, *'Miss Holmes'*.

Arabella's face breaks in relief, but Stygian wheels her away as the man lurches for her.

I see father's bowler hat still headed for two o'clock, and Stygian's now barreling in the opposite direction.

I leap off the statue, keeping my eye on the other exit.

How? *The Brethren of Large?*

It must be. The giant sent for help. Saving our carcasses a second time.

I break out of the crowd. Another colossal man blocks the exit.

Stygian whirls away; his head whips desperately back

and forth, searching for escape.

I grit my teeth and run as fast as the crowd will allow. Father falls in beside me.

"Giants," He breathes.

"Aye."

Newton's barks pierce the air as he leaps out of the fray, charging Stygian.

Bella sees him first. Ripping her arm from Stygian's grasp, she flings herself to the ground, out of his reach.

Stygian raises his pistol.

"Newton, desist!" Arabella shrieks. "No. No!"

Newton leaps, snarling, his eyes fixed on Stygian.

Arabella scrambles up, flinging herself at him. Her boot flashes up, striking Stygian's wrist.

Stygian's shot discharges with a *'Bang'*.

Newton's yelp cuts to the bone and my heart hammers. His black and white body contorts mid-air as the shot connects, as if hitting an invisible barrier. He strikes the floor and slides into the gape-mouthed crowd.

He whines, flopping like a fish out of water on the floor.

His nails tick wildly off the floor as he tries to stand, his body writhing.

Newton's back leg scrapes uselessly, unable to find purchase. He stands, teeth bared, ready to leap again.

Stygian's gaze shoots to the dog, gun swinging wildly.

"No!" Bella flies, tackling the dog, rolling with him in her arms. "Desist, desist. Oh, please, boy, please."

The second giant slips behind Stygian. I meet his eye and jerk my head.

He steps out of the way, arms extending, moving back the onlookers who are apparently devoid of common sense.

"Drop your weapon, Stygian!" father yells.

Stygian's pistol arm swings in our direction.

I see father's arm raise beside mine. I squeeze the trigger and hear his pistol fire in tandem.

Stygian's shoulders rock, one-two, as our rapid fire shots graze his biceps.

"Ah!" He collapses in pain, still clutching the pistol.

I know without any consultation, that father aimed to maim, not kill.

No matter how odious, we are trying to stop him. Others will decide his fate.

The crowd presses in, murmurs rising.

I hear someone call, "The police have arrived! Make way! Make room!"

Arabella is sobbing as she rips off her wig and I hear the inspector's familiar voice behind me, "Dr. Watson, Mr. Watson, what's going on?"

Montgomery is hot behind him.

Three uniformed guards stand above Stygian's prostrate form, pistols drawn. His eyes finally admit defeat.

His weapon clatters to the floor, and his eyes jam closed.

I drop to my knees beside Bella. She's sobbing, tears flowing and sluicing down her cheeks.

The dog is whining. "Shh. Easy boy, easy boy."

She pulls his leg up, examining it. It's a red mess of flesh. She drops the paw and swoons, her eyes rolling back in her head.

I catch her, and wrench her to me, inhaling her scent.

Words of gratitude fill my head.

Home. You are home, at last, Bella.

They echo, ringing over and over like the pealing of bells. It's like I've been on a long, long journey, and I'm finally home.

She, is my home.

"Bella. You're alright. It's alright. We'll mend him."

I bury my face in her hair, feeling the burn of stares and I hear the pop and smell of flash powder as someone takes a picture.

She opens her eyes. "Oh, Henry. I. I."

The dog lays his head on her lap, and his tail gives a feeble, welcoming thump.

I smile and nod, locking her gaze. "I know. You're both home, Bella. Home is wherever I am, from now on."

Chapter Twenty-Six

IMPOSSIBILITIES

Faculty Fund Raising Ball
Bella

I smooth the black and white striped dress and take a deep, steadying breath, and am dizzied by the sea of pirouetting multi-colored couples.

I'm grateful for the elbow-length gloves which hide the myriad of bruises and lacerations, my Stygian battle-scars.

I sigh, but it feels almost a shudder. He will be on a ship, extradited to London for a long list of previous crimes. Undoubtedly with my irate father waiting at the dock.

I try to focus on the ball, internally rehearsing my memorized small talk, but my mind keeps straying to the singular skeleton we saved from the fire.

It was one the giant had moved, hidden within the catacombs. The only Nephilim to survive.

My fingers twitch, itching to reassemble it to its full height.

The bone arrived today by post, addressed to me. Inside the envelope was a solitary line of text.

"Go in peace, small one."

I wish I could've thanked the very large man. Henry and I both owe him and the Brethren of Large, our lives. Perhaps I'll find him again one day.

A bright gown of bold crimson demands my attention, standing out from the feminine gathering of pinks and whites and blues.

I smile. It's Violet, naturally. Her perceptive eyes are tunneled on me, her hand on John's guiding forearm.

He grins, his eyes dancing as speaks to each person he passes. So easy and natural. Something I'll never master.

I smell him before I see him and gooseflesh erupts on my arms. I turn, steeling myself for the inevitable shudder of breath which comes on viewing Henry's handsome face.

A reaction which doesn't fade, no matter how often I gaze at him.

Henry bows dramatically. "Miss Holmes."

My heart box clatters to my mind's floor, leaving it completely exposed and vulnerable.

I manage a curtsey. "Mr. Watson."

He eyes my black and white striped dress, which is a departure from my usual style.

"Violet has outdone herself."

I shake my head. "I chose it myself. And arranged my hair."

His smile lights his eyes. "*Really*? Well, then *you* have truly outdone yourself. I have a surprise."

I feel my brows furrow. "Yes?"

He steps aside and my stomach plummets.

Father.

His dark eyebrows are pulled tight, his mouth so very serious.

He steps close, his fingers encircling my elbow as he leans to whisper in my ear. "Digger." He sighs, and it somehow sounds sad. "*I am so very glad* you're safe."

I pull back to regard him. His mouth opens but more words seem lodged somewhere between brain and speech. His eyes are uncharacteristically soft.

I squeeze his arm in return. "I know, father. I'm so glad you're here. I feel safer already."

And it's true.

He snaps his fingers and is businesslike once again. A young man bustles to his side. "Henry and I have spoken. He had the idea this might benefit you—open up your mind to… what was it, Henry?"

"Possibilities, sir." Henry smiles encouragingly.

Father actually smiles back, with a slight nod. "Yes."

My breath stops as my heart skips a beat.

The young man hands me a beautiful cello.

Father puts my hand in Henry's. His eyes are serious, but one side of his mouth pulls up in a very uncharacteristic tease.

"Father, have you been drinking?"

There must be an explanation for so many displays of emotion in such a short time span.

His eyes narrow. "Despite rumors, I am not Babbage's adding machine. And I endured the longest sail ever, in fear for your life. And I arrive to find you alive and whole."

John laughs, "Yes, why this is downright giddy behavior for you."

Father glares at him.

John's hand grasps father's shoulder. "Come on old man; let the young people have their fun."

Henry extends his other hand. "Might I have this dance?"

I might've imagined it, but I swear I hear my father swallow.

Out of my periphery, John and Violet's stares sear the side of my face.

My hand trembles and Henry grasps it tighter, and pulls me close. Too close for convention.

Henry stares down at me, his eyes crinkling in sheer delight. He pulls me into the fray. His hand on my hip guides me flawlessly through every turn.

The lights swirl by and the perplexed faces of nearby couples.

"Bella, look at me."

I only need to give myself to it. To him.

He slides something out of his pocket, slipping it around my neck without missing a step. I look down. It's my key, returned on a much more beautiful purple ribbon.

"I had the same idea, by the way, to use Newton. Even before I saw your key."

"Is that so?"

He nods. "And I didn't read anything. Your journal is

locked tight once again."

I blush and swallow and focus on his feet.

"Have you seen your butterflies?"

I stare above his head at a long window. Snowflakes, the first of the season, lilt and dance outside the beveled window pane.

"No. Have you?"

He shakes his head. "Not since the night Stygian took you. They…appeared to me."

I shiver. "Yes, I do wonder about them. I—"

He quietly shushes me. "One mystery at a time, Bella."

"But they do signify transformation. And I think we would both agree that's occurred. For both of us."

He is right. I *have* changed.

"And your paper? Have you chosen your topic?" he prompts.

I nod. It's painful to admit. "I. I am going to discuss the possibility of the skeleton being Nephilim."

He straightens up and smiles over the top of my head.

"What?"

He shrugs. "Nothing."

"I decided to be open to possibilities."

He drops his head to stare, and his eyes are jubilant. He spins me too fast, out-of-sync with the other dancers, which results in more off-color looks.

"Shall we review?"

"Review what? The skeletal findings?"

He laughs, briefly closing his eyes and lips, shaking his head. "No."

Our hands are joined, outstretched in dance. He lessens his grip and flicks up one finger.

"First impossibility—seeing you again. The right place at the right time. Many years later. Too many."

Heat flushes my face, but I flick up my second finger. "My butterflies."

He nods encouragingly.

He flicks up my third finger. "The gold tooth, how improbable that it survived the fire."

I shudder and nod, adding the fourth. "The Nephilim bone. How impossible it survived."

He pulls me close and desire rages. I wish to be out of this wretched room. Alone with him. To do whatever necessary to hide from chaperones.

Violet and John spin close by. "Arabella, your father's already at home." I glance around and see father chatting amiably with the police inspector.

John spins Violet close once again. He opens his mouth and blurts, "Don't forget her other present, Henry."

Henry's eyebrows pull together. "*That* was supposed to be a surprise."

Violet and he both laugh.

Violet adds, "You know your father cannot hold his tongue when it comes to Arabella."

I smile as they spin away.

"What is it?"

His face is tentative. "Cello lessons. Remember; open your mind, Bella. I'm betting it's as natural as bones."

I sigh. "Perhaps. Thank you. You shouldn't have."

The song ends. Partners part and reassemble. Henry doesn't relinquish his hold; he slowly spins me in a circle, though no music plays.

With the jerky start of a Ferris wheel, my mind spins, erupting in a whirlwind of pictures. Henry's face, the sesamoid bone, the giant's feet and a myriad of others explode in a visual tornado in my mind.

Like the cogs on a faulty film roll, unstuck.

"Henry?"

He pales looking at my expression. "Yes?"

"My mind-pictures. They have returned."

"My darling, I am ever-so-glad." He then jokes, trying to lessen my severity. "I am unaccustomed to beating you at anything. So I must admit, it is a relief."

I playfully hit his arm.

The music restarts and he alters our swaying tempo. I forget to be afraid of falling. To be afraid of the stares that bore into us like some sideshow attraction.

Henry demands my attention.

"Five?" he prompts.

I swallow as a plethora of unpleasant images skate through my head. "The giant. And his saving you, which would've been the end of me. At least in spirit."

A dark cloud passes over his face, but quickly lifts. He laughs quietly. "Definitely."

His voice drops an octave, "But do you know what six is, my darling?"

His voice is warm and tantalizing, coating my mind and heart like smooth bourbon.

My skin erupts in violent gooseflesh. I want to hear him say it again.

"Arabella? Six?"

I shake my head.

"Six is that, *you love me.*" His eyes shine, and his mouth sets seriously. "As I've loved you. Since the very first time I saw you."

I nod. One tear trickles. "I do. I love you, Henry."

And *that* was how I gave my heart to Henry Watson.

This account being the first of many, many adventures.

I believe that life with Henry will mean endless impossibilities.

Arabella Holmes

Author's Notes

- **Phrenology and L'uomo Delinquente**

Were very real disciplines in their respective times. They eventually fell out of favor as knowledge of the brain progressed and the technique of fingerprinting grew. My use and application of L'uomo Deliquente is completely fictitious, however.

- **The Mutter Museum**

Is located in Philadelphia and is wonderfully unique and strange place to visit. If you've any interest in science or oddities or medicine, it's well worth the visit. It has no connection with Sherlock Holmes, at least to my knowledge.

- **Information about the Sausage Murder**

Derived from history from the case of Adolph Luetgert, 1897. The account is detailed in the book, *Forensic Anthropology* by Peggy Thomas.

- **Si-Te-Cahs**

Sarah Winnemucca Hopkins did record legends of the Piutes and Lovelock Cave exists. Some have claimed the giants of the legends were, indeed, Nephilim. Giant skeletons have been unearthed all over the globe.

- **John Watson**

If one has read the original Sherlock Holmes stories, one quickly realizes Watson was not the bumbling, plump counterpart he was portrayed in many films. Indeed, Watson was an ex-soldier, a crack shot, an excellent physician and surgeon and able to deduce minor mysteries on his own. I stand by the screenwriter's version of the American film remakes, which portray him as a necessary catalyst for Holmes to interact with society, and while not the genius-deductive mastermind of Holmes, a force to be reckoned with in his own right.

I also contend that Sherlock Holmes had Asperger's Syndrome. One familiar with this genetic phenotype could quickly recognize his difficulty relating to people, his extreme, all-consuming passions and obsessive behavior and routines.

Holmes and Watson's relationship was symbiotic, which is consequently the case with many with Asperger's; despite their oft-great talents, they often rely on a loved one to assist them with deciphering societal cues and navigating the world of relationships.

Precisely like Watson and Holmes.

Case closed.

Acknowledgements

Firstly, to Victoria Lea of Aponte Literary. There could be no greater editorial partner, cheerleader, shrink and fellow lover of the written word. I am so very lucky to have you. To my fabulous writer friends, MV Freeman, Dan Krippene, Marlo Berliner, for reading, critiquing, and having my back. Love you guys.

Brynn Chapman

Born and raised in western Pennsylvania, Brynn Chapman is the daughter of two teachers. Her writing reflects her passions: science, history and love—not necessarily in that order. In real life, the geek gene runs strong in her family, as does the Asperger's syndrome. Her writing reflects her experience as a pediatric therapist and her interactions with society's downtrodden. In fiction, she's a strong believer in underdogs and happily-ever-afters. She also writes non-fiction and lectures on the subjects of autism and sensory integration and is a medical contributor to online journal The Age of Autism. You can find her on the web at www.brynnchapmanauthor.com